When He Finds You

When He Finds You

Sadie Ryan

Stories that inspire emotions
www.rubyfiction.com

Published 2020 by Ruby Fiction
Penrose House, Crawley Drive, Camberley, Surrey GU15 2AB, UK
www.rubyfiction.com

A CIP catalogue record for this book is available from the British Library

ISBN: 978-1-91255-036-4

Printed and bound in Great Britain by Clays Ltd, Elcograf S.p.A.

To my wonderful children, Harry and Charlotte. I love you both so much and I'm so proud of you both.

To Stephen, my muse, thank you for all your support, your belief in me and please don't stop pushing me over the line.

Lastly, to Willow (my dog) and Freddie (my cat) who give me so much joy every single day.

Acknowledgements

I would like to thank my wonderful publishers Ruby Fiction for their amazing support in bringing this book to the world and my super-duper editor for her great skills.

This is a work of fiction and I have to the best of my ability researched as much as possible, so, I hope you will forgive me if I have slipped up in any way.

I hope you enjoy reading my second novel and thank you so much for buying it. You can visit my website to see what is coming up http://www.sadieryan.co.uk or follow me on Twitter @The_SadieRyan

A massive thank you to the tasting panel and Stars at Ruby Fiction and especially to: Dimi Evangelou, Mel Appleyard, Stacey Rinnert, Yvonne Greene, Sharon Walsh, Carol Dutton, Hilary Brown, Barbara Powdrill, Alan Roberton, and Jenny Kinsman.

Chapter One

Oliver introduced Peter The Bastard into their lives as their accountant.

He stole all their money.

He didn't pay their taxes.

He screwed them good and proper.

She hated him.

She twisted the pencil in her hand over and over like a baton. Her eyes narrowed but she said nothing. How could anyone keep sane in a situation like this? She hadn't relaxed in the days since it happened. Who could? Her foot tapped on the wooden office floor sounding like a death-watch beetle. She often wasn't aware she was doing it until she noticed it getting on Oliver's nerves. It was one of her tells. To be fair, he'd endured a lot of bad behaviour from her lately. The fear was too big. She pulled the zip of her fleece up and rubbed the back of her neck to ease the tightness there. Stress. So much stress.

She used to run a lot before all this happened. It always helped clear her mind, see things in more perspective. She thought about the mess they were in and would give anything to make it all go away. The running didn't help any more, that and the fact she damaged her knee last year falling off a horse. Now she had no outlet. No way of venting the demons inside her.

In its place she'd found wine helped a lot, it blurred the edges of her ghosts. That's where she was now, desperately not wanting to rely on the drink but too scared to do without it.

Oliver knew her so well, although he knew nothing of what happened to her all those years ago. She could not bear anyone to know, especially him as it would ruin everything. The marvellous thing about Oliver was his patience. He knew the right time to take over when things began to get on top of her. She wasn't good with pressure and he was always so calm. It was one of the many things about him she adored. Right now she wanted to be held by him and wrapped up in his arms with him telling her it was all going to be OK.

Oliver, whilst taking a lot of the flack they were dealing with, had his limits. This time right now was one of them. It was stretching him very thin and she hated what it was doing to him.

She'd struggled with boyfriends before Oliver. She found it hard to let anyone in. Then Oliver turned up and it was just right. Comfortable. She knew the moment she set eyes on him that he was the one and she'd been right. Marrying Oliver had been the best decision she'd ever made.

He glanced over and gave her a warm smile. She knew he was trying so hard to keep her together. He always wanted to cushion everything for her.

Oh, Oliver, I love you so much but what is going to happen to us? She wanted to say the words. She wouldn't, though. She was too afraid of the answer.

She saw the worry in his beautiful eyes, the stress had taken its revenge on his handsome face, once bright and full of warmth now had a sallow look about it. All the colour that used to exude from him was gone. He wasn't eating properly and he'd lost weight. It didn't look good on him. She wanted to run her fingers through his hair and tell him she would sort it all out. But she couldn't. Nobody could. This was bigger than both of them. She thought of the vast numbers involved and it made her feel sick.

She wanted her Oliver back. They still had the magic even after all these years together. He still brought a tingle racing down her spine when he touched her.

Over time Gemma had learned how to mask and hide her pain. She'd had to. Her own pain she could manage. But Oliver's, that was different. Seeing him in pain broke her.

People who've never had a traumatic event in their life never understood how it changed a person. Something happened in the brain altering behaviour and attitudes. It was the way the brain coped with the trauma. Stability, for her, was the only important thing in her life. And now that was being wrenched from her.

Years ago, when she was a teenager, she'd dealt with bad situations in her life the only way she knew how. Her stepfather's abuse finally pushed her over the cliff, so to speak. By eroding her confidence and belief in herself, he stamped all over her self-worth. Years of enduring his behaviour had only been manageable because she had an end goal. To finish her education and go to university. That had been her teenage dream. She knew with a good education she could get as far away from them as possible.

She swivelled her office chair to and fro watching Oliver at the computer. He was in his mid-thirties, dressed in jeans, T-shirt and jumper. Oliver was like a swan, calm and in control on the surface. She was on edge all the time totally visible on the surface like a drowning man thrashing away in the water.

She licked her lips. That drink hadn't done much to relax her; she could do with another one. She brushed her blonde hair from her face. Oliver was so concerned about her he just didn't understand how worried she was for him. Not her. And why she needed the drink. She didn't really care about herself, it was Oliver whom she knew would take the flack for the mess they were in. That was the sort of guy he was.

Oliver was on to her about her drinking. Bless him, he had tried to not have a go at her but tried to be rational, knowing to push her would make her worse. The bottles kept disappearing. She never said anything, just bought another one and found another place to hide it. She was well aware she was verging on turning into an alcoholic if she wasn't careful. She had it under control. Why couldn't he understand that?

You see, she knew once the bloody newspapers got hold of the mess they were in they'd be in everyone's house, talked about, scrutinised over and all over social media. Everyone would know and the way they'd write it; they'd make sure that both of them looked like thieving criminals. She couldn't bear it. Because it was all lies.

She wanted to go back to bed with a bottle of wine. Crawl under the covers and sleep to make it all go away. She slept well with wine. Her tongue was parched craving the silken liquid. She ran it over her lips.

Oliver spoke and startled her out of her reverie. 'You have to open the brown envelopes, Gem, this is getting ridiculous. They're stacking up. Look at the pile. They can't hurt you. They're only envelopes. Please, you have to do it.' His voice carried an edge she didn't like. That was what she meant when she said she wanted her old Oliver back. The stress was beginning to break him. He was pulled tight like a guitar string, she knew that, only she hated seeing him that way. The thought of what would happen if they broke him terrified her. She wasn't going to let that happen. Who was she kidding? How in hell was she going to do that?

Oliver answered the questions from the bank, the tax office and the creditors; it made her head spin and she wondered how he did it. How he stayed so calm under the barrage of wolves baying for blood. If Oliver wasn't here with her, she wouldn't know what she would do. She knew he thought she was a wonky wheel in the partnership right now; although he never said as much. You heard of couples breaking up because of financial strains. She didn't want to lose Oliver. She'd do anything – absolutely anything – to keep them together.

A stillness crowded the air space in the study as she sat in the chair next to him, watching him click open email after email. The heavy silence filled the room closing in around her making it hard to breathe. The floor to ceiling windows in the office gave her a view of the world outside where people were going about their day with small worries of what to make for tea or what to wear or if the kids hadn't eaten their greens. Oh, of course she wasn't naïve enough to think others didn't have worries as bad or worse than theirs. Except, looking out of the window it seemed safe compared to inside their office full of brown envelopes and menacing emails. She took a drink from her coffee cup and wiped her mouth discreetly with the back of her hand.

Their study was designed for two people. A computer each, an in-tray each, a penholder each, that sort of thing. The answer machine blinked. They didn't answer it any more. It was a constant reminder the wolves were out there.

Her inbox showed ten new messages. She saw an email from Oliver's family amongst them. They chipped in with their little bit of helpful advice – 'You need to stand your ground with the taxman...' 'Change your number and go ex-directory...' 'Where will you live? We only have a small house you know...' All of them giving advice and making sure they didn't turn up on their doorstep. He'd been hurt by their coldness and distance. Nothing like – 'We're here to help you if you need us.'

Taking a deep breath, she flicked on Safari and opened a browsing page instead of the emails. If she got her hands on Peter, she would... well, she would know exactly what to do with him. He'd destroyed them, and they'd done nothing to deserve it. Two people making a life for themselves. God, how stupid had they been to get taken in so easily.

Oliver should never have brought him into their lives. The man had infiltrated them; she never really liked him. There was always something a little off about him she was unable to put her finger on. Oliver and Peter had become great friends. Or so he'd thought.

'Gemma don't try to disguise the smell of alcohol on your breath, I know you've been drinking, it won't help. I need you to be strong to help me,' Oliver said. 'I can't do this alone.'

She flinched at the rebuke. 'Sorry.' She shook her head dismissively. He meant nothing by it. He was worried, frightened that she was going to go over the edge with the drinking. Instead of saying any more she focused on the screen, googling random film stars and their lives; this was the limit of her brainpower right now.

He turned around to face her. 'You're upset. I get that. But you need to stop drinking like this otherwise it's going to turn into another problem we can do without. Look, I know Peter really messed us up.' She snorted. 'But we can't let him bring us to our knees, we must fight this. Don't you see how terrified I am about you? I love you, but I'm scared you're losing it.'

She burst into tears knowing he was right. Christ it didn't take much these days for the water works to start. Rising from his chair he came to her side, knelt on the floor and cupped her face, wiping the tears away with his thumb. That warm tingle when he touched her felt comforting.

'You let me take the load, darling. You just need to stop drinking and try to relax. What has happened has happened and now we need to take each thing as it comes. We will come out of this. We will, I promise you we will.'

'Oh, Oliver, I know what you're saying is right. I just feel like everything is out of control. That we have no power over our lives.'

Although she thought he was delusional if he thought they weren't already on their knees. After finding out what Peter had done to them she couldn't understand how Oliver still hadn't the smallest notion that Peter had manipulated it all to crash down on them exactly how it had.

Fucking idiot.

They were the victims but everyone who they owed money to was making out like they were the villains.

Gemma had a suspicious mind and trusted few people, Peter had been one of them but Oliver somehow managed to convince her she was overreacting. They'd spoken about it at length when Oliver wanted to employ him, but he told her Peter was a financial wiz. He would handle everything as well as invest their money in the best places.

What they didn't know was that Peter was keeping secrets from them.

He'd given them passwords to the accounts, which they checked regularly. Only they didn't know he had the authority to change them at will. Which is exactly how he had cleaned them out.

They'd worked hard to build up their company. Losing their home, the home they found together and she'd decorated was going to be agonising. The Farrow & Ball paint she spent hours choosing, the stupid number of hours she spent deciding on the tiles for the kitchen floor. The difficult decision of which Aga to get, a two oven or a four. The landscaping around the house. The colour of the gravel on the drive. And it was all so public – or would be soon. Their friends so jealous of their house and relationship, the fact they loved spending so much time together and could work together without falling out.

She scrunched up her eyes to quell the tears, then stood and went over to the window, barely visible because of the trees, she saw a van parked up on the road. Oliver came up behind her wrapping his arms around her and pulling her tightly into him. 'I won't let anything hurt you, Gem.'

Normally Gemma wasn't particularly observant, but, lately, she'd begun to notice odd things. Sometimes she had the feeling of being followed or watched. She hadn't mentioned it to Oliver. He had enough to worry about. Besides, it was probably her own wild imagination. Or the drink. Probably the drink.

She fell back into him, enjoying his warmth and protection. She wanted to crawl inside him for safety. Turning around she kissed him. 'Oliver, I'm sorry if I've been a bit of a cow.'

'You haven't, sweetheart. It's a tough time. We are together. We'll get through this together.' He kissed her and stroked her hair. 'We could always take the money we have in the Swiss account and bugger off.'

Now there was an idea.

Their business Wiggit.com, which they started four years ago as a tentative idea when Oliver was made redundant, had grown beyond their wildest imaginations, virtually overnight. *An online success story*, the newspapers said.

They sold gimmicks from phone cases to lanyards: nothing big, all easy to package and post. Who'd have thought you could make a great living selling insignificant objects on eBay and Amazon. Within six months they rented a warehouse and started buying in bulk from China. They employed four people whom they now had to let go. A horrible experience. They all lined up in the office waiting for them to arrive. Oliver explained what had happened and she sat behind him, ashamed and mortified with their admission. Three of them were understanding and compassionate. But the fourth, George Driller was nasty, an unbeliever. Calling them names and throwing insults. Telling them his family was going to starve because he now had no job thanks to them and his wife was pregnant again. Apparently, that was their fault too. Gemma watched Oliver handle the situation, calmly.

The postman arrived. He waved at her standing in the window, pushed the letters through the letterbox and whistling he left. She lifted her hand automatically to wave. He wore navy cotton shorts and blue Nike trainers, ridiculous attire for the time of year. She almost resented his happiness. How dare he have no worries. Sometimes she thought she was living in a parallel universe where the rest of the inhabitants were getting on with their lives while hers was stuck. Jammed in misery.

'We have to go through the motions, Gem, you know that.' Oliver gave her a last squeeze before going back to his chair.

She walked back to her desk and slumped in her chair. 'I can't carry on; I feel as if I'm about to have a stroke. All I see when I close my eyes is us living on the streets. It's as if the backs of my eyelids have been painted with the image of us inside a cardboard box.'

'You're not having a stroke, Gemma, and we won't be on the streets,' he said with confidence. 'I won't let it happen.'

She wasn't so sure. 'But how do you know? We have nothing left, Oliver.' She reached over to him wanting his closeness again as security. 'Oliver, don't let them take the house, please do something.'

'I am, but ignoring them will only make it worse.' He squeezed her hand.

Oliver was a true romantic. He had even planned their wedding right down to all the bows on the chairs. It had only been a small affair, she didn't invite her family for obvious reasons and Oliver's wasn't large. They had twenty guests in total but it was magical. Looking back, she knew then that she would always love Oliver and do anything for him. It had rankled him that he never met her family but to be fair to him, once she told him they were off limits and she had her reasons, he never pushed her again. That was Oliver, he'd never want to hurt her. So he did everything he could to please her.

For their honeymoon he booked Bora Bora for two weeks. 'A fairytale honeymoon for the love of my life.' She'd known those words had come straight from his heart. Her own heart bursting with love and happiness.

'Were you serious about us just taking off? You know with the money in the Swiss account?' she asked, suddenly feeling some hope. They'd never wanted to touch that account. They always said it was their ticket out if ever anything bad happened and they needed to leave. Actually those were Peter's words. They'd simply looked at him wondering what the hell he meant... dangerous.

'We might have to. I should have mentioned it before only I didn't think you could take it. But now, well, you need to know.' His shoulders stiffened and his fingers stalled over the keys.

'Oliver?'

He kept his eyes focused on the screen clearly unable to look at her. 'I'm sorry. I should have told you earlier.'

'What, Oliver?' She braced herself.

'We've had a letter from the bank.'

'The bank? What do you mean from the bank?'

'It's not good, Gemma.'

'What sort of letter? What are you talking about?'

'They're taking us to court to hoof us out of the house. And HMRC says we owe them a ton of money, much more than I thought, in back taxes, which we have to pay back asap. I don't even know how they've come to that figure.' His head drooped and reminded her of a puppet whose strings had been cut. She knew they couldn't ignore this last declaration. No matter how much they wanted to.

For a moment, the world stopped spinning. Running away seemed their only option. His pain hurt her. He couldn't crumble. No, he couldn't, he had to be strong. She depended on him. Seeing Oliver like that broke her heart.

Then, he pulled himself together, rubbed his hands over his face and straightened up in his chair. 'I'm glad I told you. I couldn't keep it to myself any longer.'

'Why did you?'

'I was afraid you'd fall into the drink even more.'

Her thoughts gridlocked. Then the cogs started turning. 'Oliver, we have the two rentals. We'll have to let the tenants go and move into one of those. It'll be OK, won't it? They can't take those, can they?' Her eyes stared into open space as she spoke. They could and they would. She already knew the answer. They really could lose their home and everything they owned. 'I don't know how to deal with what you've just told me,' she said. 'They just take what they want and we can't stop them? It's not fair. This wasn't our fault. None of it was our fault. They'll take it all, won't they? What's going to happen to us if we lose the house… oh my God.' The fear was real.

They had bought two small cottages as investments last year on the strength of the company doing so well, now they were about to lose the lot.

'The thing is, Gemma, we might have to sell to pay the taxes. I don't know until I speak with them. This is going to get worse before it gets better.' He took her free hand and rubbed his thumb along her wrist.

'But there's no equity in the houses, why would they want them?'

'I don't know, there are the deposits we put down on them so there is a little. I don't have all the answers.'

She remembered their honeymoon on the beautiful, peaceful Polynesian island, the pearl of the Pacific Ocean with the sweet scented flowers around their bungalow. The unadulterated ocean views, the turquoise water and glorious snorkelling in the lagoons. How happy they were. How contented. Their world was going to be amazing. Such plans and ambitions they had. Not a care in the world.

'Are you happy?' Oliver had asked.

She had never known happiness like it. She was in heaven and thought she always would be. 'I'm in heaven. You have brought me to heaven.'

He wore an expression of delight on his face at her answer.

'Oliver, do you think we'll always be as happy as we are right now?'

He laughed. 'I think we will always be as happy.' He pulled her towards him. 'I'll do anything for you, Gemma.'

And they had been really happy and he had done anything for her. She couldn't fault him.

'I'm sorry, Gem, I should never have brought him into our lives. It's all my fault.' He changed gears and for a moment she wasn't sure who he was talking about. Only for a minute.

'You didn't know he was a thieving bastard.' She couldn't help her resentment.

Memories massed in her head of another time and of another bastard. She could still remember the anger inside her the day she left home at eighteen, if you could call it home. Social Services weren't as hot on abuse then. Her mother was a small insipid creature. Her short thinning brown hair fell flat against her head. An unending stream of cigarettes dangled from her mouth. She threw her out onto the street. Calling her a liar and whore after she'd fought with her stepfather for the last time and threatened to go to the police. Her stepfather was a stringy looking man and a drinker who only wore trackies and sweat tops, usually with food spilt down the front. He stood in the driveway as she left. His face wore the usual odious smirk she'd seen too many times before, taunting her. Standing near him always unleashed a torrent of nerves, which caused her to shake involuntarily. But that day a rage so intense rose up inside her. Fury, you might call it, whatever it was the power with which it infiltrated her every fibre wanted to extinguish his cold eyes from the universe.

Sitting in her old car moments later, she saw him in her rear-view mirror scratching his head underneath his thinning blonde hair, his other hand down his trackie bottoms; she supposed he thought it looked a cool thing to do. He always thought himself to be a cool-looking person. But then he was always drunk. She put the car in reverse and the next thing he went down like the last standing bowling pin.

Pulling herself back to the present she tossed the pile of brown envelopes onto the floor. 'Well, I'm not looking at any more of those! What's the point?' She swiped the desk clean. The lack of control they seemed to have over their lives reminiscent of another time. Pens, paper, hole punch all toppled to the floor. 'I won't lose my home. I won't have our lives controlled by others. And live where?' Her memories of growing up in *that* council house pushed at the edges of her thoughts, like a black evil stain. Dark images, shadows and faces she wanted to forget all congregated to break through.

She jerked her hair into a tight ponytail and stood up fiercely. 'I'm sorry, Oliver, but I'm not losing everything. Where do we keep the book with the passwords?' She glanced at him. 'Nobody knows about the other bank account, do they? Oliver? You didn't feel the need to confess to HMRC, did you?'

How had this account slipped their minds? It wasn't

something they spoke about. They always felt Peter was not on the up and up about the honesty of it all, but he had a way with words and a way of convincing them they were naïve and he wasn't doing anything wrong. All big business did the same. To trust him. That was what they paid him for.

And they did.

Stupidly it would now seem.

Like lambs to the slaughter they followed, believing him.

The profit they had made from their company, Peter kindly moved into Credit Suisse, a Swiss numbered bank account. Safe, he'd told them, but you need a minimum one hundred thousand to open one. Peter had known all the ways to make money disappear, she now realised. Gemma was learning now that all his big talk about taking risks to earn big money was for his own benefit. His talk about finance was all a charade to confuse them. He'd bristled when they had questioned him on anything. Convincing them over and over he was looking after them.

'No, I haven't told HMRC. I'm not stupid,' Oliver replied.

She pulled open the drawers of the desk, searching through papers and files. 'Where's the book? Have we moved it?' She hurried over to a small cheap black laminate IKEA table in the corner and yanked the drawer pulling out the small black book

'Thank God.' She glanced at him as he stood up, ashen faced as if he'd taken root. 'You never told Peter the password?'

'I... I might have. You don't think Peter's taken that money too!' Quickly he opened a new tab on the computer. 'It was our private stash; he pulled it out for us.' She heard the echo of loss in his voice. He didn't want to believe it. Gemma tapped in the account number and password. They both held their breath as the little wheel spun until the page opened.

Balance 0.

When Oliver called the bank, they told him there was no trace of where it had gone. These accounts were anonymous. They work by numbers. No names. A set of numbers represent your identity that way you kept your anonymity.

Peter The Bastard had taken it all.

Chapter Two

A few days later, Gemma drove back from the jewellers, where she had just sold her jewellery. Through the winding country lanes of South Cheshire she sent autumn leaves scattering, small bursts flying up like confetti around the car. She didn't normally break the speed limit but today she courted danger. The sun was low, so she dropped her sun visor. She took a detour home, needing space to think and clear her mind. The orange light on her petrol gauge blinked so she headed towards Chelford to the nearest petrol station a mile or so from where she was.

She had one thousand pounds in her purse and about twelve hundred in her account. It would pay the bills for a couple of months. They had stopped paying the mortgage, what was the point, they were bound to lose the house anyway. Better to keep hold of the money for now. All the bills were overdue. The credit cards were maxed out. They had no income and no prospect of making any payments. No amount of alcohol was going to make their situation any easier.

Her mobile rang, she grabbed it off the passenger seat – there was no Bluetooth in her second-hand Mini. She'd sent her beloved Audi back.

'Where are you?' Oliver sounded concerned.

'I've been to sell my jewellery, remember I told you I would? I thought today was as good as any day.' She'd left him a note on the kitchen table. She'd not wanted to disturb him when he was on the phone to HMRC, and because she had had a little drink.

Now she felt nothing but humiliation. The whole episode at the jewellers had been unpleasant and was one she would prefer never to repeat, but knew there would be more humiliation coming up. One of their friends had walked in as she was getting a price. She wanted to run from the shop pretending it wasn't her as soon as she recognised who it was. But Gail Lomas with her poker straight blonde hair and minimalist make-up that had probably taken hours to apply wasn't going to let that happen. She'd tried hurrying the jeweller up, but Gail purposely came over and chatted, placing her handbag in front of Gemma on the jeweller's counter, all the time glancing down at the pile of goodies sat on the black velvet mat. Gifts from Oliver. There wasn't much: a few bracelets and necklaces; a couple of rings, one diamond studded; the most expensive, a beautiful diamond and pearl choker with a stunning Ceylon sapphire in the middle. He'd surprised her with it on a romantic weekend in Rome, sitting eating sandwiches on a bench in front of the Colosseum. She didn't want to sell it, but it was just stuff and eating was more important. It didn't make it any easier parting with it.

Prior to this she thought Gail was a good friend, but she was enjoying her squirming far too much. Gemma knew she would relish the gossip if she found out about her fall from grace. All this was breaking her slowly, and the hardest part was that it was just the beginning. The fallout from Peter was killing her and she was falling into the wine.

'Are you on your way back? I know how difficult today must have been for you. Come home, won't you?' Oliver knew her too well. He worried she'd stop off for a drink. It wasn't her intention. She was trying to stop. But it was really hard.

'In a bit,' she said.

After the jewellers she scouted around the estate agents, a small pokey cottage was nearly one thousand pounds a month to rent. How would they afford anything?

'What's wrong?' Oliver asked as if he could sense her dark feelings.

Why did he ask such a stupid question? What's wrong? *What's wrong!* Everything's fucking wrong! she wanted to say, then felt awful thinking so badly. Stop being such an idiot Gemma she scolded herself. 'I'll be home soon, don't worry. I'm just getting some petrol. I won't be long.' A pause. 'How did you get on with the HMRC?'

A big sigh. 'They're immovable. They're not interested in anything we say. Basically they've heard it all before.'

'Did they say that?'

'No. Not in so many words. He made me feel like I was making excuses and I was a shit for not paying my taxes and that we should have been on top of what our so called accountant was up to?'

'What? But that's what you pay an accountant for, isn't it? So you don't have those hassles.'

'I know. Look I don't want to discuss it any more. I'm going for a bit of a walk. Don't be long, sweetheart.'

They never tried to control one another; their relationship was fluid and nurturing. Neither of them needy or demanding, they welded together perfectly. They had a small set of friends they spent time with but on the whole, they spent most of their time together. Working together had also been smooth.

Oliver was considerate and always tender with a gentle caress here and there. Neither of them shied of demonstrating their love for one another in public. Of course, they were subtle about it, in a classy romantic way.

Clutching the steering wheel, she squeezed until her knuckles turned white only releasing when it hurt too much. How dare they suggest they were lying.

She swept into the petrol station and drove to the first free pump she came to. She switched off the engine, stepped out of the car, slammed the door and kicked a bottle cap on the floor. She pulled the petrol pump off the cradle and filled up. Unaware of the man at the next pump watching her, she muttered to herself about what happened to innocent until proven guilty? Bollocks, that's what. Seemed to her that with unpaid taxes you were fast tracked to the gallows. Go straight to jail. Pay up or else.

Filled up, she shoved the pump back on its cradle imagining it was Peter's head. Ooh, what she would do to that man if she got her hands on him.

The black Range Rover Overfinch at the other pump drank its fuel. The numbers on the pump's display raced round. The driver lounged against the car waiting for the pump to click off. He pulled his sunglasses down his nose as she walked past towards the shop to pay. Something at the back of her mind niggled her about him, but she couldn't quite put her finger on it. This part of Cheshire was flooded with celebrities, more likely he was one of them. She didn't glance back but walked with her head up into the shop.

For a long time, she'd relied on her ability to read people, their expressions, their emotions and what they kept hidden from view. She was pretty good at it too. But since meeting Oliver she'd let her defences down thinking there wasn't any need any more to feel scared. If she'd kept it up, perhaps she might have been able to read the man at the petrol pump loud and clear.

She might have.

She stepped into the shop and unable to help herself turned back to look at him. He was casually but expensively dressed. Designer tan leather shoes, jeans, bottle green V-neck Armani pullover with white T-shirt underneath. A heavy stainless-steel wristwatch with a large face, probably a Rolex, and aviator sunglasses. A little designer stubble. Blond hair spiked at the top and which curled up at the nape and stupid long sideburns, a popular trend right now. It wasn't a look she liked.

She wore a red fitted dress with black heels. Her mass of blonde curly hair was loose and cascaded over her shoulders. Oliver always said it was her best feature. She'd left her coat in the car and now wished she'd put it on. The sun was out but there was a definite chill in the air. When he opened the door it sent a spine-chilling trickle down her back.

When he walked in he stood close behind her. She didn't turn around but was suddenly very aware of him. Uncomfortably so. Something about him bothered her. From his reflection in the window, she observed him. He probably had one of those faces everyone thought looked like someone they recognised.

While she waited in the queue to pay, she glimpsed him looking her up and down. Men always liked to look a woman over, even if they were married, they looked. Even if they had no interest in doing anything about it, they just liked looking, just in case. Someone walked by with a Costa coffee from the vending machine and the smell of coffee wafted past.

'A bit nippy today,' he said, leaning in close to her ear. Too close. She moved forward, away from him.

She glanced back at the window; he'd taken off his sunglasses and perched them on his head. His eyes were too close together; his nose was a little crooked and he looked better with his glasses on.

'Yes, it is. I should have put my coat on,' she said, shivering and only slightly turning as she replied. She didn't know why she'd said that.

His hand reached for a bar of chocolate on the shelf next to them. He had short fingers with tufts of hair on the knuckles. She thought he sounded a little pompous. Arrogant even.

20

'I'm off to the pub for a quick lunch if you fancy joining me,' he said, casually. 'They have log fires there,' he added as if they were acquainted and he knew she loved log fires.

She whipped her head around. 'Sorry, did you just invite me out for lunch?'

The door opened, letting in a cold blast of air.

'Yes, I did,' he said and smiled. 'You look exhausted and, if I could be presumptuous, a little unhappy. Just a thought. That's all.'

She felt a sudden chill, but the cold had nothing to do with her sudden drop in temperature.

After a little deliberation with herself, she decided to answer him. 'I don't think so, thanks for asking.' Like she would go to lunch with some random guy from the petrol station!

Her reflection stared back at her in the window; how tired she looked, her hair had lost its sheen. Overall though she didn't look too bad, all things considered. He was right though. She looked miserable.

She'd cancelled her membership at the health club a few weeks ago; she now waxed, plucked and coloured her hair at home. She'd enjoyed the pampering she'd had there. She wasn't one of those women who paid for a membership and hardly used it; she took full advantage of all the perks they offered.

'Relax,' he said, whispering in her ear, so close she felt his hot breath on her skin and the smell of stale coffee. 'I want to help you. I know what trouble you're in and I'd like to help.'

Shocked by what he said, she moved away, not wanting to talk to him. There was one more person in front of her before she could pay and leave. It couldn't happen quickly enough. She certainly didn't want to discuss her problems in public with a stranger. And besides, just what the hell did he mean that he knew about her trouble?

'I'm sorry?' she said, unable to help herself.

He whispered, 'I read about your troubles and thought I might be of help.'

She felt sick and thought she would be, right there and then in the queue to pay for petrol, in front of everyone. Who was he? White faced, her lips closed tight like a clam, she said nothing.

'Join me at The Dog, and I will explain everything to you.' He grinned.

Sensing someone looking, she turned to find the cashier waiting for her. She paid and left without saying another word.

Chapter Three

JAKE

Jake watched Gemma leave the petrol station shop without a backwards glance. She was good, he gave her that. Not a single twitch showed on her face to suggest how she felt or if he'd got to her. He wondered what she was thinking and bet against himself if she would turn up at the pub. He tossed a coin in the air while he waited for the cashier to ring up his transaction. Tails she would, heads she wouldn't.

'Sixty-five pounds, please,' the cashier said.

Jake pulled out his credit card and pushed it into the slot of the card reader. Tails. He smiled. He punched in his pin number, took his card and the receipt and left.

Jake had watched Gemma for some time. He'd photographed her, followed her and kept notes on her comings and goings. He was in the Audi garage yesterday when she sold them her car back and then picked up the second-hand Mini at the BMW garage farther down the street.

Turning his attention to his car, he climbed in, turned the engine on and drove to The Dog a couple of miles away. She'd be late. He figured about fifteen to twenty minutes, that would give her time to think over what he'd said and try to deduce if he was genuine or a threat. Either way, Gemma would turn up. She couldn't not do. If for nothing else to find out what he knew and who he was.

Jake stepped inside the pub, scanned the room and the alcove with the roaring fire. She'd be on edge trying to work him out and why he wanted to help her.

As soon as she arrived, there'd be no going back for

either of them. He took an old photograph from his pocket and studied it. Three faces and she was the middle one.

He'd recognised her instantly the first time he saw her. She hadn't had the same experience, though. Strangely that surprised him; he hadn't changed that much. She'd clearly wiped him from her memory banks. Forgotten him. Discarded him like an old pair of shoes.

Her life was in danger and she didn't know it. He felt a thrill just knowing that simple thing. It would keep him amused while they talked and she struggled to understand why he wanted to help her. He wouldn't tell her who he was at first, no... he wanted to withhold that bit of information for as long as possible.

Jake Challinor wasn't like other people. He was better. He had a life of luxury and excess. People had respected him until Gemma changed that. His father had told him from an early age that he was special and would one day take over the family business. Everything worked towards that day. The schools, the introductions, the networking. Every cog was well oiled for him to slide neatly into his rightful place as head of the family business and the family. His father had told him there was nobody like him and nobody else was capable of running the business.

He ordered himself half a lager and a large glass of white wine. Sauvignon blanc, New Zealand. Her favourite. Although she was trying to quit her drinking, he knew today, she'd have to have one. He knew everything about her, and was about to pull her strings and make his puppet dance.

To take his mind off his impending excitement, he opened Facebook and read the comments to his post about Gemma's collapsing life and business. He smiled as he read about the imminent repossession of her home, the likelihood of bankruptcy and homelessness and the deliberate theft of monies owed to the Crown. His profile of Janice Littlewood, whom Gemma had friended without researching, allowed him to post and circulate to all her friends.

He looked at the three guys sat on bar stools next to him, thick in conversation and unaware of him. They'd seen him come in, registered him in their minds and promptly dismissed him. If they were asked to pick him out of a line up they wouldn't be able to. Most people don't recall most of what they see, ninety per cent of people think they remember clearly, but it wasn't true.

One of the three guys was extremely overweight but was happily tucking into a burger, the meat juices dribbling down his chin. His ruddy cheeks glowed in the warmth of the pub; he was probably a local farmer half way to a heart attack. His hands were calloused and his fingernails had dirt seeped into the edges from years of outdoor work. He scrubbed up in corduroy brown trousers, checked shirt and gilet. Jake would remember these guys if asked to pick them out. He was different to most people. He didn't forget. Anything.

Chapter Four

GEMMA

The Dog was a lovely picturesque country pub in a tiny Cheshire village with a white painted frontage. In the summer, the flower boxes were usually bursting with colour. Inside there was a wealth of period character to the place. She wasn't going to come, but she was curious about what he had to say and where he'd read about her problems.

Gemma walked in wrapped in her black woollen coat, her blonde hair a golden contrast against the muted shades of the decoration. Standing just beyond the door, she rubbed her cold hands together looking around. A few drinkers held up the bar. Three burly men sat together on bar stools, they turned to look, then turned back to their pints, more interested in their drinks than her.

Only about half the tables in the place were taken, but then it was still very early into lunchtime. The man she was meeting stood leaning back against the bar next to one of the burly men devouring a burger. He turned, saw her and gave her a smile, then beckoned her to join him.

She smiled back as she walked over, the corners of her lips twitching nervously, conscious everyone watched her walk the twenty steps or so. The man who said he knew of her troubles had ordered her a large glass of white wine. Troubles. What was she, Northern Ireland? Then she remembered what Oliver said about her drinking. This was an exception and a perfectly good reason to have a drink, she reasoned.

She followed him into the back snug where a fire blazed in the hearth, very aware that heads were turning in their direction. Was she all over Facebook? She didn't really do Facebook, she had it, but she never went on it. She had five hundred friends on there, and she knew five of them, who the hell were those people who *liked* her? What was Facebook about anyway? Who cared what they had for breakfast or who they were dating? People did it because others did it, like sheep they followed the masses, but it wasn't for her. It didn't stop her wondering if her problems had gone *viral*, that was the *in* word these days, according to her much younger ex-employees. Everything went viral, which could be a good thing if you were marketing something but crap if you were in her shoes.

Two leather armchairs stood either side of the fire. The pub, decorated in a deep blue, had a welcoming feel, with checked rugs scattered about adding to its charm. She liked the decoration.

They each chose a chair. Gemma kept her coat on for the time being, but unbuttoned it. She slid into her seat taking a sip of her wine. She took another sip and then almost half the glass.

'Perhaps I should introduce myself. I'm Jake.' He smiled and it softened his face and reached his eyes.

She watched him discard his navy seasonal jacket over the back of the chair then slump into it, resting an ankle on one knee. She was sitting in a pub with a stranger who said he knew she was in trouble. She had only just met him and nobody knew where she was. Reality began sinking in. Something nagged at her, an unshakable feeling she wasn't sure she understood. Dread? Deceit? Uncertainty? Or simple stupidity? This behaviour of hers was unprecedented.

She nervously brushed a stray hair behind her ear before answering. 'I'm Gemma. But you already know that, don't you?'

Time seemed to slow down. She locked eyes with him

and he looked right through her as though he was seeing something else, someone else. It left her feeling uneasy. And yet his body language was casual. There was no threat from there.

She fidgeted in her seat making the decision to leave but first she had to find out what he knew.

'Are you OK?' he asked as her chest rose and fell trying to get air into her lungs. She was afraid. What was it about him that made her feel uneasy? He looked so ordinary and whilst his face wasn't angelic, he looked normal. Whatever normal looked like. Which was a stupid way to describe him but she couldn't quite reach the adjectives to suit him. So why wasn't she getting up and leaving?

She nodded.

He had a casual air about him. Nothing that should really make her feel uncomfortable. She'd seen his type before; rich people with money appeared to glide through life, unlike the rest of the population who bumped along jerkily.

He narrowed his eyes, as grey as a wolf's coat, and watched her intently. She glanced around, shifting uncomfortably. Someone she knew might see her and report back to Oliver. A voice inside her head was telling her to get up and go. Go. Go. Go. And yet she continued to stay seated. What was wrong with her?

The hum of the other patrons sat close by rose and fell with the odd dash of laughter. She pretended to concentrate on her glass but was only too aware of him. The logs crackled and spat in the hearth.

'Well, I suppose you're speculating on why I asked you to join me.' He shifted in his chair uncrossing and re-crossing his legs, a waft of burning wood sat in the air.

She nodded. 'In a way. You mentioned you knew something about me. What is it you think you know?'

Another distant memory flashed in her mind. It vanished before she could grab on to it. 'Have we met before? I'm not sure, but there's something a little familiar about you, I can't put my finger on it,' she said. 'Do I know you?'

He cocked his head to the left and gave her a tight-lipped smile.

If anybody had asked her before all this mess started in her life if she would meet up with a complete stranger in a pub, she would have said there was more chance of her walking naked through the streets of Knutsford. But that was before she became desperate and about to be homeless. She was behaving recklessly. Desperation did that to a person. She could handle it; she could handle him; she wasn't a child. Whatever he was up to, she was ready for him. Besides, they were in a pub full of people. She was overthinking as usual. Regardless of what her mind thought, her body thought differently. Her legs trembled and if she had to get up right now and leave, she didn't think she'd make it.

When she lived at home, before *he* started on her, she often felt the spiders running up her back. That's what she called the tingle of dread. It began with the looks, unnerving her and sending messages only she understood. She broached the subject with her mother who dismissed it as the musing of a teenage girl. He played the long game until she began doubting herself. Then one day he began the second stage.

She took another drink. She kept her eyes fixed on him, desperate to retain a grip on her rationale. This was not the same. And if it was, she was in control this time. A million scurrying spiders sprinted up her back. Was he going to hurt her in some way? Was that his plan? Her thoughts started to fork, taking her to places that were best kept locked away.

'Well, you know. The world is a small place, isn't it? You see, Gemma, I know you're in trouble, well your business is in trouble, am I right?' He picked up his lager and drank it, slowly, watching her over the rim of the glass. His eyes still fixed on her. Locking her gaze.

An awkwardness bathed the moment. Then she said, 'Maybe. What's it got to do with you if I am?' Maybe she should leave now. How many of her Facebook friends were weirdos? Maybe he was one of them. Maybe he'd seen it all over Facebook and recognised her at the petrol station and now... what was she thinking coming here like this? She'd been so careful over the years never to put herself in dangerous situations. Christ, Oliver would blow a major fuse if he knew she was here. She'd never tell him, of course. How could she? She'd never tell anyone, this was madness. Her legs still trembled. Suddenly all she wanted to do was get out and get home to Oliver.

Jake rubbed his hand over his stubble and took another drink of his lager, his unrelenting stare not shifting. 'What if I told you I could help you? What would you think?'

She was certainly curious about what he knew. That was undeniable. Who wouldn't be in her position? But could he really help them? And why would he want to? That was the bigger question. Everyone had an angle and she wondered what his was. They had nothing to offer him in exchange for his help. And the company wasn't worth much if he wanted to buy it. Every fibre told her to just get up and leave. The problem was, she wanted to know how he'd found out and how he thought he could help. If there was a way out of her situation, she had to hear it out.

When she first moved to Cheshire, she paid attention to her sixth sense at all times. Whenever something felt wrong or the spiders appeared, she extricated herself from the situation. She relied on those feelings to define dangerous situations and it paid off. Later, meeting Oliver, she lost touch with her sixth sense because he looked out for her.

They were as one being, as close to another person as you could get. She liked that he looked out for her. Dangerous situations became things of the past because he was there to watch out for her. Today was the first time that sense rang loud inside her whole being. And yet, she chose to ignore it.

When she did speak, her words came out jerky like a phone conversation with bad reception and it annoyed her because it betrayed her nerves. 'I'm... not sure I'm grasping what you're trying to say... Jake. Perhaps you could be... a little clearer in what you think you know... and how you think you can... help me?' She stiffened her back. The last thing she wanted was to show him how desperate she was and how bad the situation really was. She took a sip to lubricate her parched mouth. Her glass was nearly empty. She could do with another.

'Well, you see when I saw you at the petrol station, I recognised you. You do know you're all over Facebook. Well, the thing is, when I saw you, I got the impression you were very stressed.'

Gemma frowned almost choking on the sip of wine. My God! So, it was out there. All over Facebook. It didn't surprise her, now all their friends would know. The thing was, nobody knew the depths of their problems, so everything out there was circumstantial. Gossip. Gossip to make anything appear worse, she cringed inwardly at what might have been posted.

'What do you mean? I didn't look stressed at all. I don't know how you can say such a thing.' He was testing her; she knew it deep down. Why, though? She prided herself on keeping a brave face; no way had he seen that on her face, she was sure of it. She learnt long ago to mask her emotions. She knew she was good at that. She knew his game, his angle, his way of approaching her so as not to scare her off. What if this offer of help was a lie? Perhaps he'd seen her on Facebook and the suggestion of help was to try and pick her up for something completely different. Idiot. How could she be so gullible?

'I know what stress looks like,' he continued without taking his eyes off her. 'I've been through it myself and I saw in on your face and can see it in you now.'

She didn't think so, but she was going to humour him for the moment. She wanted to see what game he was playing, then she was leaving. He was just another computer freak.

'Are you pitying me? Please don't pity me.' She'd wind him up and see how far he would go with this farce. 'Did you see me on Facebook and think to stalk me and hound me?' Now she had him. Liar. Those spiders were right to appear. She put her glass down and pulled the edges of her coat together, she was leaving.

'I don't pity you, Gemma. Not at all. I'm merely being pleasant. I know kindness is hard to find in our society these days; there being so many selfish people about. But I genuinely want to help you. I know how bizarre this sounds.' He flapped his hand in the air to express a puff of air.

Her first reaction was to laugh and leave. What stopped her was his tone. That was the second mistake she made. He seemed genuinely sincere. His voice was soft and he delivered his words, slowly and with apparent kindness. There was no sarcasm or malice. What if she was being hasty in judging him? She was already here, maybe she should hear him out. If he was full of bull, all she had to do was leave. Then again, if he was genuine, they might have a chance of saving themselves. She might have a chance of saving Oliver. Her rationale was twisted, she knew it. Her damned curiosity nailed her to the chair, for now at least.

'How can you help?' she asked and caught a woman on the next table looking at him. Jake was unusual looking, not odd, but because he wasn't perfect, like say, Brad Pitt, there was a quality radiating from him that was attractive. She saw that now, just as the woman at the other table saw it and was drawn to it.

'The only way I can, with money.'

She could hardly believe it. Too easy. 'Why? Why would you?'

He shrugged. 'I want to; I can't bear to see anyone go through what I went through. Besides, I made a promise to myself at the time of my own stress. If I came through it I would, if I could, help others. It's as simple as that.'

That wasn't normal, who went around helping people just because? Every red flag shot up until all she saw was a field of red flags. He kept his eyes on her. No narrowing of them. No turning up of the lips. No movement at all from his body. No tells at all. And then he smiled as if he'd read her thoughts and knew she felt uneasy. The smile softened his face. The spiders came back. Why wasn't she able to leave? That was the third mistake she made.

'Well, let's start by introducing ourselves properly, you must think me a poor gentleman. I imagine you're having innumerable thoughts, most of which won't be pleasant. And I understand that, however, there's no need. I assure you there is nothing to be afraid of. So, as I said, I'm Jake. But because I want to keep myself anonymous, for obvious reasons, I just want you to know me as Jake. Pleased to meet you, Gemma.' He leaned forward and held out his hand.

She shook his hand. 'What do you mean for obvious reasons? Why? That's not a proper introduction.'

'This has happened before. You're not the first. People, and I don't include you in this because I don't know you yet, but people have a hard time knowing when enough is enough.' His tone sounded even and measured.

She didn't detect a threat from him in any way. And

still her instinct was to get up and leave. But she didn't. She wasn't that scared person any more, she could handle herself. She'd buried that person along with the past. She'd grown lazy and dropped her guard.

'Why do you keep doing it? I mean, helping people, if it makes you feel bad?'

He shrugged. 'I only help those who deserve it.' A smile appeared at the corners of his mouth.

She furrowed her brows. 'How do you know which ones do?'

'I just do. So, will you let me help you?'

'Maybe.'

'Can I ask what happened to your business?'

She hesitated. She didn't want to explain anything to him. 'Let's just say, an undesirable within the business decided to dip his hand in the till and disappear.'

He nodded. 'I appreciate it might be painful to disclose some delicate issues. For now, that's fine. But you know, I might be able to help you with this undesirable you mentioned.'

She picked up her glass and drank the last of the wine, placed the empty wine goblet back on the table and sat back in the armchair. Years of abuse at the hands of her stepfather culminating in his death had driven a rod of steel through her. Jake wasn't about to scare her. She wouldn't allow him to. Peter had squirmed through her defences purely because she let her guard down. If, as she suspected, he was thinking of threatening her in any way, he'd picked the wrong girl. If he knew so much about her, he wouldn't be asking so many questions.

She was about to speak when he cut her off.

'Before you say anything else, let me tell you that after I saw you at the petrol station, I made a few phone calls. I've established the full extent of what your company owes and that your home is at risk. You must be terrified at the prospect of being left homeless. I know all about Peter your accountant and the private bank account he set up for you and emptied.'

She looked at him incredulously as if he'd stolen her purse from her handbag but she couldn't be sure he was the thief. He smoothed a non-existent crease from his trousers. It was a tell. She noticed.

He shot her a look. It was quick and gone before she had time to think about it. He noticed she'd noticed his tell. It didn't bother her. She knew he was hiding something and she wasn't going to take this any further. Good that he knew she had noticed his slip.

Over the years, between leaving home and meeting Oliver, she spent a lot of time studying people and their behaviours, their mannerisms and their tells. Most hadn't a clue they had any, most did. Some subtle, some not so subtle. Most would think the little insignificant gestures they made meant nothing, but if you knew what you were looking for, they meant plenty. As controlled as Jake was, he slipped up and he knew it. She wasn't afraid, he was just some guy who wanted something from her and right now, she didn't know what that something was. Maybe he even thought of finding Peter, recovering the money and taking a percentage. Who knew? They certainly didn't have anything else for him. He seemed harmless enough. Just weird. Probably a bored rich guy throwing his money about because he could. Who knew why he did what he did, she'd probably never know.

So, she was all over the internet. He had been able to find out about her and her business. She'd been a big fan of the internet, now she was discovering what an invasive parasite it really was.

'I want to help you, Gemma. Why don't you let me help you?'

'What do you want in return for your help?'

He reclined back in his chair, smiled and said, 'You know you are the first person to ask me that?'

'Surely nobody would take your help without asking what you want in return.'

His face cracked into a wide grin. 'Well be prepared to be surprised, as I said, you are the first. I knew you would ask and here is where it might get a little tricky.'

Unbidden, a memory came of her stepfather pulling back the duvet and waking her up. Standing naked in front of her. His cold unemotional voice telling her to get on her knees otherwise he would lock her in the house and she would miss her exams the following day. She'd been eighteen. She couldn't miss them. They both knew her goal. To get her qualifications and leave, without them she would have no chance of ever getting a decent job and getting out of that environment. Even then she knew she wanted better. That life wasn't hers. She was better than that. She deserved better and was going to go out and grab it. She was going to make something of herself and would do anything to get it. Surprisingly, after she walked out and into university, her life became an easy road to travel. The fear of ending up back there. No money. No self-respect. It was what drove her. She felt she'd come full circle now. They were about to lose everything. They might have to declare themselves bankrupt. The idea of being homeless wasn't an option for her.

'Define tricky.'

'Before we go any further, let me tell you what I can do for you. Oliver never needs to know. This will be between us.'

'Why can't I tell Oliver?' If it was to stay a secret from Oliver, then there was no way she was going to accept his proposal. Not that she thought she would anyway.

'I'm not sure he will comprehend the situation.'

Now he had her. What was he thinking she would do for his help? She hadn't expected this sort of secrecy. 'What won't he comprehend? What do you want from me that I can't tell Oliver?'

He shrugged and smiled with flawless bleached-white teeth. 'Nothing untoward. You do want my help, don't you, Gemma?'

It was her turn to shrug. 'Maybe, but it depends on what you want from me.'

His face dropped. 'Let me paint you a picture so you have it clear in your head. I will pay you a lot of money that will enable you to rent a house for Oliver and yourself. I will keep paying you and you will be able to maintain a lifestyle you are used to. I will help with the liquidation of your business and keep many of the nasty parts of this out of social media and the press. You can carry on living with Oliver just as you do. None of it will go public. Your reputation around here won't be tarnished. You won't need to go bankrupt and once it's all over, you can carry on as normal. Nothing there will change. You can get yourself a better car. Life will be easy for you both. I will track down your undesirable and bring him to task. Now, how does that sound? Better than the scenario facing you at home right now, surely.'

She had to admit when he put it that way it did overwhelm her. He was offering to eradicate all the stress and financial worry. She couldn't deny it was tempting. And he knew that. There had to be a catch. There was always a catch. He probably wanted sex. It usually boiled down to that.

For a moment everything became unusually still.

'Or, maybe, you'd prefer to walk out of here and carry on the good fight with HMRC and trying to track down your undesirable on your own.'

'It's what you want from me I am concerned about.' This had now focused her mind on what her real problems were and how insurmountable they were. Together, she and Oliver didn't have a chance of coming out of this unscathed. It wasn't like she didn't want the help. She did. He was drawing her in. She knew it and leaving the catch right till the last when he hoped she was hooked and the offer too enticing to turn down.

'You mustn't fear me, Gemma. Do I look as if I'm a psychopath?'

She wished he hadn't said that. Why did he have to say that?

'I haven't had much room to trust people in my life and everything has a price.'

He raised an eyebrow and smiled dimly. 'Come on, Gemma, this is a great offer, how can you refuse? Let me tell you what I want in return. But bear in mind that it might shock you, but I want you to keep an open mind.'

She waited a few seconds before she said, 'My life is complicated enough.'

'It's the best offer you're gonna get.'

'I think I'm going to pass.'

He folded his arms and leant back. 'Anyone else would kill for this opportunity to save themselves. You know it's the truth. What's the problem?'

'I think your price is going to be too high.'

He looked at her sideways and nodded. 'I get you might think that. But you haven't heard what I want in return. All your money worries will be over, just like that.' He clicked his fingers.

'It's not the money. I can't lie to Oliver and won't, besides nobody offers a free pass like this without a catch. No, thanks. There's nothing more you can do to me really, is there. As you said it's all over Facebook and the internet.

What you will want from me will cost me more than money. I'm not for sale.'

Jake put his smile away for a moment and comprehension crossed his face. 'Right then, well in that case you needn't worry. I'm not trying to buy you. What I said before is the truth. If you want to tell Oliver, you can, the choice will be yours. This really is a free ride, Gemma.'

'Really? You expect me to believe you? I'm not that gullible.'

'It is what it is.' He shrugged his shoulders.

'Tell me what you want from me then.'

'All I want from you is your friendship.'

'My friendship? How so?'

'That's it. I want your friendship. I would like to take you out to dinner and maybe away somewhere.'

'This will be a sexual friendship you mean?'

He smiled broadly. 'No. Just a platonic friendship.'

'Platonic? Really? So, you will pay me to be your companion?'

'Yes. It's important you understand. What I want from you at this moment is for you to be my companion when I ask. That is what I meant by Oliver not getting the picture. I'd like it to stay between us. I imagine you understand why. Others won't believe you just as you didn't. So, I suggest you don't tell anyone. It's best if it stays just between you and me.'

She nodded. No, Oliver certainly wouldn't be OK with it. She wasn't sure she was.

'You can tell him you have a job working for me as my virtual PA. So I pay handsomely, what of it? Tell him I'm an eccentric. He won't question it once he realises the money will be saving his situation.'

And so, like Alice, she jumped down the rabbit hole.

Chapter Five

GEMMA

Salford – 2000

She remembered arriving back home from sixth form to a quiet house all those years ago. She made herself a cup of tea and a sandwich.

He'd been there not that long ago. She saw the frying pan still warm from frying eggs thrown in the sink. There was a note pinned by the back door from her mother with a list of groceries for him to pick up. He'd taken the money and she knew the groceries would never arrive. Why did she ask him when she knew he never spent the money on anyone other than himself?

Her mother – a sad creature, worthy of no affection – was short with black hair, always greasy and un-styled. Gemma had got her height and blonde hair from her father, whoever he was. Some bloke she'd met at a club one night, her mother said. *Fucked me in the back of his Datsun that's where you came from. Promised to take me away from this place, he said, then fucked off when he found I was pregnant. Fucked my life up you did.*

She didn't hear him come back. Her bedroom door opened. He stood there with his belt wrapped around his hand. She took off her Walkman headphones; she was listening to, 'Eye Of The Tiger', she could hear the lyrics, which suddenly rang true for her. He wasn't going to touch her again. Not ever. Now her A levels were finished and her university place secure, she didn't need to worry about having somewhere to live. She had plans. Places to go.

She got up and walked out of her room. He grabbed her and tried to push her back in, but she resisted. She felt so strong with the knowledge he couldn't hurt her any more. She pushed him away down the small narrow landing with the wallpaper peeling from the damp wall and made for the stairs. He grabbed her hair and they fought. For a spindly man who was always drunk, she was always shocked how strong he was. She never really fought back; her plan was always to get school finished and with her qualifications leave and have a better life. Mattie told her she could stay with her until they started university. Mattie knew what went on in that house and tried to help, but Gemma stopped her, afraid that her stepfather would touch her too if he got the chance. They went to university together and it broke her heart they lost touch when they all left to go their separate ways.

That was her plan. But it didn't work out like that. He overpowered her and she remembered the pain when he beat her with his belt for fighting back. The buckle slashed across her breast tearing the skin through her school blouse. He threw her down the stairs and broke her leg. She was trapped for six weeks at his mercy until she finally left, exacting her revenge on them both.

Chapter Six

JAKE

Jake stood in his shower with the scalding water cascading over his skin. He drew on the glass of the shower door the picture of a hanged man only this time he added a triangular skirt. He stood under the water until his skin could no longer bear it.

Standing in his bedroom in front of the full-length mirror he dried himself off looking himself over. His skin was sore to the touch but he had to feel the pain. He was an idiot to show her that tell. He had to be careful and to resist next time, otherwise she'd know when he was nervous or lying to her.

He had photos of her that he kept in a box. Over the past year she hadn't changed much. One photo drew his attention more than the rest. He picked it up. She looked happy. Content. And so in love with Oliver. He'd cut Oliver off the photo.

Jake was a perfectionist; his plan was well constructed. It had been easier than he had anticipated; he really thought she'd have put up more of an argument as to why she didn't need his help. Maybe she wasn't as smart as he gave her credit for. That had been too easy.

Deception was something Jake did well; he always had right from being a young lad. Coming from a prominent family who were in the media a lot of the time, he was easily recognisable. Sometimes he liked the accolade. Sometimes he wanted anonymity. He learnt quickly people didn't have the same respect for him when he wasn't Jake Challinor, heir to the Challinor Electronics Organisation, which held some of the most lucrative government contracts around.

He enjoyed the attention Jake Challinor received. He liked how people fell at his feet and were all too willing to do anything for him. Mostly, he knew, it was to get a foot in the door with the company. It made him laugh how he could get them to do anything he requested, even if it was something they would normally deem to be beneath them. It gave him a huge rush knowing he held that power within him. It never ceased to amaze him how low somebody would go for money.

His mother had told him he was privileged. That he should embrace his position in life and never feel guilty for all that he had. She married his father at an early age and moved up in the world. Before that, she'd never held a job for more than a few months, she'd moved around the country in search of what she called her destiny.

She found it one night when she was twenty-one, stood beside her broken down car on a country lane. It was the day before she was due to fly out to America to start a new life. Fergus Challinor pulled up to help and she grabbed her opportunity with both hands.

Jake had a large circle of friends. Some were closer than others, he didn't regard them as best friends, he didn't have any of those.

His mother tried to clip his wings after the papers started to report the disappearance of young women in the area. Women who had been associated with Jake at some point. That was when she started sending him abroad for work purposes. He stayed away for three months at a time. Enough time for the heat to disappear.

Women threw themselves at him the moment they knew how rich he was. If he liked the girl, he usually broke the ice by being amiable and drawing them in, slowly. If he didn't like them, the ice never broke and he left them feeling used.

There were more like those than the ones that he allowed to get close to him.

The first to break his heart and hurt him was Lindsey Stott. He was seeing her for a number of months when he found out she was cheating on him.

He pulled out a cashmere black jumper from his dressing room and put it on, followed by a pair of black jeans and black Chelsea boots. He ran his fingers through his blond hair and splashed on some cologne.

He pulled the small digital recorder from the jacket pocket he'd worn with Gemma and played back their conversation. He noted the tremor in her voice when she tried to appear calm. She was good at masking her true emotions. She was like him, a chameleon, but not as good. He remembered the tell he disclosed and frowned.

When the conversation got to the part where he disclosed his terms, he noted a slight relaxing in her voice. The muscles at the back of the throat loosened allowing her voice to become smoother.

Satisfied, he went down to the kitchen and requested a light lunch. Chicken sandwich on brown malt with sliced tomatoes and cucumber on the side. A medium glass of white wine and a selection of fruit. He always lost his appetite on the build up to his next victim. The excitement tied his stomach in knots. But he knew he had to eat so he forced himself to have small meals often. His housekeeper acknowledged him but rarely spoke to him. Just as he liked it.

Chapter Seven

GEMMA

When she arrived back at the house and pulled into the drive, she saw Oliver through the hall window pacing the floor. He spotted her and walked out to meet her.

How would Oliver react when she told him they were all over Facebook? The whole village would probably know by now.

She was tempted by Jake's offer more than she cared to admit.

'Where have you been?' He opened the door for her. 'I've been ringing and ringing. Didn't you get my messages?'

'What? Oh, yes. I just wasn't in the mood to talk, sorry, it's been a horrid afternoon.' She lowered her face. She didn't want to discuss her day. She averted her eyes, but he turned her face towards him.

'Are you OK?' he asked.

She'd have to fake her sincerity. She could do that; after all it was to protect Oliver. She knew how to put on a show if she had to. But Oliver, for all his bravado that they would come out of this intact in the end, he would not understand if she told him the truth.

'Gemma, has something happened? Tell me. You know we don't keep secrets between us. Maybe I can help. Come on, babe, what's troubling you?' She sighed. 'Apart from the obvious,' he added.

She moved away a little. It felt natural for her to tell him everything. So natural in fact that the words almost leapt from her tongue. He looked so sincere, she almost believed it was safe to tell him. The words wanted to flow from her lips and she knew she wanted his blessing that she'd made the right decision. Telling the truth isn't always the right thing to do.

'Look, I bumped into Gail Lomas at the jewellers, that's all. It was humiliating. I didn't know what to say. She could see I was uncomfortable and stood there like a statue, listening to the jeweller giving me a price and handing over the money. And you know what, we're all over Facebook.'

In the kitchen plates were stacked up by the dishwasher and piles of papers littered the kitchen table. She sighed at the overspill from the study. The laptop was on. A shorthand pad lay open next to it.

'Who cares about Facebook? Gemma, it was bound to get out at some point. Maybe it's for the best. This way the sooner it's out there the sooner people will move on to something else. We can't stop that happening.'

But that wasn't good enough for her. All their friends and neighbours knowing their personal business was mortifying. She knew what he was doing. Same old Oliver, brazen it out, stand proud, don't show we're bothered by any of it. When in fact they were dying of shame inside.

He had followed her into the kitchen. 'Stop worrying about what everyone thinks.' He drew her close and wrapped her in his arms. 'Besides, you were gone four hours, where did you go after the jewellers? You look wrecked.'

For a second, she said nothing. Then she gave him a peck on the cheek. He knew she was hiding something. She had to try harder. 'Look, Oliver, I can't help it. I hate people knowing our business. I appreciate what you're saying and you're probably right. I just need time to adjust to the fact that the world knows what we're going through. Anyway, to change the subject, why are you working in the kitchen?' No, she couldn't tell him. He looked worried. Concerned for her and guilt cut right through her.

He grunted. 'I was trying to track Peter down; the office became too oppressive.'

She hung up her coat on the last remaining peg behind the stained-glass kitchen door.

'And?' she asked. Not getting her hopes up. Peter wasn't going to leave a trail for them or anyone to find him.

'Nothing. Oddly there's very little about him on the web. I thought that was strange in itself, don't you? He has no social media and no company website.'

She gazed around the room taking in all the soft furnishings, the grey painted furniture she had spent hours on. The large Welsh dresser they sourced from an antique shop in Chesterfield and fallen in love with, only to realise they couldn't get it home. They hired a van and went back the next day for it.

She opened her mouth to speak, then turned away and began loading the dishwasher instead. What the hell was she thinking of accepting Jake's offer? Lying to Oliver? She needed a drink. She needed to organise her thoughts before anything slipped out.

'I've already done those checks, Oliver. He was smart. He knew what he was doing and obviously planned it for a long while. I think we need to go deeper to find anything on him. He really set us up, you know. Right from the moment he became your friend, I'm sure of it.' He looked hurt and she had to turn away. *Oh, Oliver I'm doing this for us. You'd never believe me if I told you.*

Oliver didn't say a word.

'Don't take it personally,' she said and carried on before he interrupted her. 'I bet we're not the only ones he's done this to. I'll start looking into it in more depth and maybe, just maybe, we'll get a break and if we're lucky, something will come to light.'

Oliver closed the laptop and switched on the kettle. She

was pretty sure Peter had known what he was doing from the moment he first met Oliver. She was certain now that he had targeted Oliver from the outset. Very smart. She chose that moment to tell him her other news. 'I'm going to find a job. I can't sit around and not do anything. We need money coming in. I'm going to start looking tomorrow.'

Oliver stopped making coffee. 'Gemma, hang on, I know we're in a tight spot, but do you think you're ready?' He poured milk into both cups.

She walked down the oak floored hallway away from the kitchen. Unhappy with herself for having to lie. He had enough to worry about.

'I need to find a job, and soon, so we can rent somewhere. You do know once our credit rating is affected, we won't be able to do anything.'

He followed her. 'Gem, I know we're going to lose everything, but it's only stuff. We have each other. *I* can't bear to lose *us*. That's what's important here. Are we OK? Together we can see this through. Don't you agree?'

She did agree, but the stuff did matter. It mattered to her a lot. 'Yes, we're OK. But we still need money coming in and, well, I think I should get the job. You have to sort all this paperwork out, speak to HMRC, wrap up the company, sort out all the masses of paperwork still left to do. The last thing you need is the worry of looking for work. Let me deal with that side of things. This is what I can do to help.'

She sensed his reluctance. He was proud and old-fashioned. Too much so to be happy for her to go out to work while he stayed home. Even though he would be working. 'Don't look at me like that, Oliver. It's the best solution while you're dealing with all this.' She waved a hand around the kitchen. 'And I'm not coping well or helping, am I?'

She couldn't believe how easily she was lying to him. And

she hated it. She should tell him the truth right now. And if he didn't believe her, then sod Jake and his money. Only when she looked at him... breaking apart so slowly in front of her... she couldn't do it. Oliver had helped her get her life in order all those years ago. Didn't she owe him? Anyway, it was only friendship and only for a little while. She hoped. She could handle Jake.

'Look, Gem, I appreciate what you're trying to do, I really do. I just don't want you rushing into this and making yourself ill. You've been so stressed lately. Take a little time before you do anything. We'll be OK for a while. Don't rush into anything, please.' He followed her out of the kitchen.

She thought about what he said, but she'd already made the decision. She stared up the stairs contemplating her next words. Someone had to do something to drag them out of this dreadful situation. She put her foot on the first step. 'Answer me one thing and please be truthful, Oliver.'

He smiled. 'Of course, fire away.' He looked confused and a little worried.

'Will you answer me truthfully? You promise?'

'What do you mean? Don't be silly, you know I will.'

She stroked his face and nestled her head on his shoulder. 'I love you, Oliver. Do you promise to love me forever, no matter what?'

He rested his chin on her head. 'Why did you ask that?'

His maroon polo shirt smelt of his aftershave. Musky and earthy, the same one he'd worn since she'd known him. It was him. It was Oliver. Her pulse quickened as she thought of her lies. She fought for control before she spoke trying to keep her logical voice in her head from forcing her to blurt it out. Why did she not tell him? She was doing nothing wrong. It was a business deal of sorts. Wasn't it? Wasn't it! It was, she told herself. So then... why did she find it impossible to tell Oliver?

Because she needed to protect him from his own imagination. What could Jake even do to hurt her? She would never get herself in a situation alone with him where he might harm her. She wasn't that stupid. Or was she? She'd already accepted his deal. From a stranger. What was that rhyme they taught kids in school? Stranger danger. She was not a child and she had fallen at the first hurdle. Over and over she argued with herself.

Stop it! She'd made the decision. It was the right one. Once they were out from under the miasma of debt she would tell him. He would understand then why she had done it and why she had kept it from him.

'I don't know. I guess I feel vulnerable. I trust you implicitly, Oliver and I would forgive you anything. You know that, right?'

'I do, but I'm not planning on doing anything illegal if that's what you're worried about. I know I mentioned us running away. I might have considered that but that avenue is closed to us. Stop worrying so much, Gem, please.'

He held her tight, stroking her hair, nuzzling her neck. 'I want us to grow old together.' She looked up into his kind, strong face. Those blue eyes like the bluebells they had in the garden crinkled at the edges when he smiled reaching deep into her soul. 'There is nothing I wouldn't forgive you for.'

They kissed long and luxuriously. Their passion hot and desperate. He held her face in his hands as he kissed her and she melted at the touch of his flesh on hers. She needed him right now. Needed to know how much he wanted her. Desired her. She brought her hands around and undid his trousers. He pulled off her jumper. He groaned deeply and moved them both back closer to the front door onto the patterned rug. They kicked off their shoes, her hair spread out around her like a fan. He cupped her breasts out of the bra, coaxing her nipples with his tongue as he kissed them and ran kisses along her collarbone. Slowly stroking her skin, making her brown eyes melt like pools of warm chocolate. She ran her hands over his back, then up to his head where she grasped his hair and held onto him. She sensed his urgency to make love to her. He entered her slowly, taking his time. When he was finally deep inside her, her body clasping him close, he moved up and down. She wrapped her legs around his hips and felt a quiver run through his body. Together they moved in a lovers' rhythm and she surrendered herself to the feelings he invoked.

Chapter Eight

A few days later she received a text message from Jake.

Le Manoir aux Quat'Saisons, Oxfordshire. Thursday evening.

She texted back. *That's miles away.*

I'll see you there at 8 p.m.

Le Manoir aux Quat'Saisons was the biggest and oldest house in the quiet village of Great Milton. The classical English honey coloured manor house enjoyed an idyllic view across the beautifully kept lawns, orchards and flower borders.

Gemma arrived early evening, full of apprehension and an uneasiness she could not shift. The more she thought about it the more she thought she was walking into a nightmare. A very smart middle-aged man approached her taking her bag and escorting her to reception. He was pleasant enough, he gave her a small nod and courteous smile. The knot in her stomach had begun tightening little by little on the journey down, forcing her to stop at virtually every motorway service station to go to the loo. She also desperately needed some Gaviscon. She popped a pill to try to ease the acid reflux burning a trail up her oesophagus. What if she changed her mind? What if she just got back in her car and went home? Would Jake let it go? Or would he be so angry he'd tell Oliver?

'Mr Jake is expecting you,' the receptionist said.

Gemma nodded and said nothing; she didn't know what to say because she wanted to become invisible and travel to her room wrapped in an invisibility cloak. Christ, the shame of what they probably thought. She thought about Oliver and what he'd think if Jake turned up at home and told him she was willing to meet him in a hotel hundreds of miles away, for companionship.

Oliver would be destroyed. Especially if Jake told him he was paying her. That would sound so wrong and he'd immediately get the wrong idea. But Jake wouldn't turn up at home. He'd said to her that Oliver needn't know. He even suggested not to tell him because he wouldn't understand.

They asked if she would like to look around the boutique hotel or take a stroll around the gardens before going to her room. They then informed her that Jake would not be arriving until later; she chose to go straight to her room. Did they know why she was here? Maybe they thought she was here for more than companionship. Perhaps he did this a lot and they were used to it so turned a blind eye. Colour rose in her face and she took off her coat, suddenly feeling hot and uncomfortable. Her phone pinged. A message from Jake flashed up.

I will see you soon. Enjoy yourself and order anything you like.

She was hungry, but she doubted she'd be able to stomach much.

There were three ground-floor suites located in the Garden Courtyard. One of them was to be hers for the night. The Opium room was fourteen hundred pounds a night. She had looked up the prices. She walked into a hyperbolic oriental extravaganza. Her bag had arrived before her. She walked in, uneasily, the wood panelling on the walls set off the scarlet fabrics. The king-size bed was lower than normal and a Ming stone carving stood in the room. She kept away, well away.

She stepped out into the private walled garden with an oriental style water feature. The day was dry with a crisp chill in the air. The place was idyllic. It had a charm all its own. The sort of place she would love to bring Oliver. Of course, it was never going to happen. She could never return here.

The thought of *companionship* snagged in her brain each time she revisited it. She pulled at the plausibility of this companionship like a thread that might unravel and show something ugly. She felt it deep in her bones. And yet, despite all her sensible warnings to herself about how this could turn out, she never pulled on that thread hard enough because she needed the money so badly. She didn't want to see the plausibility fall apart. Christ, what was she even doing here? Was she out of her mind coming away with a stranger and nobody knowing where she was? A whirring sound overhead caught her attention. She looked up to see a helicopter landing, this was a world so removed from hers.

The bathroom was all marble with a separate bath and shower. She ran a bath, pouring in some interesting looking liquids after making sure the bedroom door was locked. Unpacked, she poured herself a glass of Madeira from the decanter so invitingly placed nearby. She drank one, then poured another to settle her nerves. She caught sight of herself in the mirror; she looked shockingly older than she had a month ago. Tentatively, she touched the lines at the edges of her eyes then looked away, placing the vase of flowers directly in front of the mirror.

There was a knock on the door. She opened it to find a waiter carrying a silver tray. Relief flooded her to find it wasn't Jake.

'Mr Jake ordered this for you, madam.'

'Oh!' Curious, she moved to one side to let him into the room. He placed the tray on the coffee table, bowed and left. With trepidation she lifted the domed lid to find a glass dish full of caviar standing on a bed of crushed ice.

Her hand shot to her chest. She helped herself, scooping the little silver spoon into the black velvet bubbles and savouring the nectar. Oh God, she adored caviar, and this must be Beluga. The best. Her eyes rolled as she let the glorious black bubbles roam over her tongue, the salty ocean taste making her taste buds zing.

She docked her phone and switched on a smooth jazz radio station before taking the caviar and another glass of Madeira to the bath with her. Although she felt guilty eating the delicacy and enjoying the luxury of the bath, she thought she might as well take advantage while she was here.

As she soaked in the scented oils, ate the caviar and drank her Madeira, she let the warm highly scented water caress her body. She blocked everything from her mind. The gentle sound of a saxophone filled the room. Leaning her head back on a fluffy towel she forced herself to relax. She imagined being there with Oliver, in a time when they had no worries and their lives were good. No, they'd been better than good, they'd been bloody brilliant. She let the tears run free into the bath like a river running to join the ocean. They flowed freely and a part of her knew the tears were for the loss of her and Oliver. How would they ever be the same people after this monstrous lie?

She had informed Oliver this morning that she was going to stay at an inexpensive spa hotel with her girlfriend, Karen, who was paying.

She hadn't seen Karen in years and why think of her now? How strange that the one name to shoot to the tip of her tongue was Karen when she was thinking of someone to act as conspirator. It must be eighteen years since she'd seen Karen. A shiver ran through her at the memory and she dropped her caviar-laden cracker in the bath.

Oliver was surprised, asking a lot of questions. *Who was she? Why hadn't he met her? Where did she live?* That kind of thing. Thinking on her feet she fluttered around the answers keeping them simple and with no detail colouring them. Thankfully, he was so engrossed with the emails that he did not press her further.

Climbing out of the bath and wrapping herself up in a huge fluffy towel she perched on the side. That's when she noticed the curtains drawn in the bedroom and the warm flicker of candlelight.

Jake reclined on the bed watching her. His head was propped up by the deep pillows, his arms folded behind his head as he gazed at her. He wore chinos in a deep brown colour like the bark of a tree and a lighter shade in a V-neck sweater, with a white T-shirt. Gemma stood motionless, her daydreaming coming to an abrupt halt. How had he entered her room? And what was with all the candles! There was an air of creepiness about the room and his collected manner unnerved her.

'Come here, Gemma.' His voice was low and steady.

Reluctantly, she lifted herself off the bath and shuffled towards the bedroom, very aware she was wrapped in just a towel.

She kept away from the bed and leaned against the door frame. There were so many candles in the room, she must have been away with the fairies not to have sensed or heard him enter the bedroom. A mass of goosebumps covered her skin. How long had he been watching her? The candles spooked her, was he going to perform some sort of ritual with her? Nobody would know. She glanced around for bags that might contain some gruesome tools, but saw nothing. The creepiness of the situation grew rapidly as if it had been dosed with Miracle Grow. Why did her mind have to go there?

'Did you do all this?' She motioned to the candles with her hand, her other hand holding her towel, tight.

'Yes, while you were dozing.'

'How did you get in?' She looked around again for a bag or something to tell her he was planning on staying in the same room. Something she hadn't even thought of. It hadn't even crossed her mind. Why? What was wrong with her, had she had a brain malfunction? How had she not thought he might want to stay in the same room? 'Why did you let yourself in? I mean without knocking?'

He shrugged. 'Did I need to? I'm paying for the room; I simply got a key card. I was enjoying watching you bathe. You looked exquisite in the bath. Your blonde hair clipped up and falling in gentle stands around your face. I know this has been a big decision for you. You can leave if you decide you don't want to do this.'

She shivered. She'd pulled the lock across the door so he couldn't have come in that way. Then she saw the adjoining door. His compliments were a little too personal. Too intimate. Too far over the line. She saw him look at the scar above her breast and quickly placed her hand over it. Leave. He knew she wouldn't do that.

'You don't mind me complimenting you, do you? The last thing I want is to make you feel uncomfortable. Can I ask you where you got your scar? It looks as though it would have been very painful.'

'No, I don't want to talk about it.'

Silence filled the room as he watched her. 'Don't worry; I've got the room next door. Does that put your mind at rest? I can see you're wondering where my bags are.'

She smiled, nervously. 'Yes.'

His eyes burned a hole in her with their intensity.

To escape, she turned and walked towards the French windows. She fumbled for something to say. The leaves whipped up by the wind look like mini cyclones.

She opened the French windows and a faint smell of a fire burning close by drifted in. She bent down to pick up a deep blood-red leaf and caught sight of her wedding ring on her finger. How is it possible you make all those promises when you get married and truly mean them? And how bizarre that life then pushes you into situations where you must break some of them to keep others. Her husband was at home dealing with all the crap surrounding their lives. She was here, a companion to a stranger who was willing to pay her handsomely for her company. One vow versus another and never the twain shall meet.

'I want you to relax, Gemma. I want you to enjoy this experience. Sometimes experiences are what make us who we are, don't you think?'

'Maybe,' she said. 'Are you married?' she asked, suddenly curious.

'Nine years,' he said, proudly. 'I don't wear a ring; I don't like jewellery on men except a watch.' He flashed his hands up so she could see. He wore the same big stainless steel Rolex. 'Do you think life is full of opportunities, Gemma? Each big event is either a negative or a positive, don't you think? Sometimes a positive for one is a negative for the other, don't you agree?'

'I don't understand what you mean, but I guess so.'

'Let me try to explain. Take you, for example. The big event happening to you right now with your business that is a negative. But a positive to me. Meeting me has turned your event into a positive for you and a negative for Oliver. Do you see what I mean? A bit like the movie *Sliding Doors*, did you ever see it? Great film and very true if you think about your situation.'

She had seen the film. 'You mean the choices we make can alter our paths dramatically.'

'Yes, but the choices others make for us, sometimes without our permission, can also have profound changes to our lives,' he said. Flinging his legs off the bed, he sat for a moment. 'Forgive me, I'm rambling. I do that sometimes.'

Gemma hesitated. 'What are you doing?'

'I'm going for a shower. I'll be back in thirty minutes.

Will you be ready for dinner? I'm assuming you've brought a change of clothes, if you haven't I can have something brought up for you.'

She clung to the towel around her body. 'I have something. Thirty minutes will be plenty. I'll be ready.'

'Excellent. What a wonderful evening we're going to have.' He smiled warmly. As he walked out of the door he turned and said, 'I want you to feel comfortable, this is not the time for you to be afraid.'

Chapter Nine

They entered the thickly carpeted, softly lit dining room at quarter to eight. Her black velvet body hugging dress fitted in well with the formal diners and she was glad she had chosen to bring this one. Her hair flowed free like a lion's mane as requested by Jake. He even told her how to apply her make-up, right down to the colour of her lipstick, which she felt was weird but she did it.

Earlier Jake had knocked on her door and entered holding a black leather box. 'Something for you to wear tonight.' He put the pearl necklace around her neck and closed the clasp. 'There, perfect. I want you to wear them. They're yours.'

'Oh, no, I couldn't possibly keep them.'

'I'll be hurt if you don't accept them.'

She fingered the pearls, embarrassed and unsure what to say, so she smiled meekly.

'I want you to have them, let's not discuss it further.' He offered her his arm and escorted her to the restaurant.

The maître d' sat them at their table. Diners glanced at them. They made a handsome couple.

'How are you keeping, sir?' asked the maître d', his heavy-lidded eyes careful not to look at her.

'I'm very well, thank you. You know, Gemma, this is my favourite hotel. I never tire of coming here. We'll have a bottle of the Rosé Brut, Pol Roger Champagne to begin with,' he said to the maître d'.

Jake wore a bespoke dark navy suit, impeccably cut. As she watched him talking with the maître d', she questioned what was behind his kind façade. Although he wasn't saying as much, she had a feeling deep inside this was all for her benefit. And there it was again, that thread she wanted to pull. Why? Why would he do this?

Oliver loomed large in her heart and mind. She didn't want to be here or lie to him. She wanted to leave. Oh God, it was horrendous to be dependent on another person for her livelihood. This would have to be a one-off. The ten grand she'd been promised by Jake for this evening would have to see them through until she found real work. She wasn't going to be his PA.

He watched her and she felt as if he read her mind. 'You look very beautiful tonight,' Jake said as the maître d' poured the champagne.

His compliment again made her uncomfortable. 'Thank you,' she replied, nervously. It wasn't the compliment as such, more the way it was wrapped up with hidden connotations. She was glad he couldn't see her heart beating faster.

The maître d' kept his eyes fixed on the glass of champagne he was pouring. Soft classical music filtered through the hushed restaurant.

'Are you thinking of Oliver right now?' He smiled kindly at her.

She blushed. 'I am.' What was it about him that irked her so much suddenly? There was a definite undercurrent between them now.

'Would he be devastated if he were to find out about us?' He paused before continuing. 'I do hope our little arrangement doesn't spoil your relationship.' He drank slowly from his glass.

His question frightened her. 'He would, yes. But you know this, Jake. I don't think any husband would understand what is going on here,' she said, calmer than she felt. She looked down at the tablecloth not wanting to make eye contact.

He nodded thoughtfully and his brow furrowed, then he opened his hands in a gesture of friendship. 'I'm sorry, I didn't mean to unsettle you. Silly of me to ask, so we had better do our best not to let it happen, hadn't we.' He smiled, pulled the champagne bottle from the ice bucket and topped up their glasses. 'Cheers, Gemma, to opportunities and paths crossed.' He looked at her curiously across the table, waiting for her to join him in the toast.

An uneasiness settled in. 'Cheers,' she said.

'Have you considered what I said about working for me? You know as an explanation for where the money comes from?' he asked. 'Oliver is bound to want to have a plausible reason for you having this money.'

'I've mentioned to Oliver I'm thinking of getting a job.' In her mind this was a one-off, but clearly Jake was thinking differently. She wished she had stated at the beginning this would be a one-time thing instead of allowing him to think it had any future. She should have been stronger. But her worry had been, and still was, that he would back out and she'd lose the money.

'Good, good. Only if you're comfortable, of course. I don't want to *force* you into doing anything you don't want to. Don't you think forcing someone to do something they don't want is wicked?'

'Yes, absolutely.'

He was silent for a moment as if considering what to say next. Then he drew air in through his nose and said, 'You look uncomfortable, are you sure you're OK?' When she nodded, he continued talking. 'You could say you are working as my virtual secretary as I suggested before.'

'I could.'

'Splendid idea, I think,' he said. 'I'm glad you already seem to be thinking in that frame of mind.'

'What frame of mind?'

'Deceit.'

'Deceit?' she asked. 'I'm not quite sure I understand what you mean.'

'I don't mean anything at all by it. I'm merely making an observation. You are now lying to your husband, easily, which is a good thing because he wouldn't understand our little arrangement.'

'No, no, he wouldn't.'

'How will you explain your whereabouts the next time we meet up?'

She dropped her gaze so he wouldn't see how shocked she was by his suggestion.

'Good, good, I can see you're working on that too,' he said, his face lit up and he raised his glass. 'To deceit.' He laughed.

She raised her glass, reluctantly, this was not a toast she wanted to drink to.

They both had the à la carte menu. Gemma chose the Cornish crab, coconut lemongrass sorbet and passion fruit oyster leaf, to start. Followed by the fillet of brill, scallop, cucumber, wasabi and garden vegetables. It smelt and looked delicious, but her heart wasn't in it and she played with her food more than she ate. Jake started with terrine of garden beetroot, horseradish sorbet, buckler sorrel. Followed by the pan-fried Cornish sea bass, langoustine, garden carrots, fennel, anise. He ate greedily leaving nothing on his plate. He didn't mention her lack of appetite, which she thought was odd. But she was pleased she didn't have to account for it. For dessert, he ordered for them both the seasonal pear Almondine, caramel croustillant, ginger sauce and sorbet. Gemma's stayed on the plate; the knot in her stomach twisting and making her feel sick more than hungry. The drink went down well though. She had plenty.

To lighten the conversation a little she changed the

subject and asked, 'Whereabouts in Cheshire do you live, Jake?'

'Oh, not far from where we met.' His tone was playful.

'And what sort of companies do you own?' she asked, trying to hide her oncoming nerves of the evening ending and what he might want from her, despite his promises this was a friendship.

He leaned back in his chair regarding her. 'I have a few different companies, but primarily I'm a property developer. I used to be CEO of a big company a long time ago,' he said, stonily.

She nodded her head. He seemed edgy talking about himself. 'Oh, why did you leave?'

He laughed. 'I didn't leave, Gemma. As we discussed earlier on that was my big event. Somebody came into my life and turned it into a negative one.' His eyes darkened although his smile continued.

Gemma fidgeted in her chair. She didn't like the way he looked at her but it was there only briefly. 'Right, and what was their positive?'

He shrugged. 'Who knows, they came into my life fleetingly and left destroying what I had in their wake. I doubt they ever knew what they had done, people rarely do.'

'Right.' She nodded, feeling very uncomfortable as though his words were cryptic in some way. 'So, don't you feel vengeful. I would?'

'Would you, Gemma? Would you want to destroy somebody if they had destroyed you?'

'Yes, I bloody would, I would destroy the undesirable who tore my life apart, for sure, and my ste— well, someone from my past.'

He nodded and grinned in approval. 'Good, good, I'm so comforted you recognise the full meaning of wrath. Would you stop at anything?'

She shook her head vehemently. 'No, I bloody wouldn't. If I could, I would destroy him. I don't forgive.'

The next hours passed very slowly. She was exhausted from smiling and pretending to enjoy herself. She longed for her bed and her home and couldn't wait for tomorrow to come and for all this to be over. And now Peter The Bastard had been mentioned she fumed with rage. She was here because of him.

They left the restaurant and had coffee in the lounge. She didn't want coffee but Jake insisted and she was so close now to getting the money she really had no choice but to go along with it.

Idly, she twisted her wedding ring around her finger.

'Gemma, you seem nervous.'

'Oh, well... to be honest, Jake, I am. What will you want now the meal has finished?'

'Want? I told you... aah, you think I want sex. You needn't worry, at the moment, Gemma, all I want from you is what I have previously told you, companionship. You can trust me to do the right thing, after all, we seem to think along the same lines.'

She gave a vague smile. 'OK, good.' Her wedding ring slipped off her finger as she played with it. She stared at the gold band as it rolled under the table, she quickly picked it up and slid it back on.

In the morning, she was up early and dressed when he called and asked if they might have breakfast in her room. She had little choice but to acquiesce. A breakfast tray arrived and was set up on the table holding the Madeira. She grabbed one of the small croissants before he arrived.

'Sit down, Gemma, you need to eat before you leave.'

They sat facing one another.

'I think we've found we're quite compatible, don't you?'

Gemma paused for a second as she ate another pastry. 'I don't know if we are or if we're not.' She noticed he was taking his time over his breakfast. She looked at the time on her phone; it was five after eight. She wanted to get on her way.

If judgement day existed, she would imagine this would pretty much be the scene she'd be faced with.

She wanted her money and to go. Now, about that. How to ask him for it.

'Err, Jake?'

He smiled while he buttered his toast. She watched him choose the jam from the selection and spread it on his golden toast. He wore jeans and a blue shirt, which hung loose.

'About the money,' she said. Her foot tapped out an even beat on the carpet.

'Yes?' He took a bite. 'Would you like it now?' His whole demeanour made her feel small.

Her face suffused with a deep-red flush. 'Please. I need to get off.'

He curled his lip into a smile. 'I have an idea, Gemma.'

'What sort of idea?' Her phone vibrated on the table. The display showed. Oliver. She spoke to him last night, briefly, and told him she was leaving early in the morning. He probably wanted to know if she'd set off. She started to feel guilty all over again. Not that the guilt had ever gone. Just subsided. It weighed heavy on her. Pressing on her chest. Crushing her. As long as she was here with Jake that weight increased. She hoped and prayed she'd put all this behind her and Oliver would be none the wiser.

'How about I drive back with you and you can introduce me as your new employer to Oliver. It would make you having a job more believable, don't you think?'

Her phone vibrated again. It cut through the silence in

the wake of his words. Oliver. Two missed calls. He'd start worrying soon and that was the last thing she needed. He'd phone the spa if she didn't get back to him.

She got up from the table. 'What are you talking about, Jake? You can't come home with me. That's ridiculous.'

There was a pause as they both looked at each other.

'Oh! Why not? I thought it would help you,' he said.

'How the hell do you think that will help me?'

'Like I said, you can introduce me as your new boss.'

'But I haven't even told Oliver I have applied for a job yet!'

He shrugged. 'Just a thought. Never mind. We'll do it another time.'

She put her coffee cup down. 'Jake…' She was bringing trouble to her front door. She knew it. She felt it. This was going to lead to trouble. Oliver didn't deserve any of this. What had she done?

Jake held up his hand. 'It's OK, not to worry, I was trying to help. Don't look so worried, Gemma, you know worry ages a woman a lot. Trust me. You can trust me to do the right thing.'

Jake finished chewing his toast. He wiped his hands on the napkin, folded it and placed it on the table beside his plate. He drank his orange juice, wiped his mouth with the same napkin and replaced it back on the table. Then he got up and went over to his jacket and pulled out a fat white envelope. It was full of fifty-pound notes bursting out of the top.

'Sorry about the envelope, the other size was huge, I thought you'd prefer it like this.'

She shoved the envelope inside her already full handbag then turned to face him.

'Goodbye, Jake. Thank you and thanks…' She pointed at the envelope sticking out of her handbag.

He leaned over and kissed her on the cheek. 'A pleasure, Gemma. I'll be in touch for our next extravaganza.'

She left the room. What he said about meeting Oliver disturbed her.

It was time to go back to her real world.

She was never having anything to do with Jake, again.

Chapter Ten

JAKE

He always managed to get a discreet parking spot near to Gemma's house. Always in a rented car. Occasionally in one of his. Always a different car. She was smart and he supposed she'd soon notice the same car parked on the road. What made it worse was the lack of cars on their road. This way, it would always look as though the cars were visiting.

He took the helicopter back to Cheshire, then drove the rental to her house and now waited for her to arrive. She had visitors. Perhaps that was why Oliver had kept ringing her.

He sat in the driver's seat drinking hot tea from a flask. He had a pretty good view into their house. The office boasted a large window and with his binoculars he was able to see right in. Oliver looked distressed with his visitor. From this vantage point he'd seen a lot of their relationship over the weeks and months. They were close. Too close for his liking. The kitchen was on the opposite side to the office, again with an overly large window, easy to look in. Here he saw Gemma sneaking her drink away from Oliver's prying eyes most days.

More importantly here he saw them together, intimately. They liked doing it wherever the fancy took them. The kitchen seemed their favourite spot.

He managed to get a listening device into the house by entering through the back door. They never locked the back door when they were home. Remarkably he managed to take their key, get a new one cut and return it within the hour without them knowing anything about it. That had been two weeks ago.

Jake listened to all their conversations now so he was one step ahead at all times.

He watched and listened to their squabbling and fights, then their making up afterwards. Their lack of money was putting a great strain on their relationship. HMRC were putting them under intense pressure. Oliver wanted to go by the book. Gemma wanted to run away. The money she thought they had stashed in the Swiss bank account had failed to secure that possibility.

Jake was jubilant.

There was no guarantee that Gemma would continue to see him. If that was the case, he'd have to go to plan B. As he thought about this, he saw Gemma arriving home.

Oliver met her at the front door almost bolting out. He spoke to her urgently and took hold of her hand trying to keep her from the front door. Oliver showed signs of resistance when she tried to walk in the door. Another man came out. Jake watched and switched on the digital recorder pushing the earphones tight into his ears.

Jake was irritated he didn't know who this other man was and why Oliver was behaving erratically. It could only work in Jake's favour if the other man brought more bad news.

Although Jake was careful to always be fully informed, life sometimes threw a curveball. He picked up the burner phone he used and dialled a number. The voice on the other end answered, her tone curt. She sounded stressed.

'I can't talk long. What do you want now?'

'I need you to find out if you're paying my friends a visit and, if so, what exactly is involved.' He listened in case she showed signs of resistance or reluctance to finding out the information. He held the power in this relationship. They both knew it. Fear could control anyone. He used it to his advantage every time. He always had. He needed to put the pressure on them with HMRC and the only way he could do that was to infiltrate one of their workers. Miss Thompson fitted the mould perfectly.

There was a slight delay before she spoke, that for Jake suggested reluctance.

'Do I need to pay your mother a visit?' asked Jake.

'No, you don't. When do you need the information?' said the voice.

'ASAP, of course. I'll be waiting.'

'I'll text you what I can find out.'

'Make sure it's everything. Don't think to leave anything out,' said Jake and cut the call.

Jake mostly liked to work by himself when stalking someone, but on occasion he needed help with information to infiltrate their lives plausibly. He liked the chase. He liked to drop the breadcrumbs and be the rescuer. Sometimes he hit obstacles along the way. He usually dealt with them in a direct manner. Miss Thompson could access databases and gather information inaccessible to most people. She had proven herself very useful over the years. Each time he promised her it would be her last. They both knew now after so many years together that he never kept his promises.

He derived great pleasure from destroying his well-chosen victims. And, of course, from utilising Miss Thompson's help. They weren't friends. Jake was subtle in his dealings with her. The threat. The tiny but significant clues he left for her to let her know he was a very real threat.

'Mrs Palmer? We've been waiting for you. I'd like a few words with you, if you don't mind. Just a few things to clarify, if possible,' said the voice through the mic. Jake closed the window, switched off his phone just after reading the text from Miss Thompson and pulled out his binoculars. Gemma sat facing the window. The man sat with his back to it. Jake smiled watching her cling to her handbag stuffed with cash. Oliver gripped her shoulder, the whites of his knuckles showed. Gemma was clearly too desperate to conceal what was in her bag to notice the pain in her shoulder.

Chapter Eleven

GEMMA

The gravel crunched under her wheels as she parked up. An unfamiliar blue car stood in their drive. The radio died when she cut the engine. In silence, she sat staring at the front door unable to think of an excuse for where the money had come from.

She would just tell Oliver to trust her and not ask questions. He wouldn't buy it. But, for now, it would have to do.

As she walked towards the front door her racing pulse belied her steady pace.

Oliver rushed out to meet her, the rigid lines and colour of his face expressing something was wrong. She stood on the threshold one leg in and one leg out, her knees buckled, did he know? Oh... my... God, but how? How had he found out? Her eyes glazed over, what did she say? How could she talk herself out of it? Oliver caught her before she hit the floor. A sharp sting travelled through her leg where her knee caught the edge of the door frame.

'There's someone here to see us, Gem.' He tried stopping her going in. She pushed forward, she didn't want to do this here, outside. He attempted to remove her coat and handbag in the hallway, but she held onto both, tightly.

'Me? Who's come to see me? I'm not expecting anyone.' Was it Jake? Had he beat her home and decided to introduce himself to Oliver? She looked over at the car in the drive, no, that wasn't a car he would drive.

'I saw you arrive and wanted to get to you before *he* knew you were home. Let me take your bag and coat, darling. I need to speak to you before you see him.'

'No, I'll hang onto them.' Sluggish with dread and before he could answer, a tall man appeared in the hallway. His grey suit was badly cut and the collar creased, jacket pockets misshapen from too much detritus. Who was he?

'Mrs Palmer? We've been waiting for you. I'd like a few words with you, if you don't mind. Just a few things to clarify, if possible.' His voice was devoid of any emotion as though he was reading from a tired script that he'd read a thousand times and really didn't care any more. What was happening?

Oliver let go of her arm. Gemma obediently followed The Suit into the office. He had taken over most of the desk and asked her to sit down. She sat with her coat on and her handbag on her knee, her hands tightly clenched around the strap. Her eyes staring like a rabbit caught in headlights.

'Where are the computers?' she asked.

'We've taken those, Mrs Palmer, we will need them for information,' the hollow voice said, firmly.

'What about all the other stuff? What about the files and…?'

'Gem, just answer the questions as he asks them,' Oliver said, standing beside her. He rested his hand on her shoulder and squeezed. The familiarity of his touch kept her panic stable even though his grip was painful.

'Let me introduce myself, Mrs Palmer. I'm Mr R Fox an investigator for HM Revenue and Customs. I am here to investigate and collect evidence of alleged fraud by yourself and your husband, for non-payment of VAT.'

Stay calm, act normal, don't panic. Don't give any more information than what they ask for. Keep it simple, that's the key. Simple answers to the questions. Simple. Simple. Keep it simple. Don't think about what they might know. They probably don't know as much as they pretend to know. Keep it simple. Her left foot tapped on the floor; she pushed her left hand down, hard on her thigh to stop it.

She couldn't catch her breath; her lungs burning from the strain. Inwardly she was struggling, but she was reassured by the calmness she projected to the hollow-voiced man with the ugly suit. Why would anyone wear such a disfigured suit?

'Are you all right, Mrs Palmer?' The Grey Suit asked.

Was his question a deliberate way of trying to make her believe he cared? But she knew better than to fall for it. Her hands held her bag so tightly they were turning white from the lack of blood circulation. She tried portraying calm, composed and distant. Impenetrable. She straightened her back and lifted her chin. What did these people want with them now?

'Yes, thank you,' she said.

The Suit gave a curious look at her handbag and continued. 'We have written to you on countless occasions. We've requested for you to get in touch with us but have had no reply from yourselves. As you are aware, as a partnership, the liability of debts for the company fall on the partners.'

Gemma nodded. Her pulse throbbed in her neck. Their letter probably came in one of those brown envelopes she didn't open any more.

'Our records show you haven't paid any VAT. Your husband informs me you weren't aware this hadn't been paid.'

'Yes.'

'Yes, Mrs Palmer? Yes, you haven't paid your VAT, or you weren't aware it hadn't been paid?'

'Yes, that one. The second bit. We didn't know.'

'You are aware ignorance is not an excuse, Mrs Palmer.'

'It's not ignorance. Our accountant did the books. We left it to him.'

'May I suggest a lack of judgement there, Mrs Palmer?'

'Not really. We paid him to take the pressure off us.'

'We have the name of a Peter Hayes.'

'Yes, that's him.'

'Mrs Palmer there is no record of a Peter Hayes at the address you gave us as an accredited accountant. You look very hot, Mrs Palmer. Would you like to take off your coat?'

'No. No, I'm fine.' She watched his face. It never changed expression. All his features were pointy, his nose and chin and his cheekbones sharp enough to cut you. He wore a wedding ring. What did his wife look like? Would she too be thin and pointy or contrasting, short and round? She always thought it was odd when couples so opposite got together.

What if she didn't answer his questions? Refused to speak to him. He would have to leave her house. But, of course, she knew only too well that was not an option for her. They'd probably arrest her. Lock her up. Handcuff her. Throw her in the Tower. After all, tax evasion was more punishable than murder, wasn't it?

'Gemma give me your handbag.' Oliver reached for her Tote. The white envelope visible inside, partially sticking out.

'No, Oliver, it's fine. I'll hang onto it.'

'Gem, please, you're red in the face. Take off your coat and put your bag down.'

Gemma gripped the bag tighter. 'No, Oliver. Leave it, please.'

'Christ, Gem, calm down. I'm only trying to help.' She sent him a sharp look.

The Suit cleared his throat. 'Can I ask you to describe your relationship with this Mr Peter Hayes, Mrs Palmer?'

'I didn't have a relationship with *Mr Hayes*. And you make it sound like he's not real. He's very real. He stole our money,' she said, looking down and seeing a tremor in her hands.

'Please try to stay calm, Mrs Palmer. Tell me how you know him, this Mr Hayes.'

This man was not a fidgeter of any description. He was motionless, the only moving part was his mouth. Even his eyes were still, watching her, staring at her as if forcibly trying to look inside her brain to see if she was lying.

She sucked in her breath, the colour in her face heightened. 'He was a friend of Oliver's. I only knew him from working for us.'

'And how did he steal your money, Mrs Palmer?'

'He took it from...' She looked at Oliver, who shrugged his shoulders. In her nervousness she nearly let it slip about the Swiss account.

'Took it from where, Mrs Palmer?'

'The bank account,' she said and looked at the window as if it was the first time she had ever seen it. Absentmindedly she noticed a car in the distance, but thought nothing of it, her mind too focused on the here and now to take it in.

'Which bank account, Mrs Palmer?'

Gemma looked back at him, he wrote everything down. Didn't Oliver say they knew about the other account? God, she couldn't remember now.

There was a momentary silence.

'Is there something wrong, Mrs Palmer?'

Idiot. Clearly there was a lot wrong. 'The one with the money in it.'

The Suit looked up. 'And which account exactly was that?'

How did his voice have no rise and fall in pitch? How did anyone know how he was feeling with a flat, boring voice and what if his wife was monotone too?

'I don't know the account numbers off by heart, do I?' She sounded petulant. She didn't care, his voice was grinding on her nerves. The Suit ignored the crabby response.

'Was it a British bank account, Mrs Palmer?'

'I guess so. I'm afraid I don't follow you.' She was so hot now, she thought she'd pass out any minute but she daren't move. Oliver noticed and tried again to take her bag. She clung onto it.

'You guess so? Did you know you had a bank account in Switzerland, Mrs Palmer?'

'No. I don't know about any bank account in Switzerland.'

'I hope for your sake you don't, Mrs Palmer.' His words didn't ring true, he sounded as though he hoped for his sake she was lying. 'I'm aware you may not know all of the details of these accounts, but we need to check everything out thoroughly.'

In one quick movement, Oliver ripped her bag from her hand placing it on the table right next to The Suit. She gasped. 'Just take off your coat, Gem, I'm really concerned you're going to pass out.'

She was suddenly enveloped in a wave of panic. She spread both hands flat on her legs in order to stay calm. Fear fitted itself around her body like a coffin.

One second, she was holding her bag, the next it was next to The Suit. A second later, Oliver helped her take off her coat and hung it on the open door. The white envelope stood a little proud of the handbag. The edge of it torn with the unmistakable colour of a fifty-pound note underneath. The only thing in focus was her bag. And the fact it was right next to an HM Revenue and Customs investigator.

'Mrs Palmer?'

'What?' she snapped, realising she wasn't doing so well at holding onto her composure any more.

'The bank account, Mrs Palmer.'

'What bank account?' She'd lost the thread of the conversation. He could turn his head and see what was in her handbag.

'Gem?' She didn't respond.

The Suit adjusted his position then moved her bag further along the table so he could rest his elbow. Her hands turned into fists on her knees and she let out a tiny yelp.

'Did you know you had a bank account in Switzerland, Mrs Palmer?'

Why had her brain seized up like a rusty wheel?

'Did we? I wouldn't know,' she said. Oliver's had squeezed her shoulder, again, pressing on the already bruised area. His fingers dug in, hard. What the hell was he trying to convey to her?

'Mrs Palmer, are you saying you had no idea this Mr Peter Hayes had moved your money into a numbered account in Switzerland?'

Her face darkened. Why was he on this line of questioning? She thought nobody knew about that account. Damn Peter, he told them it had been untraceable. 'Yes.'

'Mrs Palmer, can you be more open with your answers. Do you mean, yes, you did know? Or, yes, you didn't know?'

She raised her head. 'The second.'

The Suit stopped writing and drew in his breath, then slowly exhaled. 'Mrs Palmer. I am assuming you are aware by lying or withholding information from HM Revenue and Customs it is a criminal offence.'

She wasn't listening. All the signs were there. They'd have to go bankrupt to get out of this. For seven years they'd be unable to get credit of any sort. It would take something extraordinary to get them out of this mess. Jake had said he could make all this go away? Was it true? At what price though?

The VAT amount they owed had floored her. They'd never cover it. What little equity they had in their property portfolio wasn't enough.

She shook her head. It was more devastating than Oliver had led her to believe. Life was going to be immeasurably difficult. The ten thousand would help initially, but it wasn't going to last long.

Chapter Twelve

Sometime later sat in the office Oliver said, 'It looks like there's no way out of this, Gem. They've frozen all our accounts. Yesterday they informed me we will have to sell the houses, even though there's very little equity in them. They want what they can get.' He placed a china mug of hot coffee on the office table next to her.

She had sat in the office since The Suit left unable to move. Wondering if she'd ever be able to move again. It was as though her life had stopped. As if she had no control over what was happening. Others around her were now controlling her.

'Thanks, Oliver, just what I needed to hear,' she said, sarcastically, looking at the coffee. 'How did you make the coffee?'

'With the coffee machine.'

'The one in the corner that's been sat there for six months untouched? The one we couldn't get to work because all the instructions were in Italian?'

'That's the one. Yesterday, I decided if I couldn't work it out, I was going to smash it up. I even managed to froth the milk. Do you like it?' Oliver's idea of smashing something up would be throwing it in the bin or taking it to the tip.

She laughed. 'I do, it tastes lovely, thank you.'

She wanted to stop thinking about Jake. About what he'd said when she left. She didn't want to consider the possibility of seeing him again. But she couldn't help it. The draw was too powerful. What he offered was too desirable. She knew there was more to him than he'd revealed to her. And that might be a bad thing. But it might not be so bad. Nevertheless, the harder she told herself she was letting it go, the more intensely she was drawn to it. He could make all this go away.

Oliver was the love of her life. She'd known it the moment she met him. Such an intense feeling of wanting to be with him was like no other she'd ever experienced.

Always the sceptical one, always the one to look for the flaws in a person, it usually stopped her enjoying who that person was, faults and all. But not with Oliver. She loved him. She wanted to look after him. Never had she ached for someone as much as she did for Oliver.

Oliver didn't judge her, even when she drove him crazy with her strange ways. He laughed with her not at her. He paid her beautiful compliments, even when she was sick as a dog with the flu or some other ailment. He told her she was beautiful and that he loved her.

She clung to him as though he was her life raft on the stormy sea of life, always there to steady her, protect her, guide her and, above all, love her. He'd given her a home and security, and total unconditional love. And never raised a hand to her.

They met on her birthday ten years ago. She left the pub where she was celebrating with her friends. It was late and they were the last few to leave. Unbeknown to Gemma, Oliver tried all night to catch a moment with her. So, when she found she had a flat tyre, he was there at the rescue.

'Are you with the RAC or AA?' he asked.

'Neither, but I know how to change a flat. The problem is I can't get these damned wheel nuts loose.' She'd propped her car up on the jack. But the wheel nuts weren't budging.

He waited until she exhausted all her attempts and flopped against the car. 'You try then,' she suggested.

He gave it a shot, but his attempts were as futile as hers. 'Look, don't look so fed up, these things are tightened with an air gun, few people can release them. Besides, have you checked if you have a spare?'

She thought he was laughing at her, so she opened the boot and removed the floor revealing what should have been the home of the spare wheel. 'Oh my God, there isn't one. Where is it?'

'I think you'll find you have to squirt some gunk into the hole.' The gunk was for puncture repairs on run flat tyres.

He offered to follow her home because she didn't believe the stuff would hold and she was worried she would end up stuck on some country lane. Then the next day he came back to take her to the garage to get a replacement. It was that simple. They fell into each other's life as though it was meant. She loved his consideration and concern for her. And it was a relief to let go and let somebody else take some of the burdens life threw at her.

'Sit down, Oliver.'

Oliver sat in the chair The Suit had occupied. She leant over and grabbed her bag, took out the envelope and thrust it at him.

He looked at her questioningly.

'Open it.'

'What is it?'

'Just open it, Oliver.'

He looked at the envelope, felt it, turned it over in his hands.

'Just open the goddamned envelope, Oliver,' she yelled, irritated he couldn't see what it was. There was a fifty-pound note virtually poking out of one end.

When he opened the envelope, the fifties burst forth. 'Oh my God. Gem, what is it? Where did this come from?'

'We have it, Oliver, that's all you need to know. There's ten grand there. We can rent a small house and live off it while we sort out our next move.'

'Where did it come from?'

'It doesn't matter, does it? The point is we have it. And for God's sake don't let HMRC know anything about it.'

'Your bag! Oh my God. I put it right next to him! Christ.'

'Yes. You did. I thought I was going to go into shock. I can't believe you couldn't read my face. I was clearly telling you to leave my bag alone.'

'But you looked so hot! I thought you were just panicking. How was I supposed to know you had ten grand stashed in your bag? Where did you say you got this from?'

'I didn't. Well next time try to read my face.' They both started laughing. The strain of the day taking its toll. It was either laugh or cry. The tension seeped out of her and her walls, the walls holding her together... just collapsed. She pressed her eyes shut, but the salty tears ran down her face and dropped from her chin, soaking her jumper. Trembling, unable to stop them, the raw emotions and her pain were ready to burst open like a water-filled balloon dropped from a height.

With the money still in his hands, Oliver came over to her and cradled her head in his shoulder. He said, deflated, 'You know Peter Hayes is untraceable? They can't find him. I can't believe it. I don't even think he was a real accountant. It's incredible, he had other clients, how did he get away with it?'

She sniffed. 'A cunning liar, people don't ask questions, do they? If you advertise yourself as an accountant, people assume, don't they? I don't suppose you would have reason to doubt him, would you?'

'Thinking about it, you know we never went to his office. He always came here. He was so convincing,' he said

'You remember a while back, he mentioned to us that he had a good size client list? Do you recall any of the companies he was working for?' she asked.

'I can't off the top of my head, but I'm sure one or two will pop up. Wait, there was one he mentioned a lot, I think it was something like Butler or Cutler Homes in Carlisle. I do recall him talking about going up there quite a bit.'

Chapter Thirteen

February – Two Months Later

The thing about stress is that it doesn't come and go like grief. With grief it comes out of nowhere. Bang. And paralyses you on the spot. It doesn't care where you are, the car, the supermarket, the toilet or even getting on the bus to go home. It just comes and you burst into tears, your chest hurts and breathing becomes an issue. It embarrasses you because you have no control over it. Stress is different, it's with you all the time, 24/7. Like an ominous presence it lurks, skulking around your ankles waiting for you to dare to forget it for even a second. Then it trips you up, giving your heart a jolt of remembrance.

In the morning, Gemma arrived at the estate agents to sign up for a house rental. Closing the door behind her, she noticed a man lurking on the other side of the street. He wore a baseball cap, black hoodie, black jeans and his hands thrust in his pockets. She couldn't see his face. His baseball cap was pulled down low. He turned away as soon as she looked at him. She froze in the entrance staring at him. Glued to the spot. Concentrating on him. Sure it was Jake. She hadn't heard or seen him in two months.

The weather had changed in the last few days in to real winter. On the pavement there was a smattering of snow now turning into sludge and she could see the warm breath escaping her.

She couldn't be certain it was him, but her instincts now on high alert told her the chances were high that it was.

He turned and left, pulling the baseball cap further down. She took a lungful of air and closed the door, watching him disappear down the busy street. She hoped he'd moved on.

The estate agent's office was a small uninviting place, with four desks facing the entrance door, so all four heads looked up when she entered. No chance of a private conversation here, for sure. The dull colours of beige and sage green carpet and seat cushions added to the atmosphere of a care home. Everything screamed! Dull! Boring! Old granny did the makeover!

Chapter Fourteen

Arriving at the house some time later for a viewing, she found it to be a pleasant little cottage even on a cold February afternoon. Located down a single-track country lane outside Knutsford it was very appealing, away from people they knew.

The road to the cottage needed a lot of attention; you couldn't drive quickly but had to snake down the lane or prepare yourself for a hefty repair bill. It was the only affordable property she had found. It was old-fashioned and needed a bit of TLC, they told her.

She checked her watch after pulling onto the drive. The landlord was meeting her to show her around; he wanted to hand over the keys and run through some temperamental issues associated with the house and its age.

Rents in this part of the country were through the roof. Apparently, because she was paying six months in advance, the landlord had dropped the rent, considerably. The estate agent, a remarkable Margaret Thatcher replica, right down to the heavily lacquered hairstyle, said she'd never had such a situation. 'After all, landlords were there to make money; they weren't charities.' Gemma took offence; *she* hadn't requested the drop in rent.

'You have such a lovely manner about you,' Gemma said to the rude woman who wore pink lipstick, some of it stuck to her front teeth. She didn't tell her.

'Oh, thank you, I do try to look after our landlords,' she replied, bursting with pride and a bright smile. Clearly missing her sarcasm.

The cottage was isolated, standing beneath a thick canopy of trees. The paved path around the house was a little wonky and mossy in places, but not too bad and they would have to put an outside light in; otherwise she could see somebody taking a tumble on the uneven flagstones.

It was one of those beautiful winter days where the sun shone but it was cold. The light covering of snow had melted, but the forecast was for more snow on the way.

She called Oliver from her mobile, wanting to hear his voice. 'Shall we grab some lunch at the pub after I've seen the house?'

'Good idea, what time do you think you'll be finished?'

'Oh, I don't know, the landlord hasn't arrived yet. I can't see it taking more than half an hour. Then half an hour to get home,' she said, checking the time on her watch.

They hadn't been to the pub for food for over a month. They had stayed away because of the looks they were getting. But it was time they got out. Being stuck in the house was driving them stir crazy.

She was glad of her boots today; the wind had picked up since she arrived. She fastened her woollen coat up against the cold.

There wasn't much security around the house. The isolation would serve them well. She was well aware they were cut off. Jake was out of her life and so in reality there really wasn't anything to feel worried about. They lived slightly isolated now, but this house was really cut off. There weren't any other houses down the lane apart from the two right at the bottom. The thick canopy of trees shielded the house from the outside world. It suited Gemma because she didn't want to mingle and make friends with new neighbours. Too many questions.

She made her way around the back of the house through a small wooden gate. Again, the patio was as uneven as the front and the patio flagstones slippery.

Gemma peered through the patio doors. The kitchen was

small and no Aga, sadly. But then again, they wouldn't be able to afford to run it any more.

A car pulled onto the drive. The deep, growling engine sound of some sort of expensive 4x4. She picked her way carefully back around to the front.

A one hundred and twenty-five thousand pound black Overfinch Range Rover with blacked out windows and private reg. T8 JAK stood in the drive. She knew the cost of these because Oliver had wanted to buy one before it all happened. Gemma moved towards the front door with her arms bound around her to keep warm. The driver's door opened.

Her steps slowed as the driver got out of the car until she stood still, just staring. Her eyes flicked to the number plate and back to the driver. Her first thought was; how could this be? First, she thought she'd seen him in the street and now this. She tripped on the uneven flagstone when she moved and fell backwards into the slumbering, climbing Jasmine, which hung over the front door. It had been him after all. He wore the same black top and jeans, but carried the baseball cap.

Jake moved stealthily towards her.

'Hello there. Do you think it's fate that has brought us together, again?'

'What are you doing here?' she said, surprised. Shocked.

'It's my property, Gemma. I thought you wanted to rent it. Have I got it wrong?'

He put the baseball cap on and dug in his pocket for the keys. 'You OK with that?'

Pale-faced she looked at him. 'What? No.' She stared at him uncomprehending. 'Have you been following me? Was that you earlier on?'

'I've been keeping an eye on you. Was today the first time you noticed?'

'You can't do that!' Her mind was all over the place. 'Why?'

'Can't I? Why? I was simply in the same place you were on numerous occasions. There's no law against it.'

Something occurred to her. 'Did you know it was me wanting to rent this place?'

'You mean did I lower the rent because I knew it was you? Of course. The agents called me. They told me they had somebody wanting to take a twelve-month rental with six-month's cash up front. I asked for some information. What a pleasant surprise when your name popped up.' He smiled. 'We don't take that much cash any more, it has to go through the bank. I had to insist on this occasion, seeing it was you.' When she didn't reply he added, 'Well you might be a little more grateful, I don't suppose you wanted to pay the higher rents. That ten grand wouldn't last you long if you did.' He pulled the Jasmine away from her face.

'You didn't have to help us out. We'll manage.'

He helped her out of the Jasmine, picking the odd dry leaf and brittle branch out of her hair, slowly, deliberately taking his time about it. 'This is so beautiful in the spring.' He lifted her face up with a finger beneath her chin. 'The smell as you enter the house is really something.' His finger casually stroked her cheek. 'It's a shame you can't smell it now. It really is delightful.'

She shivered. She wanted to step away from him, but the Jasmine bush on one side and him on the other trapped her. The wind slackened for a moment as if it too was unsure what to do.

'This was my first property, you know. I bought it years ago after I left the family business to start on my own and build my property portfolio. I own a vast number of properties around here. Some commercial ones too.'

His look was a little intense and made her uncomfortable.

She really wasn't interested. Right now, she just wanted to leave.

'Shall we go inside? I presume you'll want to have a good look around.' He took the key from his pocket and opened the red front door with the tiny diamond shaped window in the middle. 'After you.' He smiled as she hesitated but he gave her a gentle push inside. 'You remember I mentioned I would look into your undesirable?' he said and locked the door behind him, putting the key back in his pocket.

When Jake hadn't been in touch for such a long time, she thought their lives had been moving on. The ten grand was slowly depleting and she was getting concerned.

She needed a job really badly. She never realised how difficult it would be to find one after being self-employed. Even something boring was unattainable. Nobody was interested. It was as though she'd fallen off the grid. All her experience amounted to nothing. She was feeling totally demoralised about ever finding something. The supermarkets were the worst. She didn't pass the online test. That was the worst feeling of despondency she'd felt in a long time. Oh, she was smart enough to know it was probably that she was over qualified. It still didn't answer the question of how did you get work?

'And have you found anything on him?' she asked, with a self-conscious laugh trying to hide her nervousness.

'I was thinking of phoning you and inviting you out to dinner to discuss it. But now you've made contact...' He ran his finger over the surface of a small table standing against the wall with a dried-up plant on the top and checked for dust. 'This place hasn't been rented out in a while. It needs quite a bit of work doing to it. I really should get round to it.'

'I wouldn't have gone out with you again anyway. You know that. I told you that last time. And besides; I didn't know you owned this. I wouldn't have agreed to come had

I known.' She wasn't going to allow him to twist things. 'So, what about Peter? Have you really found something on him?' she said, hoping to change the subject. She was here to rent a house. Nothing more.

He shook his head. 'Such strength of character, Gemma. Even with austerity staring you in the face.'

She stopped in the tiny hallway unwilling to walk in any further. She wasn't getting into a conversation with him like this. He seemed strange. Different. He was right about one thing. She needed to rent this house. He'd made the rent so cheap she couldn't refuse. It was the only affordable property in the area. If he wanted to show her around he could. Then she'd sign the papers, collect the keys and be done with him. There was no need for any more contact with him.

She suspected he didn't have any information on Peter and was stringing her along, perhaps trying to unsettle her by mentioning phoning her. He knew she'd fear that happening.

She didn't want to rent his cottage, not really. The fact he admitted to following her unnerved her. A lot. God, if there was anything else available at this price. But she had to be realistic. They couldn't afford anything else.

They had to economise. Besides, there was nothing wrong with renting this place, she thought against her better judgement. It was going through the estate agents. Not him. She'd deal with them over any issues they had. She'd tell him. From here on. There was no need for them to stay in contact.

The winter sun flooded in through the Venetian blinds next to the front door throwing slanted lines on the stone floor around them.

He held a sheet of paper out in front of her. 'Do you want to know what this is?'

She looked at the paper. 'Maybe. What is it?' So, he did have information on Peter. What if she was wrong about him and he did genuinely want to help? But why follow her? Again, a coincidence? Even as she said it, she knew she wanted to know what information he had. If it had to do with Peter she wanted to know.

Jake ran his fingers through his hair.

'Well? Aren't you going to tell me?' she asked.

He gave her a big smile and looked at the floor while he spoke. 'I'm sorry. I suppose I'm a little hurt that all you want from me is this piece of paper.' He flapped the paper in front of her face. Goading her.

She scoffed. She doubted that. She smiled at him trying to make her smile reach her eyes. He was messing with her head and she wasn't about to let him.

'The thing is, Gemma. Why would I simply hand you this information? What do I get out of it?'

She stood up straighter giving him her complete attention. 'I already gave you my time and you implied the information on Peter was part of that.'

'Because you wanted to hear it like that. I didn't actually say that now, did I?'

She paused. 'OK, what is it you want from me?'

'Gemma,' he said, and leant back against the wall giving her his full attention. 'You seem to forget that to me you are an expendable asset. I don't need to help you. I want to. I could pull this house away from you. In a few months with no job and no way of paying your rent, you'd be out of wherever you rented. So, I ask myself, why is she not being nicer to me? I haven't done anything to hurt you; on the contrary, I've done everything to help you. Now, as things stand, you also get to keep your reputation intact. But that could easily change. Could it not? If Oliver found out? If Facebook were to run a little gossip?'

'Stop messing about, Jake. I've asked you what you want in exchange for the information and now you're evading.' A threat? She'd ignore it for now. First, she wanted to know what kind of information he had. Then maybe, and that was a big maybe, she'd see what he wanted from her.

'It's not good news, I'm afraid.' He waggled the paper in front of her.

She said nothing waiting for him to continue. He would when he was ready. She'd already noticed he liked to drag things out for maximum effect.

'He left the country a few days after you told me you discovered the theft. The fact is he flew to the Middle East. We have no trace of him there.'

'I don't believe it. How can someone vanish like that?'

'Money can buy you a lot.' He shrugged. 'I suspect there are plenty of people looking for him so he's probably gone into hiding. You're not the only one he's swindled. My sources tell me you were small fry compared to the others. So, it figures he's disappeared.'

'Why didn't you just tell me that? Why all the drama waggling that piece of paper?' She took a minute or so to gather her thoughts. Annoyance built inside her for letting herself be duped so easily.

Part of her wanted to storm out and tell him where he could shove his house and his information. Another part wanted her to stay because maybe, just maybe, Jake might actually be able to find Peter.

'You're not going to find him, are you?'

'We might. There's every possibility. It will take time, that's all.'

'What about all your contacts that you spoke about?'

'It takes time, Gemma.'

'You made it out as though it wouldn't be a problem for you to track him down. Seems to me you make false promises.'

'It probably looks that way.'

She so desperately wanted to find Peter and watch him go to prison for embezzlement. She wanted him to pay for what he'd done to them. She was never going to do that on her own.

'Gemma, I'm here to help you. Look, I've brought some more cash with me, I thought you might be needing a little extra.' He pulled an envelope out from the inside pocket of his coat, smiled and walked past her into the kitchen, then over to the back door and checked it was locked. He did the same with the windows which all had locks on.

She thought of how far she'd come in her life. The moment she left that miserable house in Salford she knew she would have to work hard to never be without. Her first job was working for a life insurance company in administration. She slogged her guts out. She put in the extra hours just to be noticed. When she thought she never would be, she was, and then she was promoted to office manager. What a relief and a boost to her self-esteem. Then a position came up in HR, she moved into that field and eventually left the company, took a conversion course and worked in HR from then on.

Her life moved on an upward spiral. Her dreams came true. She had a great job; her money was her own. She depended on no one and feared no one. No one intimidated her any more. Then she met Oliver and her life improved even if at the time she thought it couldn't get any better. She was on a roll and everything kept getting better and better. Until that day, when Peter came into their lives.

She was suddenly conscious of Jake behind her, the warmth of his body close to hers. She saw in front of her on the black granite worktop the envelope filled with money. His hand traced a line down her spine ending on the curve of her hips. Her hands gripped the edge of the granite. Both his hands clasped her on either side and he pulled her back into him. Memories of her stepfather danced in her mind. The times he dared to touch her, presumed he could. She stiffened, unable to stop the shiver that shook her body. Fear and hatred ran a close match inside her. She became aware of his breathing close to her neck. She daren't move, afraid of what any movement from her might do to him. Turn him on? Anger him? She knew he was unpredictable.

'What are you doing?' she asked through gritted teeth, trying to turn around but he held her firm. Her instinct was to push him away and run, but she knew she wasn't a match for him and that behaviour might trigger the wrong reaction in him.

She'd been here before, too many times. *He* would push her to run or fight giving him an excuse to hit her. She forced herself away from the past and back to the now. But the anxiety she dragged from the past sat alongside the present.

She squirmed to free herself. 'Jake, let go of me.' She pulled at his arms to free herself but he was too strong for her. 'Let go of me,' she insisted, still trying to break free.

He let her go suddenly and she stumbled into the granite-topped island, quickly moving around it, putting it between them.

'I'm sorry, Gemma, it wasn't my intention to scare you. I think you've overreacted. Please don't be afraid of me. There's no need. I simply wanted to make you feel safe.' He moved away giving her space.

Her eyes followed him, not for a second did she release him from her gaze. Feeling claustrophobic she wanted to get out of the house and into the fresh air. Was she overreacting? Was her past colouring her present?

He strode towards her again. She flinched and stepped back. Her eyes on the front door.

'There's no need to fear me. I keep telling you that. Why won't you believe me?'

'Oh, I don't know maybe because you're acting a little weird right now and you've locked the doors.'

'Just habit. I'm not keeping you here. You can leave at any time.'

She pushed away from the granite island. 'Open the door. I want to leave, Jake.'

He raised his arms and she flinched, again. 'Gemma, what are you afraid of? I know you've never told me about your home life. But I did some checking and I understand why you're so jittery around me. You don't trust me, do you? Not all men are like your stepfather.'

She stalled on her way to the front door. 'You had no right to do that.' She whirled around. 'My life is private. How dare you go snooping around? Who gave you permission to do that?'

He looked at her curiously. 'I don't need permission. I simply want to understand you, that's all. Trust is a funny thing, isn't it? Don't you see I care about you?'

She snorted. Looking at him through narrowed eyes, not seeing him but seeing her stepfather repeatedly telling her that what he did was because he loved her. Annoyed with herself for going there. To that forbidden place she never allowed herself to visit.

'Open the door. If you don't…'

'What? What will you do? Gemma, really, you need to calm down.'

Then she thought of her phone and pulled it from her coat pocket. She dialled 999 and looked at him. 'Open the door or I call the police.' Everything from the past came at her. She had no understanding why. Why now? Maybe it was the look in his eyes, or the sarcasms or the intent that she felt fuelled it. She didn't know. She ran to the door. A desperate need to get out. To breathe fresh air.

'Really?' he said. 'And say what? That I have locked you

in the house. Would they believe you, do you think? After all, when they arrive, if they do, I will open the door.' He indicated the door and showed her the key. 'Take it. I'm not stopping you.' He came to stand in front of her and put out his hand, palm facing upwards. 'Give me your phone. You don't need to call the police.'

'Why would I give you my phone?' She moved away from him. Out of his reach.

He unlocked the door. 'Just think before you bolt. Think it through, will you? Now this is an interesting scenario. I mean, if they came to your rescue and I denied it then I could, for example, if I was as nasty as you suspect, say you were angry because I'd called our affair off and you were trying to hurt me. What do you think they would say then?'

'Affair? What are you talking about? We haven't had an affair. You're talking rubbish and you know it.' She moved to the open door, her breath catching in her throat. She needed air. She was confused. He made no sense and neither did she.

'Yes, but they don't.'

She laughed. 'What are you going to tell them? Lie and say I slept with you? Don't be so ridiculous. It's untrue. Nobody will believe you.'

'Are you sure about that? Are you one hundred per cent sure *nobody* would believe me? Why would you have gone away with me? For money? Why would I pay you anything, if not for sex? Doesn't stack up, does it, Gemma?'

'But you did pay me not to have sex with you. You paid me for companionship.'

He laughed. 'Really? They'd believe that! Are you sure? After all, we're not in the last century, Gemma. Who pays for companionship these days?'

There was silence. Gemma considered what to say. What exactly was he implying?

'Let me go.'

'Gemma, just leave, I'm not keeping you here.'

Her eyebrows twitched. Her thumb hovered over the call button on her phone.

'I can go?'

'Yes, you can go. You could have gone at any time. All I wanted to do was show you the house.'

'Yes, but you touched me.'

'I held you, Gemma. As I said, I wanted to make you feel safe. I'm sorry if I spooked you.'

'You shouldn't touch people like that.'

He held up his hands in surrender. 'Sorry, my mistake. I should have thought it through. Look, I'll get the paperwork sent over to you and you can move in as soon as it's convenient.'

She walked out to her car, fishing her keys from her handbag.

When she was ready to pull away, he stopped her. She dropped open her window.

'I'll be in touch. Oh, just a quickie, before you leave. Think back to your university days, to a fun-filled night with your girlfriends in the summer of your graduation. Fast forward to the end of the evening where you meet two young men a little older than yourselves. You go out drinking and dancing. They spend a lot of money on you. They all get very drunk and you girls promised lots of sexual favours you had no intention of giving. You left them tied up on a roundabout, promising to come back. But you never did.'

Her mind raced backwards in time. The colour draining from her face as though someone had pulled the plug. Had that been him? Jake Challinor?

Chapter Fifteen

Chester University 2003, Fifteen Years Earlier

The evening of May 12th 2003, Gemma, Karen and Mattie drank for most of the afternoon. Gemma made a jug of Martini and lemonade and by six o'clock they were well on their way to getting very drunk. Blotto. Pissed.

They had finished their last exam at lunchtime and decided to celebrate by getting drunk and going out on the town one last time. There was an eighties party at one of the local clubs. Mattie hadn't stopped crying for the most part. She couldn't bear the thought of them all going their separate ways.

'Don't cry, Mattie. We'll stay in touch,' Gemma said, hugging her tight. She for one was ready to take on the world.

Karen was going back home and sweetly asked Gemma if she needed a place to stay. 'You come and live at mine. Mum and Dad won't mind; you can sleep in my room until you decide what to do with yourself. Come along, it'll be fun.'

Karen and Mattie were the only people who knew about her home life, and Karen took it upon herself to act as protector most of the time. Having said that, it changed her view on men, she now perceived them all as predators.

Gemma wasn't going home. She never wanted to go back to Salford as long as she lived. But it was kind of Karen, nonetheless. Tea and sympathy weren't her thing. What she wanted to do was reinvent herself. Start her career and make something of herself so the ghosts of her past stayed buried.

She wanted to develop a new past. One which included loving parents, alright they'd have to be dead parents, but dead was better than living child abusers.

She had no solid plans though. She would probably stay in Chester for a while; she knew the city and liked it. She felt comfortable and was able to lose herself there.

She'd look for work, maybe get a house share to begin with, then her own place. She looked forward to that. Her own place. Her safe place. She saw some advertised in the local paper and with the money she saved from her part-time work she'd have enough for a few months. She wasn't worried. She was free. Free!

The night out was Karen's idea, at first Mattie and Gemma were against it, but they didn't need much persuading thanks to the Martini. Karen had finished with her boyfriend a few days previous and was out to punish all men in general.

'Bastards the lot of them. Bastards! I'll show them. I'll fucking show them.' It had been her mantra since the day he dumped her. They, as her best friends, agreed and joined in with the idea that all men should be humiliated for being... well, men. What that humiliation was to be, none of them knew. But when Karen was on the warpath for anyone, it never ended well for them.

The three of them sat on Gemma's bed, heads spinning and resting against the wall. Karen spilled her idea to them as well as her Martini on Gemma's duvet.

'Don't you think they might work out what we're up to?' Mattie said.

Mattie, sweet, angelic Mattie always raring to join in on any conspiratorial mayhem. But cursed by fate, if anyone was to get caught, it would be her. Like the time they decided, again on another mad drunken evening after a Christmas party, to shove holly leaves in Steve's bed.

Steve house shared with them and adored himself, always looking in the mirror and checking out his hairstyle. But, worst of all, the crime he committed over and over, was to hog the single bathroom for ages before a night out.

So, the holly leaves were dumped. When Steve bellowed in the hallway, 'The motherfucker who thought it was funny had better own up or I'll make everyone's life miserable,' Mattie came out to soothe him. As she would, with her big, kind heart. Unfortunately, Mattie couldn't stop laughing at Steve, standing in undies and T-shirt on the landing covered with holly leaves. He assumed it was her and went to her bedroom and trashed all her make-up. Poor Mattie cried for days and they had to share their make-up with her because none of them had enough funds to replace it all in one go.

'No? Let's make it our challenge not to let them work it out! Come on, let's see how far we can go with it,' Karen insisted. 'I reckon we can get free drinks all night, a meal and maybe they'll buy us something. Cool, I want some new jeans.'

'Buy us something?' Gemma questioned. 'How can they do that? Everywhere will be closed.'

'Oh, yeah, forgot that bit.'

Mattie and Gemma suddenly found that hysterical.

'OK, well we can get the other stuff.'

Gemma and Mattie nodded.

'I think it could be fun; we have nothing to lose so let's do it, let's take Chester by the horns tonight and show it what we can do,' Gemma squealed. 'What you wearing?'

Gemma got up off the bed and tripped over her shoes scattered all over the floor. She'd run out of cupboard space yonks ago and now just left them anywhere. Which wasn't good when you were drunk.

Karen shuffled on her bottom off the bed and grabbed Mattie. 'Come on, Mattie, stop worrying, let's get a sexy outfit together. We're going to that eighties do, it'll be fun. We're gonna pick up some rich guys tonight and spend their money for them. We're gonna go out with a bang!' She giggled.

Mattie's head lolled to the side. 'I feel sick.'

Chester was buzzing when they finally arrived in town. They headed for the most popular bar, Baccarat. Inside it was full of bodies, they pushed through to get close to the bar to the sound of 'Raspberry Beret' by Prince.

'I'm glad we had a snooze before we came out,' Karen said, her eyes like radar scanning the room. She wore a tight pink satin jumpsuit. Her long, black hair falling loose over her shoulders and spiked at the top à la Cher.

'Christ, me too, I don't think I could make it if we hadn't,' said Gemma. She wore a red dress, dangerously short and close to being indecent. Her fake tan had a hint of sparkle and she wore her big blonde hair loose tonight. She caught a glimpse of herself in one of the smokey mirrors behind the bar. Maybe she'd used too much hairspray, but she couldn't quite focus to be sure.

'Did you add vodka to it?' asked Mattie, who had rimmed her eyes with kohl eyeliner. Her dark blonde hair in the style of Madonna, she wore armloads of bangles and mismatched clothes.

Gemma giggled. 'Maybe a little, along with some gin I found in the kitchen. I think I got overexcited because it was the last day.' She hugged Mattie and her heart tore a little at the thought of not having her friends around her every day. But it was new beginnings for all of them.

The girls laughed and for the first time she realised there was a tremendous bond between them. Bonded by living together for three years and this would probably be the last time anything like this carefree night out would happen again.

In the nightclub, everyone danced and chatted each other up. It was hot and sticky, but they didn't care, they were having fun. Where would they all be in twenty years, Gemma thought, probably not where they imagined.

That vision for herself didn't extend so far, she didn't want it to. She wanted no plans. She was living each day as it came along. OK, she had goals, to be independent and financially secure on her terms. A man? Perhaps, but it wasn't at the top of her agenda. A good one would be hard to find.

'Over there, look, can you see them?' Karen shouted. They could barely hear each other over the sound of the music. The mirror balls hanging from the ceiling cast little dots of light over everyone. Gemma sipped her Malibu and Coke. The drinks at the club tonight were all popular eighties favourites. Too sweet and too easy to drink.

They zigzagged their way through the throng of people towards the *Miami Vice* lookalike duo propping up the bar, Karen in the lead.

Before they got there Gemma stopped them, putting a hand on Karen's shoulder. She shouted to be heard over the music. 'Let's decide what we're going to do. What exactly is the plan?' Now that Karen had her target in sight, Gemma wasn't so sure any more. It sounded like a rubbish plan.

'What do you mean? We're going to get them to spend lots of money on us, silly,' Karen said, giving some guy who fancied his chances a dirty look. Gemma steadied her, catching her before she fell over in her heels. 'You're not chickening out, are you, Gem?'

'No. But are you sure about this?'

'Err, yes, and you are too. Come on. What's up with you?'

'I don't know, just a bit unsure.'

'Oh, come off it, Gem. Where's your spirit? We're not going to do anything terrible, just have a bit of fun with them. You're not going all sissy on me, are you? What's the worst, that can happen?'

She relented. 'OK, in that case let's do something really mad and play a prank on them,' Gemma said. 'This will be the last time we will probably be so uninhibited. So, let's go for it. Let's do something so crazy we can remember and laugh about it in the future. Just the three of us. Something naughty. Something bad. Something out of our comfort zone.'

'Like what? What you thinking, Gem?' Mattie asked.

Karen thought for a moment then said, 'Let's get them really drunk and drive them out to that clearing, you know the one near the roundabout. It's quiet at night but roaring busy in the morning and tie them up to the signpost. Let's strip them to their underwear. Or better still, naked.' She fell about laughing.

Two sets of startled eyes looked at her.

'What! Wow, that is crazy. How do we drive them?'

'We'll get a taxi.'

'We don't want to hurt them,' said Mattie, looking worried for the first time.

'Oh my God, Mattie, we won't hurt them. It'll be just a bit of fun.'

Karen took the lead and moved in on the *Miami Vice* boys. Gemma and Mattie either side of her.

The duo bought them a bottle of champagne straight away. Introduced themselves. The taller of the two, Jake, eyed up Gemma and handed her a glass. He moved in on her, pushing his way into her personal space, something she disliked. She stepped away but came up against the bar. Then he put his hand around her waist; she felt a prickle of irritation as he chatted her up. He was pleasant enough looking. His hand moved over her back and bottom and hips as if he was a security guard. She drank her champagne and pushed further into the hardness of the bar already digging into her to get away from his roaming hands.

Karen was on form with the other boy who was better looking than Jake and appeared less touchy-feely. Mattie stood with them but danced on her own with her eyes closed, it wasn't much of a dance, more rocking from one foot to another.

The floor was sticky beneath Gemma's shoes.

Jake pushed up the sleeves of his jacket and kept filling their glasses up.

Marco's Restaurant on a Friday night was packed. Normally you needed a reservation to get in, but Jake flashed the cash and before you could say *where's the loo*, they sat at a table with red checked tablecloth and a candle stuck in a bottle of Mateus wine. Menus and a couple of bottles of wine were plonked down in front of them.

The room had a welcoming feel to it lit only by candle light. Italian music mixed with Frank Sinatra played in the background. The colourful waiters were all Italian, flirting with the women and charming with the men. They made their job seem seamless and organised in the bustle of service.

They hadn't eaten here before, who could as a student, the prices were out of their reach. They lived on baked beans. When they got bored, they spiced it up to baked beans and sausages. When they got bored of that they moved the bar up to baked beans on toast. It was a rarity because beans on toast involved buying bread and they didn't always have enough money.

'You're very sexy,' Jake said, his words a little slurred. His slightly glassy eyes slid down her body stopping at the hem of her short red dress riding high, virtually to the top of her thighs. She pulled it down and wished she'd worn something else.

'Thanks,' she said, pulling the hem down a second time. He made her feel uncomfortable. She had some more wine and glared at Karen. This wasn't such a good idea. His hand moved up her thigh and then towards the inside. She slammed her legs closed. He didn't remove it.

A loud shriek of laughter came from Karen who slowly unbuttoned Jake's friend Liam's shirt and played with his chest hair. She was really pissed tonight. Some of the other diners started looking at them.

Gemma stuck her fork into Jake's hand. Irritated with him.

'Ouch, what the fuck!!'

'That was rude, don't do it again,' she hissed, and stared daggers at Karen struggling to get her attention. It was no use she was too pissed to notice anyway. Mattie was no use either as she was the third wheel engrossed in the wax covered Mateus bottle. When the food arrived, Gemma watched her attempting to twirl the spaghetti on her fork and get it inside her mouth. Each time she got close it fell off back on to her plate.

He didn't do it again, but he moved his chair closer. She couldn't put her finger on it but something felt off with Jake. She forced herself to stay calm. She drank another glass of wine. Her head felt a little woozy. She glanced at the other diners enjoying their food and company. A party of women a few tables away laughed raucously, they wore party hats. Must be a hen party, she thought.

Eventually the bill was paid and they stumbled out of the restaurant. Too inebriated, she wobbled on her heels. Mattie trailed behind them, her shoulder bag dangling from her hand, trailing on the ground. Gemma linked arms with her pulling her along with them.

They took a taxi, four of them falling in the back with Gemma sitting in the front. Karen directed the driver in her usual bossy way. Turn left, now right, right, right, turn now, I said right what's wrong with you, now straight ahead, at the end go right again.

In the back, Jake tried it on with Mattie by shoving his hand up her dress. Mattie shouted for him to stop, slapping at his hands but he just laughed like it was a game. Karen pushed him off.

Gemma's head snapped round, she leant over the seat and punched him in the balls. Pain etched itself into each pore and crevice of his face. He lashed out to punch her back, but she moved and his Rolex caught her skin, opening up an old scar. Blood seeped through her dress.

'How does it feel? Painful? Then think how it felt to Mattie,' she hissed, rubbing her chest and remembering the countless times her stepfather had molested her. What a twat. She wanted to shove him out of the car. Just who did he think he was doing that.

Maybe Karen was right, all men were bastards. And they deserved what was coming.

When they were dropped off, she was the one who took charge. It was quiet, not a soul about. Nobody used it at night, but in the morning it was a cut through to the main road and mega busy.

Maybe it was the drink talking or maybe she wanted to cause pain to these idiots who thought women were just a commodity. Whatever it was there was no way she was going to let that bastard go unpunished for his behaviour tonight.

At first, the men resisted. But they were drunk and it didn't take much persuading, especially when they had sex offered to them. Karen was the one who offered. 'Come on, are you chicken?' She convinced them to strip and allow themselves to be tied up to the signpost by the wrists while she danced in front of them in her underwear.

'Look what I found in the glove compartment of the taxi.' Gemma pulled the blue nylon string from her handbag the sort you tie parcels with, tough and easy to use.

'How did you find that?' Karen asked.

'Looking for tissues to wipe the blood off my dress where that idiot caught me with his watch.'

'Ooh, make a criminal of you yet.'

They tied both men to the signpost by the wrist then tied their ankles and stripped them to their underwear. At first they wouldn't undress but Karen soon convinced them with her raunchy dancing.

As soon as they realised the girls weren't going to go through with their promises they got angry. Very angry.

'Undo us, right now. You'll be sorry if you don't,' Jake bellowed, pulling at his wrists to free himself.

Gemma shrugged, pulled their underpants down to their ankles. 'We'll come back later and let you go. Teach you a lesson not to grope girls.'

They ran off giggling, tripping over as they went and hailed a taxi a few streets down nearer to the centre.

When they got back to their digs they had every intention of going back before the rush hour, only they fell asleep waking up late morning.

Chapter Sixteen

JAKE

Present Day

After Gemma left, Jake drove around for a while getting his breathing back under control. His body no longer felt heavy and stiff from the pent-up rage he kept hidden. His pulse began to slow down; he no longer heard the thud of his heart or felt the pulse in his neck.

Half an hour passed before he felt OK and back to normal.

He drove home, changed cars and drove to Gemma's. He parked up the lane, in a different spot than the last time. He saw her inside the house. He pulled the earphones from his pocket and switched on the recorder. His heart rate climbed again reminding him how much he wanted to settle the score with her.

He'd told her to jog her memory. He'd wanted to have a confrontation with her. He'd wanted and needed to show her what he wanted to do to her.

Too soon. He had to bide his time. She wasn't drawn in enough yet. He needed to really mess with her head to screw her up. And break them up. With Oliver out of the way, his job would be easier. He did like a challenge.

He watched her through the binoculars making them both a drink and listened to her story of the house they were going to rent. She spoke with ease and no hesitation, no sign of what had gone on. It surprised him; he thought she might have pulled out. Clearly, her money situation was forcing her to take his offer. He didn't go back inside the cottage after she had left, so he wasn't sure if she took the money. She wasn't saying so to Oliver.

He ground his teeth thinking how close he came today to getting satisfaction.

Their conversation was boring him to death. He gauged she wasn't going to tell Oliver anything interesting and as far as he knew nothing new had happened.

He switched the engine on and turned the car around. He headed out of the lane and on to the A34 heading home. He had another appointment to keep.

This part of Cheshire had a healthy selection of millionaires. Plenty of the older properties were getting knocked down and replaced by vast monstrosities. You needed money to live here. Even buying a first home required a big deposit and that would only get you a two up and two down if you were lucky. Jake owned a lot of properties here; he'd been buying up for the last fifteen years.

It was money that made people who they were. Avarice. It made them do things they wouldn't normally do.

When he was twelve years old, he realised he had a knack of making people do just what he wanted. His mother told him he could charm the birds from the trees. He hadn't understood what she meant then. To him, he was just Jake Challinor. What he wanted, he got. Every time.

In the beginning it was easy, those friends who didn't have as much as him were easy targets. He befriended them, then found out what they really wanted badly enough to do just about anything for it. Then he bought it for them, only they had to do something for him, to prove how badly they wanted the item.

Initially it was easy. Then he raised the stakes. As the gifts got bigger and more expensive it didn't take long for word to get around that if you wanted something, he'd get it for you.

He found this worked better on those friends who were middle class. Those parents bought them the majority of what they desired, but there was a budget and a limit.

One boy, Sam, pestered him for a long time. They were sixteen by then and dabbling in drugs: cocaine, weed, nothing more. Jake really didn't partake. He liked keeping a clear head. Sam wanted to go bigger. Jake realised that if he did, he would eventually be so indebted to him because of his addiction, he'd do almost anything to get it.

When that time came, Jake told him what he wanted in return. Sam shied away for a few days, insisting he'd find another supplier and that Jake was sick and he'd kick the habit before he did that.

Sam went everywhere with his dog, a Jack Russell called George. Jake didn't care for him, he growled at him every time they met. Once, when Sam and he argued, the dog went for him, leaving a bite mark on his leg that he still had to this day.

He asked Sam to kill George.

Sam said no. He said no, ten times. Then one day he came to see him in tears and told him it was done.

Jake knew then that desperation will drive anyone to do pretty much anything to survive. That desperation was different for everyone. But everyone had a breaking point. Kids. Finances. Hate. Almost anything.

He didn't give Sam what he wanted. That was Jake's prize.

A car horn brought him back to the present. He turned down a suburban road packed with parked cars leaving a narrow channel down the middle.

All the houses were identical two up, two down terraces. Some had freshly painted front doors in pastel colours; others had the paint peeling off. He stopped outside the house of his informer. He texted her and it wasn't long before she came out and jumped in the car. He drove down the road until he found somewhere to park.

Carol Thompson was a small woman in her mid-fifties. Life wasn't good to Carol. She looked hollow and drawn as if her insides were being sucked out, slowly. She lived with her invalided mother. Jake had done his homework.

Of all the people working at the HMRC office, he picked her because she was desperate. She received a nominal wage for her administration work. Some extra benefits for her invalid mother and she occasionally worked at the local pub for cash to make ends meet. Tut, tut, her bosses wouldn't approve of that.

Jake's contribution was home help. He paid a nurse to visit her mother and look after her until Carol returned from work. He knew this was invaluable to Carol.

At first, she thought she was only acquiring bits of non-consequential information for him.

But Jake went beyond the non-consequential.

Chapter Seventeen

GEMMA

They moved into the cottage. She hadn't heard from Jake since that horrible day.

She knew she would hear from him again, just not when.

She waded through the moving boxes, throwing out lots of stuff that a) they had no room for or b) needed binning.

Over the last few days, Oliver made several trips to the tip to de-clutter their lives. The new house was small. OK for first-time buyers, but not for those who had a life to drag into it. Their wardrobes only just managed to get up the stairs and around the stair bend. Downsizing, that's what they were calling it. Trying to squash your life into a shoebox was a bit like trying to get into a size eight pair of trousers when really you were a twelve. It didn't seem real that they were getting booted out of their lovely home.

They stood on the drive of their old home, the car full with the last of their possessions. Oliver pulled her to his side. 'Well, Gem, I guess this is it. I can't believe it's come to this. Everything we worked for just gone.' And together they held onto one another. He wouldn't make eye contact with her but she detected tears. She wrapped her arms around his waist and hugged him close.

It was amazing how Jake had got inside her head. It would have been easier to tell him to stuff his offer of help. But she was too far down that road now. She wanted to find Peter. Each time she packed one of the boxes it was a reminder of what he'd done to them.

Keeping a smile on his face, Oliver said, 'Do you

remember when we bought this place? We had such high hopes for the future.'

She looked up into his face. 'I know. Do you remember the dreams we had? The two of us together. Oh God, Oliver, do you think we'll ever be the same after all this?'

He looked at her hesitantly, drawing her closer to him. 'I'd like to think so, Gem. I can't love anyone else. Not the way I love you. We'll get through this. I wish you would tell me what's bothering you, though. You've been acting kind of odd recently. Gem?'

'What?' She tried to pull herself together and push Jake from her thoughts. 'Oh, sorry, I was just thinking about what you said. That's all.' She smiled up at him hoping it would stop him pressing her for answers she wasn't ready to give.

'Why don't you drive the car to the new house? I'll sort out the last few things here and lock up and call for a taxi.'

'Oliver?' She screwed her eyes tight. Bracing herself for the lie she was about to tell him. 'I found out today I've got a job. Are you OK with me taking it? It's with some property developers. I'm to be their virtual secretary.' She hated lying to him. Hated it. He didn't deserve it. She kept her eyes closed and her head turned away.

'Wow! Yes, I think it's great and how superb you can work from home.' She heard the slight hesitation but he covered it up quickly. 'I always said you were smart, didn't I?' He kissed her head and pulled her in a little tighter. 'Why didn't you tell me you were going for it?'

She shrugged. 'In case I didn't get it. It's a bit of a fluke, I think they were desperate.'

'Well, it's money coming in, and that's the main thing, we can pay the rent and the bills and things will improve. Just you wait and see. I told you the two of us were a team.' He squeezed her. 'Things will be OK, Gem, I promise.'

She wasn't so sure. They decided Oliver shouldn't look for work right now, he needed to keep on top of everything that was going on in their life. There was enough paperwork to keep him busy for a long time. She knew he hated the idea of her going out to work because he didn't see what he was doing as working.

'It's amazing you found the cottage with such a reasonable rent.'

'Yes, probably because it's not great inside.' She blushed and kept her face turned away. 'The agents said it wasn't moving that's why they dropped the rent. I was lucky. Right place. Right time.' What a load of bullshit. How could he believe her? She wouldn't believe such a stupid excuse as that. She supposed he was simply happy they had an affordable home to go to. Knowing Oliver, he'd think about it and come back with more questions. She'd been stupid not to have prepared for this eventuality. She'd better get her answers right in her head. The last thing she wanted was to rouse suspicion.

'Ah, I see. There you go, then. A bit of luck coming our way.'

If anyone had shaped her life, it was Oliver. He was her husband and best friend and it killed her that she was lying to him now. 'Oliver? I hope one day you'll be able to forgive me.' She pulled out of his embrace. Pulled the car keys from her handbag and turned away from their beautiful home.

She caught the puzzled look that came over his face. 'Well, that goes for me too, Gem. Don't you think this is down to me? Don't blame yourself, if anything you were the one with the reservations about Peter.'

She gave him a crooked smile and nodded. 'Yes, I suppose. But I mean it.' She had never told Oliver about her childhood. She couldn't bear that he might judge her. She wanted to open up on so many occasions. But she chickened out. Just like she was doing now. The horrors of that life had left their mark. The stress and horrors of the last month or so were now taking their toll on her and she knew there was much worse to come. If only she had the guts to tell Oliver, then Jake would have no power over her.

'Now you're being silly. Come on, let's get moving towards our new life.' His eyes found hers. He paused only for a second. 'I love you too, sweetheart. We'll get through this, don't worry.'

Gemma said quietly, barely audible, 'I love you.'

Chapter Eighteen

The next morning, in their new home, in their new kitchen, Gemma looked at Oliver across the breakfast table. He read the newspaper on his phone, his toast and marmalade by his side and a cup of tea in his hand. They had thrown so much stuff away that they were pretty much straight in the house. Amazing how little one needed. The amount of stuff they'd binned had staggered them both. They stayed up until late getting most of the house straight. To be fair it was such a small house that if it didn't fit it was tossed. Outside the kitchen window she saw the empty cardboard boxes thrown out carelessly last night ready to be taken to the tip today.

When she'd walked into the kitchen earlier the door was closed. They never closed internal doors. A pet hate of Oliver's. He liked to think if anyone broke in, he'd be able to hear them.

She sipped her tea and found herself wondering what he would say if she told him she thought somebody had been in their house.

Nothing was immediately apparent when she came downstairs this morning. Apart from the door. She flicked on the light and although the kitchen looked just as she'd left it, something was wrong. As she scanned the room, nothing was obvious, but then she realised objects had been moved around. The fruit bowl, which lived on the pine kitchen table was on the worktop by the cooker. The kettle was on top of the bin. The coffee machine was turned on, and she distinctly remembered turning it off. The bread bin was open.

She checked the back door. It was locked. Then she turned back into the kitchen and saw the footprints. Muddy footprints marked the tiles and on the path outside leading to the side gate and no doubt to the drive. He had left them to let her know it was him.

Sensing her looking at him Oliver glanced up. 'Shall I make some more tea?' He smiled, his blue eyes crinkling at the edges. 'You OK?' He gave her a curious look and from his expression she thought he was reading her mind.

'I'm fine, yes, if you want to.' She toyed with her toast unable to eat it.

'OK, so what have you planned for today? Oh, when do you start your new job? Wasn't it this week? I can't remember which day you said.' His words were full of the harsh reality of the mess she was in and digging herself in even deeper.

'I'm waiting for an email confirmation.'

The post arrived with a clatter. She got up to fetch it but he beat her to it. 'It's alright, I'll go,' he said. 'Finish your toast. You need to eat. You ate so little from the takeaway yesterday.'

She took a deep breath trying to quash the bad feeling she had.

'Ooh, lucky you. You have a red envelope, looks like a card,' Oliver said, doing a quick mental calculation. 'Thought I'd missed your birthday for a moment. But nobody knows our new address, do they?' He sorted the post out into two piles on the kitchen table. 'Aah, it's been re-directed, I thought it was odd we had post.' He handed her the red envelope then took it back. 'Hang on, this has this address on?'

'Can't think why someone's sent me a card.' She looked at the red envelope in Oliver's hand not wanting to touch it. How the hell could she relax knowing he was out there. And she suspected he'd sent the red envelope. On purpose. Handwritten too just to make Oliver even more suspicious.

She thought of him plotting his revenge. Enjoying putting her through the stress of not knowing what his next move was going to be.

'Who's it from, darling? Aren't you going to open it? I'm really hungry this morning. I'm going to grab some more toast. You want some?' he asked, dropping the card in front of her then moving to the toaster and popping in a slice of bread, and pouring himself another cup of tea. 'Oh, have we run out of butter? I had the last little bit.' He looked again in the fridge searching in case he'd overlooked it. 'I don't understand it. Didn't you bring the contents from the fridge at home?'

'It's just a circular. Rubbish.' She pushed the card to one side. 'You know the sort of thing.' She looked in the fridge for the block of butter she knew was in there, but there was none. 'I did bring everything from the fridge.'

He smiled kindly. 'A circular? In a red envelope?'

She looked at the back door suspiciously. Jake was playing childish games now. For what purpose? 'Hell, you don't think we took the cardboard boxes with the food to the tip by mistake, do you?' she asked.

He shrugged. 'I suppose it's possible but I don't understand how some of the food is here?'

'I'll pop out later and restock. I've had a lot on my mind.'

'Don't worry, I'm going for my walk in a bit, I'll fetch the bits we need until we do a proper shop again. So, who's sending circulars in expensive red envelopes?' He wasn't going to give it up no matter how much she avoided the damned red envelope.

'I said it was rubbish,' she snapped, unintentionally. She shoved it in her pocket and sat very still, staring at her phone pretending to read the paper. Hoping he'd give it up.

Oliver came over to her and brushed the back of her hair with his hand. 'Do you think you'll get an email this week about the job? Maybe starting work will be good for you.

Take your mind of what's going on here.' He kissed the top of her head. 'You need to stop being so tetchy, love. If you want, we can leave everything today and go out for a long walk. You know clear the cobwebs a bit. How does that sound?'

She wanted to take reassurance from his words. She drew in a deep breath. He pulled her up out of the chair turning her around to face him and wrapping her in his muscular frame. Oliver wasn't tall, he was average for a man. His lean, muscular body from playing football felt safe. She buried her face in his jumper breathing in his scent.

'I don't know. Soon I imagine.' She didn't have the answers for him and she wished he'd stop pressing her. One thing she did envy was his naivety that everything was going to work out well for them both. Once she might have believed that.

He nodded. 'Didn't you want to go into town today?' he asked, looking at her. 'Why don't we go together later and grab some lunch? Might help you relax.' He leant over her to clear away her dirty plates.

'I'll do that,' she said. She couldn't relax. Not knowing he was out there and not until she saw what was in the envelope.

'It's fine, no problem,' he said.

'Lunch would be lovely.' She smiled and made an excuse to leave the kitchen, rushing up the stairs to their bedroom and locking herself in the bathroom. She dropped the loo lid and sat down. There wasn't a card inside the envelope only photos, she pulled one out.

They were pictures of her. Driving. Looking pensive crossing the street. Walking into Raymond Blanc's place in Oxford. God, he must have arrived before her to take them and then pretended to turn up later. Sitting nursing a drink at The Dog. Leaving her house wearing sunglasses. Having a coffee in Starbucks the day she got soaked by a sudden downpour.

Checking her phone. Taking a drink at the Cross Keys pub, alone. Buying bottles of wine from Booths supermarket. Walking around his cottage before she knew it belonged to him. Why had he taken these? How had he taken these?

She called him from the bedroom but it went straight to voicemail.

She suspected this was what he wanted. To keep her on the edge, not knowing what he was going to do next.

He probably wanted her to panic and chase after him. Scared of what he would do next.

Well, she wouldn't panic. She needed to think how to get herself out of the stupid jam she was in. She started to feel claustrophobic. Oliver had already noticed a slight change in her. He was being extra nice at the moment.

She wondered if they could spare some cash and go away somewhere. That was stupid. Funds were too tight, and besides, Oliver would think it frivolous.

She hurled a cushion across the room. Damn him!

Sitting on the end of the bed, she slipped off her tartan woolly slippers and kicked them with her heal under the bed. One went under the other didn't. She gave it a shove with her heel. It resisted.

On her hands and knees, she peered under the bed; a brown box stared back at her.

'Gem?'

She shot up off the floor. Guilt written all over her face. 'Hi!'

'What are you doing under the bed?' Oliver asked, coming over to where she was.

She spotted her slipper. 'Just looking for my slippers. One was stuck under the bed.' She pulled the throw back over the end and pulled the slipper out.

'But you had them on when you came upstairs?'

Jittery laughter poured from her as she tried to think

quickly of an excuse. 'I know I kicked them off and one shot under the bed. No big deal.'

'Not hiding anything from me, are you?' he said and laughed cheekily. 'Hope you haven't done something silly and bought me a birthday present. You know we said no gifts. We need all the money we have to live off.'

She looked at him confused.

'My birthday?' he said, with a raised eyebrow.

Christ. His birthday, she'd forgotten all about it. 'Maybe, so don't go looking around for presents,' she warned and laughed a more natural laugh, grabbing hold of her slippers and putting them back on. His birthday was soon. She mustn't forget. 'Have you finished your breakfast?'

'Yes, why?'

'No reason, just wondered when you were going for your walk to the shop.'

'Well, I thought I'd come and see if you were all right first, you seemed a little preoccupied this morning.'

She stood up and wrapped her hands around his waist, pulling him tight into her warm embrace away from the end of the bed. 'Shall we go to Manchester for lunch and treat ourselves?' She kissed him gently, sucking his bottom lip as he liked. 'What do you say?'

He pushed her onto the bed, kissing her neck and moving down her chest. 'Do you know how sexy you look in those tartan slippers?' He moved back up to her throat then kissed the length of her neck. 'Gemma? What's going on, are you OK?' His soft voice, tender and full of worry.

'I'm fine; I just need a change of scenery.' She brought his face up to meet hers and kissed him. Her words sounded insincere.

'Great,' he said, quickly rolling on top of her laughing gently. 'Because I want to make love to my wife because I've missed her.'

They gazed at each other in silence for a few moments. He reached out and stroked her face. She kissed his palm. He pulled her slippers off. They undressed each other. She sat on top of him, kissing him tenderly. Placing the tip of her tongue inside his mouth, enough to arouse him. He caressed her body. Feeling the warmth of his skin under her touch, the heat from his body filled her with desire. He was beautiful to her, the dips in his chest and the downy hair covering it. The maleness of his torso lying beneath her, so strong and masculine. She loved looking at him while she made love to him.

Quietly, while Oliver was downstairs getting himself ready for his walk, she pulled the box from underneath the bed and took it into the bathroom, closing and locking the door behind her a second time. She flicked on the light, put the box down on the tiled floor and crouched next to it.

The box was lighter than she expected. Though she really didn't know what to expect. A box of spiders wouldn't surprise her.

She looked at it for a while before nervously reaching out to it. It wasn't taped up, only the flaps tucked in to keep them closed. She slipped one of the flaps back, then the other. As she opened the box, unbidden, an image of Jake's face, smiling gruesomely, came into her mind.

She peered into the box half expecting something to jump out at her. The memory stick sat taped to the centre of the bottom of the box. She peeled it off and held it in her hand as though it was a grenade. She didn't know whether to bin it or not. Of course, she couldn't bin it; she had to see what was on it. She sat on the tiled floor holding the stick in her palm.

In the spare room, she woke the computer, pushed the memory stick into the USB portal and sat down to wait. As the screen came to life, she gasped and fell back into the leather office chair. 'Oh – my – God.'

Her phone lit up with a text message from Jake.

What are you thinking of?

She sat up straight and looked at the message astounded he knew she'd found the box.

What do you mean? she texted back.

Was he watching her somehow? She glanced around the room. Had he hidden cameras in the house when he broke in last night? Oh God, he must have been in their bedroom. Last night. As they slept. And shoved the box under her bed. She shivered at the thought of him watching them both sleeping.

A blast of wind slammed the bedroom window shut causing her to jump with fear. She got up off the chair and pulled it closed. The window latch was loose; it didn't hold very well. She'd have to tell Oliver to fix it.

He'd filmed their time at the hotel. All of it. And edited it to make it look more salacious. Including the payment. There was no sound, so it all appeared like a cheap film noir. She stared at the screen unable to stop herself.

I think you know what I mean. You're very photogenic. Your hair looks amazing.

She gasped in shock and sat back in her chair feeling used and creeped out. How far was he going to take this? Would he never let her go? She picked up her phone and her thumb hit the keys.

Why? Why are you doing this to me?

Nothing came back.

She closed the computer down, deleted the history and pulled out the stick putting it in the back pocket of her jeans.

As she walked out of the room a reply came back.

Because I can.

She could do nothing to stop him. Apart from telling Oliver. And she wasn't doing that.

Chapter Nineteen

While she waited for Oliver to get back from a meeting with the bank, she sat in the kitchen watching a song thrush in the back garden. She'd put out a fat ball for him that morning. He came to the garden most days. She called him Robert.

If she lost Oliver, what would she do? How would she survive? He was her world and her reason to get up in the morning. There was nothing in Oliver's behaviour of late to suggest Jake had made any contact with him. He was his usual helpful and loving self or he was a magnificent actor.

He should be on his way back by now. The inevitable was unavoidable.

It was three o'clock; his meeting was at one o'clock. She poured herself a drink and tried his phone again, it went to voicemail. She didn't leave another message. She drank the wine she'd poured and filled the glass again.

She'd not heard anything from Jake since the text messages. That was three days ago. She was living on the edge. Getting up early each morning to be the first to catch the post. Nothing else arrived. It couldn't be long now before he sent something else or did something else.

Unable to settle, she went into the lounge and flicked on the TV, the news came on. She wasn't really listening but something caught her attention. *The Cumbrian house builders, Butler Homes might have to go into liquidation after thirty years in business.* She turned up the sound. *Butler Homes have been prosecuted for non-payment of taxes; a spokesman for the company has said they are in talks with HMRC.*

Immediately she picked up her laptop and googled Butler

Homes. Drumming her fingers on the keys, she wracked her brain for a way to find out who their accountants were. She was sure Peter mentioned a large house building company as a client up in the Lakes; it was too much of a coincidence. The name, she was sure, was Butler.

She was shocked, in a good way, because now they had another lead. Why didn't Jake know about this with all his connections? If she could prove Peter Hayes was the accountant for that firm, then HMRC might believe they were telling the truth.

Suddenly she thought they might have a chance of turning all this around. But the words of the grey-suited man came back to her. *Ignorance isn't an excuse.* Fine words indeed. A get out clause for them, because what it ultimately meant was they would still be liable for the debt. But they had to try. If they got proof, they might be able to hire a lawyer to help them fight this.

She remembered something Jake said at the cottage. There was something odd in the way he told her that Peter had disappeared. And, of course, she never looked at the paper he flapped in her face to check if he was telling the truth.

A thought popped into her head – if this lead led them to finding Peter, then they might not have to lose everything, he would be responsible. She and Oliver might be able to walk away from it all. It was a long shot. They'd have to prove they weren't in it with Peter. She knew that was going to be near impossible to do. But it was something, nevertheless.

Oliver walked in some time later, looking beaten. She poured him a drink and made herself another one. Quietly putting the empty bottle behind the bin.

There was something in the way he looked at her as he crashed on the sofa that told her the meeting had gone badly. His look of defeatism annoyed her for some reason.

Oliver never showed weakness. He couldn't break. Not Oliver. Annoyed with herself for thinking so selfishly, she chased it away.

'Do you want to tell me how it went?' she asked, unsure if he was ready to talk. She sipped her wine waiting for him to open up.

They sat drinking their drinks in silence. There were so many different types of silence she thought. This was filled with fear and pain.

'It was busy on the roads; sorry I took so long.' She heard the tension in Oliver's voice, he looked uneasy. Whatever he wanted to say to her, he was struggling with it.

She asked again, 'What did they say? Are we losing everything?'

He clenched his fist. 'The bank manager was no older than twenty-five, Gem, with no life experience and the personality of a tiny organism,' he hissed. 'He was a parasite only wanting to claw back everything. There was no remorse.'

He looked deflated. Not her Oliver. He took the knocks but they never really knocked him down. Her anger was wrapped up tightly. The intensity of those feelings shocked her as much as the rage she felt towards Jake and his stupid games.

His look of alarm frightened her.

'We expected that, didn't we? We never really thought they'd give any more extension to the loans,' she said. She swallowed, her throat parched and took a long drink of her wine. Her heart hammered in her chest. There was something he wasn't saying. She couldn't think what more they would have to endure.

He reached out to her and wrapped her in his arms. 'I know, Gem, but it's real now. The house is lost. It's final. It's that finality that's broken me.' And then he cried.

Shocked by his breakdown, she held him tightly to her, trying to pour her strength into him. He was her rock, her steadfast. He couldn't break. Not her Oliver.

She said gently, 'Oliver, it's OK, we'll be OK, you said so. I believe you, please be strong.' She didn't know what else to say. The future looked bleak and bleaker still if he found out about Jake. Now that fear was very real.

It wasn't the right time to mention Peter and Butler Homes.

'Gem, I was pretending, for you. Deep down, I really hoped they'd give us some hope. Some extension. Something. It was all so cold. Ruthless. We've lost everything.'

She pulled away and looked at him. 'Look at me, Oliver.' He raised his face. She wiped the tears away. She was the strong one now. She looked him in the eye. 'This isn't you. You're better than they are. Better than this. This isn't going to break you or me. We will come out of this.' She had no idea where all this was coming from or even what the hell she was suggesting because she had no clue how to get them out of this mess.

He frowned. 'I'm scared. For us and what this might do to us. Financial worries and pressure break couples.'

'We'll be fine, Oliver. I promise.' She pulled him into her arms and held him, lost in her thoughts and nightmares. 'You scared me for a moment there, Oliver.'

'I'm OK now. As long as I know we're together. I can't lose you, Gem.'

'You won't. We're for life,' she replied.

Unless Jake interferes, she said silently. She knew she had no choice but to see this through. She had to find Peter The Bastard.

Chapter Twenty

She still hadn't heard from Jake; it was driving her slowly mad. Oliver was locked in the study going through the process of closing the business down every day.

To fill her time, she spent long hours in the garden. It was back breaking but it took her mind off the business, the bank and Jake. She tried to help Oliver, but each time she froze when she thought of the huge debt knotted around their necks and was completely useless to him.

'Have you not heard from that company yet?' he'd asked her that morning.

'No. Maybe they've changed their minds. If I haven't heard by next week, I'll go and look for something else.'

Jake was deliberately keeping his distance. She knew that. Making her more and more desperate. The money they had wasn't going to last forever. They'd already had to pay out for a car for Oliver, second-hand and not great, but it had cost them more than they'd intended to spend. His had been repossessed.

'Where did you get that money from, Gem?'

He caught her on the hop with his question. She'd been unprepared and stumbled over her words, staring at him open-mouthed. Swallowing the tightness in her throat she said, 'Don't ask me, Oliver. I just have it and let's be grateful for that.' She gave him a watery smile and left the room.

Now she opened the freezer, pulled out two ready meals, stabbed the packets several times ready to put in the microwave when Oliver got home. He was out food shopping and would be back any time. Her thoughts drifted to Jake. She didn't doubt he watched her all the time. For now, as long as she heard nothing from him, she sort of hoped he would get bored and leave her alone. She hoped he'd had his fun with her. Those photos bothered her though. What he might do with them. After the initial shock of the meeting with the bank, Oliver was in a more positive frame of mind. She wondered if she might not try to reason with Jake the next time he got in touch. The man had to understand that his behaviour was unacceptable, and she wouldn't take it any more. She could not be held accountable for a prank that happened years ago.

She pulled down the shoebox, which she kept on top of the fridge at the back. Usually full of rubbish, string, glue, paper clips that sort of thing. Underneath the detritus, she pulled the photos Jake had sent of her.

What do you really want from me, Jake? she asked herself. What happened was a long time ago. A stupid prank. No big deal. Why are you behaving so irrationally about this?

Although she told herself she was going to confront him the next time he got in touch, she wasn't convinced she'd be able to stop him. He appeared to be on a mission of some sort. Perhaps she should get in touch with Karen and Mattie. But she didn't know where they were or how to find them. After all their keen words of staying in touch forever, they had all soon lost touch. Facebook was an option but *he* would be monitoring that and she didn't want to bring him into their lives if she could help it.

She was setting the table when the doorbell rang.

She thought Oliver must be laden down with shopping. He'd arrived back sooner than she thought. She glanced at the wall clock. From the time he texted her to say he was on his way home, it was too quick. She pulled the front door open. Standing on her doorstep was Interflora with a huge bunch of flowers, all white; lilies, roses, carnations and those pretty little daisies she liked. Surprised, she took them from the delivery man and was about to close the door when he told her there was more.

He brought them into the house for her, all twelve bouquets of white flowers, all identical.

'Isn't there a card?' she asked, looking inside the last bouquet. Wondering what on earth had possessed Oliver to spend so much money on flowers, her first reaction was annoyance and anger that he'd done it. Then she thought about it for a second and understood that the gesture was sent with love and she'd better hold her tongue. What a silly man, didn't he know she didn't need flowers to know how much he loved her? Still, it was a wonderful surprise.

'Yes, just the one, it's in the first bouquet.'

She pulled the card out of the flowers and opened the small envelope. A smile pulling at her lips. *It's terrible to hear about your loss. Ps. 12 days left.* Her hand shook as she read the words. 'Did you see who ordered these?' she snapped.

'No, it was done by phone.'

'Was it a man who ordered them?'

'I don't know, I'm just the delivery man,' he said, heading out to his small blue van.

What the hell was going on?

Just then her mobile rang, it was Oliver. 'Hi, darling, I'll be with you in ten minutes, got caught up in traffic, sorry. I hope you've rustled us up something delectable with the microwave.'

She looked at the flowers on the kitchen table. All twelve bouquets. 'Yep, I'll turn it on as soon as you get back.'

'OK, darling. Good job I've bought some proper food now. Fancy making a curry from scratch tomorrow?'

'Sounds a good idea.'

'I've got a lovely pud they were reducing at the

supermarket, a white chocolate Bakewell that should make up for the ping ping meal. You OK, Gem? You sound weird.'

A text message came in.

They're your favourites, aren't they?

She didn't reply. Her heart thumped, again. What a sick bastard he was. She had to get rid of them before Oliver came home.

I've decided. You have 12 days left.

She smiled down the phone and put on her best chirpy voice. 'No, no, I'm fine, I'll see you in a bit.' She cut him off.

All the bouquets were in a little water filled balloon bag secured at the stems.

She threw them in the black wheelie bin outside. Placing some of the black bin bags over the top to hide them. Checking they weren't visible, and when she was happy Oliver wouldn't see them, she closed the lid and went back inside. Twelve days left? For what? He had to be joking, right? Surely, he wasn't threatening her?

Her mobile rang. His number flashed up. She grabbed her glass of wine and answered it. 'What the hell do you think you're doing?' she hissed before he had time to say anything.

He replied, laughing. 'You got my gifts, then?'

'What are you trying to achieve? And what's with that stupid message?'

'Gemma, you seem to be getting a little anxious. Is that your first glass of wine of the day?' It wasn't. Was he guessing? He must be, there was no other way he would know she had a glass earlier on. She wanted to stop. She really did, but right now he was making it impossible. She topped up her glass.

'And how would you like me to react? You've sent me a heap of flowers with a stupid message about loss. Why?'

She took a large gulp of her wine. Scrunched up the card and tossed it into the bin.

'For the loss of your home and business, what else would it mean? Nobody's died, have they?'

A sickly dread washed over her. She pushed away from the kitchen worktop and headed for the window in the lounge. Was he watching her? It was dark outside. She put her glass down and went outside to look down the road. Nobody. Only a car parked a little way up the road. Was he in there? She stared at it for a good few minutes until she convinced herself there were no signs of life inside. She breathed in a large lungful of air before going back inside.

'You need to stop this,' she said, striding back to the house.

'I like your fire. I like that I'm getting under your skin, but you're not running this show, Gemma.'

She slammed the front door and walked back to the kitchen to check the time. Oliver would be back any second. 'I wasn't aware there was a show, Jake,' she yelled, unable to control her rising anger and panic. She whirled around at a sound outside knocking her glass of wine off the counter. Glass shattered all over the floor spraying wine up the cupboard doors, her shoes and across the tiled kitchen floor. Dammit. She didn't want him to know she was riled. He would have heard that.

'What's the point in all this?'

'What's the point?' he repeated, hissing the words with a menacing tone that stopped her in her tracks.

She hesitated before answering back then chose to not say anything.

She was beginning to understand Jake Challinor. He wanted her to lose her control. She wouldn't give him the pleasure, again. If she did, he wouldn't know about it. That was for sure.

In front of her she saw the Japanese, laser sharp kitchen knife she used to prick the microwave meals. Picking it up, she stabbed it into the wooden chopping board in front of her to stem her anger.

In a controlled and level voice, none of which she actually felt, she said, 'Right, you need to listen to me, Jake. Whatever you're thinking this is, it's not. Get over your past. We had a business transaction that suited us both. But now you're taking it to a whole different level. Stop threatening me.'

'Had?' he cut in.

'Yes, had.'

There was an intake of breath, and she imagined him stemming his fury. She'd rattled him, again. She smiled knowing it would grate on him, this ability she had to make him lose his control.

'What?' he sniggered. 'Are you saying you want to stop seeing me? I will tell you when it stops.'

She pulled the phone from her ear and counted to five. It really was taking all her self-control to stay calm. The man was a sick bastard. And she was stuck with him. He'd changed. She never would have agreed to anything with him if she'd sensed he'd be vicious. Then a voice inside her head said, *but you chose to ignore the red flags, you idiot. Because you wanted the money. And now he has a hold over you.*

Quietly, but firmly, she said, 'Yes, Jake, I do.'

'Well, I don't agree. By the way don't you think you should clean up your spilt wine? Oliver won't be long now.'

She raced around the house looking out of all the windows to see where he was. He must be watching her. But from where?

'You're mad. Where are you?' She looked around for hidden cameras.

Silence on the other end of the phone.

A few moments went by before he spoke again. 'What if I don't want to stop it?'

'Where are you, Jake? Are you watching the house?'

He laughed. 'That would be telling, wouldn't it?'

She squeezed her eyes shut, ran her hand through her hair in desperation. She had no idea how to put a stop to this and she most definitely had to. It was out of control. How could she have been so stupid?

'Stop it, Jake. Stop this stupid game you're playing. This isn't a movie. It's real life. You can't control me or keep me as your pet. You can't force me to do anything. You've already pushed me to rent this house of yours. But that's it!'

'Aah, yes. I heard you were making the rounds of the estate agents, pity they have nothing for you.'

'Well you'd know, wouldn't you? I don't know how you've done it, but they won't talk to me, always busy, apparently. I know it was you who put them up to it.'

'Yes, well, money does talk and I do have many rental properties. I guess they got the idea I might remove them from their books, funny how people interpret things, isn't it?'

'You have to stop this, Jake.' She hated the pleading tone that had slipped into her voice. 'What happened all those years ago was just a silly prank. Get over it.'

'Stop it? Stop what? Stop reminding you of your past misdemeanours? Tut tut, Gemma. Maybe I'm not over it.'

'Look, we all have stuff happen to us we need to get over. Christ, go get some therapy if you need to get it out of your system. And why did you feel the need to take those photos or make a film? What's that all about?'

'Funny you should mention therapy. My therapist tells me to face my demons, so I can get closure.'

'I don't think she means torment them and blackmail

them. I'm pretty sure if you asked her to expand on *face your demons*, her answer would be very different to yours.'

'But I find it's helping me, thanks for asking. You just told me to get help and that's what I'm doing.'

'Look, this is getting us nowhere. If you don't stop creeping into my house and following me around, and threatening me, I will go to the police.' Maybe if she threatened *him*, he would back off. After all, she knew his name and any bad publicity would harm him and his business. He wouldn't want that, surely.

It was a long moment before he spoke.

'Be my guest. But remember, curiosity killed the cat. You know, you might not like what you find.' He laughed as if he was goading her. 'Skeletons in closets sometimes shock.'

She hung up, fed up with his cryptic one-liners. He was playing with her head and doing a damned good job of it. She stabbed the chopping board, again. So hard it skidded across the worktop, incredibly missing all the dishes and glasses in its trajectory to the floor.

A text came through. *I'm closer than you think.*

Chapter Twenty-One

JAKE

He emerged from the bushes down the side of the house. As he passed the kitchen window, he stole a look inside. He pulled his cap down and smiled. Content with the bewildered look on her face, he walked up the road to the parked car, and slid inside in one swift movement.

Oliver arrived as he slipped down in his seat. He pulled out the binoculars and watched him unload the boot and carry the shopping to the front door.

It was the first time he'd had a good look at him. He turned the car on and slowly crawled down the road to get a better view. Today he was in a different car. Different colour. Different model. He focused his binoculars and increased the magnification. The 60mm objective lens and 16mm eye lens allowed more light to enter the monocular, making the image brighter and clearer.

He wasn't bad looking, taller than he thought. But not as tall as Jake. He had his coat collar turned up against the weather. He had dark hair cut fairly short.

On an impulse he got out of the car and strolled up to Oliver. He startled him and that pleased Jake. Oliver's face wore a hardened expression until Jake smiled, then it softened. The initial shock having worn off, he was helpful when Jake spoke to him.

'Sorry to frighten you. I thought you heard me walking on the gravel.'

'No, it's a bit windy, the trees are thrashing a bit.'

Jake nodded, careful to hide most of his face with a scarf pulled up and his cap pulled down low. 'I'm sorry to bother you but I am a little lost. I'm trying to find some friends who I think live around here. The Fletchers? Their house is called Malvern Lodge? I've been driving around in circles when I saw you pull in. Satnav's a joke telling me I've arrived at my destination. Stupid things sometimes, don't you think?'

'Oh… no bother. Yeah, they can be a pain sometimes. But I can't help you. We've not been here long, and we don't know anyone around here… sorry. I can ask my wife if you want to wait a moment.'

'No that's OK, I'll have another drive around. A bit isolated here, don't you think?'

The light from the house didn't penetrate too much outside, he was confident Oliver wouldn't recognise him again. Jake stood close to Oliver. How easy it would be to tell him.

Oliver closed the boot and picked up the shopping bags. 'I guess, but we like it.'

'Here, let me give you a hand.' Jake picked up two bags and took them to the front door. It would be so easy to tell him and destroy her life right there and then. But he didn't do quick and easy.

'Thanks, you sure you don't want me to ask my wife? It's no bother.'

He shook his head and said thank you. A gust of wind blew his scarf off his face. He turned quickly and left, walking out of the drive just as the door opened and Gemma came out to help.

Gemma finished laying the kitchen table for two and put out the rest of the bottle of wine, not before taking another glassful herself. She felt a little drunk now and needed food to soak it up. She grabbed a handful of peanuts and jerked the kitchen curtains closed against the dark evening, then took out the bin bag full of broken glass.

His cryptic messages kept rolling inside her head. She pulled out the plastic food containers from the microwave, stirred them and banged them back on for another couple of minutes.

When Oliver arrived, she went out to help him with the shopping. He walked straight into the kitchen, dropping the bags on the kitchen floor and gave her a huge bear hug.

She put her bags down and melted in his arms, letting herself absorb his love and the warmth. He felt solid draped around her. He felt real.

'You look weird, are you OK?'

'Oliver,' she began. 'I…' It was on the tip of her tongue to tell him.

'What's wrong?' he asked, urgently, pulling back and taking a look at her face. 'You look terrible.'

'Oh, I'm OK,' she said, quickly. 'It's nothing.'

Surely, Jake hadn't really threatened her? But what was the thing with the 12 days? Was it a countdown? If so, to what? No, he was just trying to get inside her head, that's what he was doing. He had no need to threaten her like that. No, she was overthinking it. She was wound up by the stupid flowers. That was it. She was reading too much into it. It probably meant until he wanted to see her again.

Oliver pushed her into a kitchen chair and fetched her a glass of water. She realised he thought she was ill. She played on it to cover her nervousness.

'I had something to eat, some leftovers from the fridge. I thought they smelt odd, but we have that smelly cheese in there and I thought it was that. I guess I was wrong.'

'Well you go to bed, have a lie down. I'll put all this away. I'll heat up some soup for you later. Nothing lost with the dinner tonight, is there.' He gave her a concerned smile.

His kindness almost smothered her. How had she done

this to him? 'I will if you're sure you don't mind putting all this away. The dinner's in the microwave.'

He laughed. 'Nothing wasted then. I'll sort this lot out. You lie down and I'll come up and see you when I'm done.'

If only he knew he was married to a stupid bitch whose mad idea had turned into a Hitchcock screenplay. Oh, for the love of God. Why had she been so stupid?

She got up. He folded her in his arms. 'You go and relax, go on.' He kissed the top of her head and shooed her out of the kitchen.

But her mind was full of Jake, not relaxing.

He walked her to the stairs and said, 'Shame I didn't take up that guy's offer of help, he might have helped put all this away.' He laughed to himself walking back to the kitchen.

She stopped dead on the stairs.

'What man?'

'In the drive. He was lost. Looking for the Fletchers. I've not heard of them, have you? He said the house name. I think it was Malvern. I don't know it, do you?' He looked back at her.

She frowned. 'No. What else did he say?'

'Nothing, apart from offering to carry the groceries to the front door. Nice bloke, I think his satnav brought him down the wrong road.'

She looked hard at him. It couldn't be Jake. 'What did he look like?'

Oliver shrugged picking up the single bag left in the hallway. 'Couldn't say. Wore a baseball cap pulled down low and a scarf. Scared me to death when he appeared, though. Didn't hear him coming up the drive. The wind's blowing a gale out there.'

She watched his face carefully to see if he was lying, but he gave nothing away.

'That's weird, don't you think?' She wanted to ask more, but hesitated and stopped herself. He'd done that to spook her. Why? To show her how easily he could get to Oliver?

'Not really, the guy was lost. Stop worrying. Get yourself to bed.'

Chapter Twenty-Two

Later that evening, propped up in bed, as he moved around the bedroom putting laundry away, he asked, 'Have you managed to get any rest?'

She shook her head. 'Sorry, no.' She watched him opening and closing drawers and wardrobes.

'Can I tell you what I found out in Cumbria?'

He stopped what he was doing and turned around.

'Cumbria? What were you doing in Cumbria? I didn't even know you'd been up there?'

She blurted it out without thinking how to explain it properly.

'It's to do with Peter.' She let the words hang in the air. 'Something came on the news a few days ago.' She shifted her position. 'A house builder called Butler Homes is in trouble with HMRC. I remember Peter mentioning them.'

'You're right, he did.'

She sat up. 'So I drove up there. I didn't tell you because I found out the day you got back from the bank and didn't want to raise your hopes.'

'You drove all the way to Cumbria? Did you get to speak to anyone?'

'Not really, only reception, but I got a lot out of her.'

'What did you find out?'

She shrugged. 'It was Peter who managed their accounts. He was a consultant Financial Controller on the finance team. I don't know how he did it. It's a big company, not huge like Barratt Homes, but bigger than us and he's taken hundreds of thousands. The receptionist only knew a little of what went on. But from what she heard he was brought in two years ago as this new whizz-kid who was going to

142

turn the business around.' She laughed wryly. 'She said he blindsided them all. They all fell under his spell.'

'So, he's done this to others. It's not just us then. Gem, do you know what this means? We have proof we're not lying.'

She nodded. 'And get this.' She looked straight at Oliver. 'He had an affair with the CEO's wife. Probably how he got his foot in the door, you know, befriending them both then took advantage. You can just see him, can't you? His blond floppy hair and all year-round tan, those soft blue eyes looking at you, reassuring you, telling you to trust him. His brilliant white smile and manicured fingernails.' She shook her head. 'When I think of it now, how did we not think he was too suave?'

Oliver didn't move a muscle for a few moments then said, 'Did you tell her he'd done the same to us?'

She shook her head. 'No.' Her face looked suddenly hopeless.

'Why not? Maybe we can go see the CEO, tell them it's happened to us. HMRC will then see we're not making it up and Peter Hayes does exist. Don't you see that, Gem?'

'I already made tentative enquiries and she said they had closed ranks, especially since the press knew about it. You can imagine can't you how much damage this could do to their business.'

'Yes, but they won't go under, they're probably solid enough to ride it out.'

'I think what he's done is taken from a lot of businesses, not enough to sink them...'

'He sank us, why? We... I was his friend.'

'I don't know, the receptionist said that when the CEO's wife didn't want to go off with him, he turned nasty.'

'Christ, you mean violent?' He looked shocked. 'I really didn't know him, did I?' Oliver dropped his head. 'But why us? He didn't have an affair with you, so why sink us? It makes no sense.'

Peter Hayes' suave tanned face skipped in front of her eyes, smug and full of it.

'Do you think we should get a lawyer?' he asked.

'Oliver, we can't afford a lawyer? What for anyway? To write a letter? No, you do that. Write to HMRC and tell them, better than ringing up, that way it's in writing and we have proof we informed them.'

She hated the limbo they were now in. A tiny bit of hope always just out of their reach.

She hadn't been able to settle since she found out about Butler Homes. Now it was out, it was a relief in a way.

But why hadn't Jake with all his contacts found that information? She tried not to let her mind go there. She tried not to imagine him keeping that and possibly Peter's whereabouts from her on purpose. For what? Had he spun her a web of lies? Was the whole thing a hoax? Was he even Jake Challinor? Her mind fragmented into a multitude of what ifs.

'I think it would have more power behind it if it came from a lawyer,' he said.

'But we can't afford a lawyer,' she snapped unable to find her composure in time. She'd not told him of the extra money she had. She'd hidden it. She didn't want it, and she wasn't able to think of a plausible reason why she would have it. They were still living off the first lot of money.

She took a moment, then turned back to him, but nothing prepared her for the look on Oliver's face that said so much.

'What?' she said bewildered.

The colour dropped from Oliver's face. 'I'm only going to ask you the once, Gem.'

'Ask me what?' she cut in.

'Don't lie to me, please. I couldn't bear it.'

'Lie about what? What are you talking about?'

He closed his eyes. Took a moment. Then asked, 'Did you sleep with Peter?'

Nothing came from her. Not a squeak. Not a nod. Nothing. How had he come to that conclusion? How? 'No, of course I didn't sleep with him,' she said outraged.

What the hell had made him ask that?

'Sorry, Gem. I don't know why I even asked it. I'm sorry. Stupid of me to even think it. I must be going mad to have thought you could do such a thing. I'm sorry. I'm truly sorry.'

She couldn't stand it. She got out of bed. She had to do something. She felt devastated he had thought she was capable of sleeping with Peter. Feeling deceitful and dirty about Jake she was unable to face him. Count to five. Count to five before you say anything, she told herself.

'Oliver? What made you ask that?'

'Just what you said about the CEO's wife. I… I'm sorry. I know it's crazy to even think you'd do that, but for one moment, I wondered if that was why he did it.' He dropped his head into his hands. 'You should hate me for thinking that. I know you'd never do something so awful. I don't know why I said it. Christ. I didn't believe it even when the thought popped into my head.'

'Oliver… I don't know what to say.'

'I thought maybe you'd pushed him aside or something and that's why he did it. Stupid I know. I think I'm just grasping at straws and nothing makes any sense. It's all going round and round in my head.'

'Oliver, I'd never do that to you. I can't believe you even asked.' Now she would never be able to tell him. If he thought for even just one tiny second she'd have slept with Peter, he'd never believe what was going on with Jake. Never. Shit. What a mess.

'I feel so bad now. Gem, will you forgive me?'

Chapter Twenty-Three

She ran through a forest; it was dark, and the moon was shrouded by the thick clouds, very little light filtered through. Far ahead in the distance, she saw Oliver running towards her. To her left she saw their house and the sun shining over it.

She tried to run to him, but she was stuck and her voice wouldn't work to call out to him.

He stopped and looked around. There were dogs, wild dogs snarling behind the trees. Oliver ran towards her, but it was as if he was running on the spot, no matter how hard he ran he never reached her.

She tried moving her legs, but she couldn't shift them.

Then Jake appeared and he ran towards them from the side. He had something long like a sword in his hands and waved it about. He ran faster and faster, unlike Oliver.

She screamed when she saw what it was, but Oliver couldn't hear her. Her legs ached from pulling them out of the treacle pulling them down.

The sky darkened with her terror. If she didn't get to Oliver, Jake would kill him.

Jake was nearly upon him, but Oliver still didn't see him.

She screamed but nothing came out.

Then Jake was upon him but he didn't stop. He ran right through him like a ghost and then Oliver was gone and she was all alone in the woods.

The silence was thick and loud. She never got to say she loved him. She couldn't save him. She tried, but she couldn't save him.

The stabbing pain in her chest was so strong, it woke her

up breathless. But she hadn't died and neither had Oliver, he lay breathing gently beside her.

She lay in the darkness, sweat dripping between her breasts and on the back of her neck, her heart pounding. It took a few moments for her to settle. She switched on the light, and the horrors were gone.

Or were they?

Chapter Twenty-Four

Walking through Knutsford the next day, all sorts of thoughts flooded her mind. Crazy ideas. Outrageous plans. Fantastic plots to rid Jake from her life once and for all.

The way she was feeling things could spiral out of control if she wasn't careful, but she couldn't stomach him in her life a moment longer.

She didn't trust Jake not to come banging on the door and getting full satisfaction from telling Oliver his fabricated lies.

She had awoken this morning with such turmoil in her stomach; she was now popping Gaviscon tablets like sweets. Not good. She pushed her hand inside her handbag and searched for the packet, located it and popped another pill from the blister pack.

The village hummed with people. Most of them were young mums with children and lots of old folks, and downright annoying folks who milled in and out of the shops. All glad to be outside after the wet weather even if it was cold. It always happened after a spate of rain. Everyone came outside, gasping for air as though they needed to see for themselves that the rain had really stopped.

She had to stop walking and grab hold of a lamp post as the sheer impact of her situation with Oliver hit her. She had no idea what to do and how to get out of her predicament. Her eyes brimmed with tears. Dread wormed through her that this was all going to end so badly.

She had to get Jake out of her life before he destroyed her. But how?

The narrow pavements made it difficult to walk as a pair. So, everyone tended to walk in single file. She cut through the throng of mothers and buggies and old people ambulating at a snail's pace through the village.

She looked behind her, sensing she was being followed. Crossing the narrow street, she headed straight into Boots on King Street.

At the medicine section she checked out all they had on show. Her lips puckered while her eyes scanned the shelves. She picked up a few bottles, read the labels then replaced them. Did she think she would really find a solution here? What on earth was she thinking?

This was not a Victorian England apothecary where she would find the solution on the shelves. She had to be smarter. She had to be smarter than Jake. She had to outsmart him.

Christ, was she really thinking along those lines?

Wind Relief – not going to do much harm. She looked at the side effects of taking too many, diarrhoea or constipation, well she might make him unable to leave the house but it wouldn't be permanent. Vapour chest rub – nope. Maybe if she shoved it up his nose it might burn its way up to his brain. Breathe right nasal strips – not unless they had Breathe wrong nasal strips. Night Nurse – yes – potentially. Nytol – mmm possible but not strong enough.

She smiled at the shelf stacker in case she read on her face what she was thinking and quickly headed out of the shop.

She zigzagged through the milieu of shoppers on the pavement to get back to her car.

A car hooted making her jump. She stumbled across the pavement tripping on a loose paving stone and caught sight of someone who looked like Jake scurrying down one of the side streets.

Cutting through one of the narrow side streets which ran parallel with the main street, she walked past the back of a small row of terraced houses, squeezing between the wheelie bins and slipping back onto the main street.

Standing outside the newsagents, she looked back along the street. Sure enough, there he was. A movement inside the newsagents caught her eye. The window display was full of business cards and adverts of people looking for work. But one of the business cards caught her attention. She took a photo of it on her phone.

'Gemma?' a voice behind her said.

She whirled around startled. 'Yes?' She recognised the face but it was older and tired-looking and the hair was different, but she knew it. She just couldn't place it. Her mind raced trying to photofit the face with a name.

'It's Karen. Karen Loomes,' the woman screeched with a huge smile on her face. 'Fancy seeing you after all this time. I can't believe it.'

'Oh my God, Karen! I was only thinking of you just the other day, how weird! Your hair! It was so beautiful and you've cut it all off?'

'You were always rubbish with faces. But yeah, it had to come off once the kids arrived. I wanted something easy to manage. Do you like the colour?' She did a little twirl.

'Well, from black to auburn is quite a change. I love it. But you can't blame me for not recognising you. It's a drastic change. I can't believe it. I can't believe it's you.'

They hugged and hugged until people passing began to tut loudly because they were obstructing the pavement.

'You haven't changed, though,' Karen said. 'Look at you. Still sexy as ever. And your hair, still so amazing. I can't believe you haven't changed your hair and it still suits you! Look, do you fancy a coffee? Let's have a coffee and don't tell me you have somewhere to be because I'm not having it. After all this time you owe me a coffee! God, how many years is it, Gemma?'

They were a few paces from a coffee shop at the top end of Princess Street. 'Go on then,' Gemma said, she wanted to get off the street anyway. This way she could sit near the window and see if Jake went by. What were the odds of bumping into Karen? She wanted to tell her that her stupid idea all those years ago had now come back to haunt *her*. But then she'd have to admit what a gullible prat she was. She popped another Gaviscon pill.

They ordered two lattes. Gemma grabbed the high stools by the window, giving her a great view of the street. She was about to say something about Jake but paused remembering that at the moment Karen wasn't in trouble and was it really fair to distress her about it?

'Look, we'll do all the catchy up stuff in a mo. I have to ask you. Do you know who I saw in town a few months ago?' Karen said, full of excitement.

Gemma frowned. 'Who?' She already knew the name she was going to say.

'Jake Challinor.'

Gemma said nothing.

'What? Don't you remember? Sure you haven't got Alzheimer's? Don't you remember when we were at uni; we met him and his friend, Liam? They were older than us. We picked them up in a nightclub for a laugh. The three of us, you, Mattie, and me, remember Mattie? Matilda Whitehead? We dared each other to do it. We had no money. Christ, we were pretty wasted at the time.'

'I remember, but I don't remember it the same way. You were the one who had the idea to raid the rich boys.' How could she forget Mattie? She felt awful she'd allowed them all to lose touch. Why had it happened after all their pledges to stay close forever?

Karen nodded enthusiastically as she spoke. 'Aah, my idea, your idea, who cares, but you remember what we did. Christ, if my kids did anything like that, I'd belt them 'til they were black and blue.' She laughed trying to convey she wouldn't really hit her children. 'Do you remember we went to a very smart Italian place full of toffs on the corner of Brad Street, what was it called?'

'I can't remember.' She didn't want to talk about it. It had been so innocent they'd thought. Her smile now gone from her face as she thought about what was happening in her life because of Karen's stupid prank.

'Funny when you look back; it wasn't posh really, was it? Mind you anything was posh to us if it wasn't baked beans. Christ I can't stand the stuff now.'

Gemma tried to pull a smile out and nodded. 'No, I'm not partial to them either, but we were smashed and anywhere would have looked upmarket to us.'

'Oh my God, I know, we were so poor. Surprised we didn't get scurvy or something?'

'We lived off beans for years. We didn't have our five a day for sure.'

'Couldn't afford fruit and veg.' Karen shook her head in disbelief and took her latte from the waitress. 'Remember we promised them all sorts of kinky sex; I can't believe we had the gall to do that, can you? And then we made them strip naked.' She hooted with laughter. Some heads turned in their direction. Gemma dropped her head. She didn't remember Karen being this loud?

'We tied them to the signpost at the roundabout just outside the centre of Chester where it gets mad busy in the day but it's deadly quiet at night, remember? It's not like that now, you know. Traffic is chaotic around there. Loads of new build and there's a small retail park there now too. You wouldn't recognise it if you saw the place. Have you been back?' Karen sipped her latte looking over the rim at her.

'No, I haven't. I haven't been back.'

'Really? How odd. Every time I go past there I remember. Hard not too, considering.'

Gemma resisted the temptation to ask what she meant.

'Jake was such a dick. Remember he tried to shove his hands in Mattie's pants. Dirty bastard. I think that was Jake, not his friend.' Then she spluttered, her coffee shooting out of her mouth spraying the table and Gemma.

Gemma wiped the table and her face. 'Bloody hell, Karen, watch out.'

'Sorry, but Christ, you gave him such a whack in the bollocks. I can still see his face turn white. Freaked me out. The look he gave you. I was glad we tied them up.'

Gemma shook her head numbly hating being forced to remember that night.

'Remember his anger? Christ, I still remember his yelling, '*"Untie us. You'll pay for this, don't think you won't."*'

'We made Mattie tie them up and you helped. Then we buggered off and left them,' Karen said, laughing.

Gemma moved away avoiding another possible spraying.

'He made Mattie cry,' Gemma said. She remembered how upset and confused Mattie had been and how angry it made her. 'Remember how he kicked her when he got out of the car? I felt so mad I wanted to smash every bone in his body and cut off his balls.' She remembered how dark her mind had gone that night. The same dark she felt towards her stepfather. Jake's yelling echoed resoundingly in the night. All she heard were the same threatening words from her stepfather. She didn't remember much after that, the red rage consumed her. She'd tied them up with Mattie's help and made sure the knots were unyielding.

'I know, you were so mad at him. You know, we were crazy. I can't believe we got away with it. These days we'd be locked up.' She lowered her voice. 'We were so drunk; you were screaming what you wanted to do to him. You couldn't stop yourself. We couldn't stop you. We had to drag you away. We thought you'd go back later and do something stupid to him so Mattie slept on the floor against the door.'

Gemma didn't laugh. Now she remembered Mattie lying on the floor and wondered why? Sweet Mattie looking out for her. She remembered all too well how terrified she was that night of what she wanted to do.

'We rang the police and told them where to find them, then called the local paper to piss them off for being such prats,' Karen said.

'I didn't know you'd done that,' Gemma said. That explained a lot.

'You were so cross with him calling you a whore and prick tease.'

Karen was right. If she hadn't been so drunk, she would have gone back regardless of Mattie blocking the door. All the way home to their digs she contemplated going back, beating him up and dragging his body into the woods. But she passed out. Thankfully. Big talk for a drunk.

'It was only later we found out they were from Knutsford. It made the *Daily Mail*. "*Prominent businessman's son found naked and drunk by roadside.*"' She laughed. 'Served him right, really. Imagine us moving here to the same town as that prat. I've not been here long how about you? I'd forgotten all about it until I saw Jake in the town. Luckily, he didn't recognise me. Thank God I've changed my hair so drastically.'

'Lived here a few years but I've never seen him, not that I would have remembered him anyway.'

Gemma drank her coffee considering whether to say anything else. Her mind was so full of Jake she felt if she didn't say anything to Karen she'd burst. She had to vent, to talk to somebody about it. Somebody who knew him. As wrong as she thought it was to open up, she needed to. Why should she carry all the burden? It had been Karen's idea in the first place.

'What's your address? We must stay in touch,' Karen said.

She didn't have time to answer. Suddenly, he was right in front of them. She froze. 'Karen, look out of the window, but don't move.'

'Ohmygod.' She turned back around rapidly on the stool, facing away from the window. 'Gemma? How is this even possible? A coincidence?'

Gemma ducked her head down. 'I don't believe in coincidences.'

'I can see him in the reflection in the picture on the wall. I think he's leaving. Yes, he's looking around again as if he's looking for someone... and now he's walking away,' Karen said, turning back and searching the crowds. 'This is so weird, I mean, we're talking about him and then he's here! Right outside the window! It must be a coincidence.'

Gemma cleared her throat. 'Look, Karen, I have to go.' She felt light-headed. She stood up and moved past Karen to get out of the shop. It was as if the walls of the coffee shop were closing in. It wasn't fair to burden Karen with it all.

Karen grabbed her arm. 'Wait, you're right, that's too much of a coincidence, Gemma.' She could see the puzzlement in her eyes. 'What's going on, you know something? Tell me.'

'Alright, sit down. It's not easy to say any of this, Karen, but I do need to speak to someone about it.' To hell with it. She'd asked and she needed to speak about it.

The coffee shop had gone quieter. There were only a few tables in use now, the rush of lunchtime having died down. She told Karen everything.

'Are you telling me he's blackmailing you?' Karen said.

'I suppose in a way, yes.' The waitress cleared their plates, and they ordered another couple of drinks.

She scrutinised Karen's face carefully as she cogitated what she'd told her. She realised she was hoping Karen would come up with a solution. But all she saw was fear in her eyes and disbelief.

'Wow, I don't know what to say, Gem. Why the hell did you do it?'

'I felt I had no choice at the time. Look, don't judge me, I made a mad choice thinking it was a good choice. That's a lie, I knew it was wrong, but I was so bloody desperate, that's why. Don't pity me about my finances, that's the least of my worries right now. What worries me more than anything is if Jake tells Oliver.'

'Mmm, I can see why you'd worry. Oliver wouldn't believe nothing happened between you. Especially after getting ten grand for the night.' She gave her a hard stare.

'No! I didn't sleep with him. What do you take me for after what I went through? You think I'd do that?'

Karen reached out and took her hand. 'Sorry, sorry, I didn't mean that. I do believe you.'

'But you wouldn't have done it, would you? I'm an idiot. But I was so desperate and didn't know who he was at the time. I would never have done it if I had. You know, there were so many red flags that day. I knew something was odd about the whole thing. I knew it.' She stressed the last words to get her point across. 'But I chose to ignore the warning signs because I was scared and desperate. You won't understand unless you've been in that situation. I felt as if I had nowhere to turn and just like that he was there offering help.'

'I'm not judging you, Gem. I'd never do that. You know I wouldn't,' Karen said.

'I know, I know. I'm judging myself. That's the problem. And now I'm stuck and I don't know what to do. Any suggestions?'

Karen gave a sad laugh. 'No. I don't, I'm afraid. Go to the police?

Gemma hesitated. 'No, no I don't think so. It's too messy. There has to be another way. I just needed to talk to someone about it to give me some perspective.'

'The countdown. You have no idea what that's about?'

'No. It came out of the blue.'

'And he sent you a dozen bouquets?'

'Yes, what you thinking?'

'I'm not, that's the problem. But twelve days, why twelve?'

She considered what Karen said. 'I can't think of anything.'

'Think, Gem. Is there anything? Anything that happened years ago to do with the number twelve? Something that perhaps you didn't share with us?'

She bit her thumbnail as she thought. Nothing came to mind. 'I can't remember anything. No.'

'There has to be something you're not remembering,' Karen said.

'Seriously? If it was something significant, I'd remember, surely.'

'He's giving you a clue. To make you remember. The countdown must have some significance to you both.'

Gemma's eyes widened. 'This is so sick. But why would he want to do this? I never saw him after that night.'

Karen looked at her hard. 'To make you work it out. Something happened back then that links you to the twelve days.'

'So, what happens if I don't figure it out?'

Karen's blue eyes looked deeply into Gemma's. 'I don't want to think about it.'

And that's when she realised, she had to get ahead of him. 'I can't do this on my own, Karen.' She fished out her phone from her pocket. 'I took this before.' She showed Karen the photo of a business card she had seen in the newsagent's window.

'Really? You think you need them?'

'I do,' she said, vaguely. 'I need to get ahead of Jake to stop him. I need information about him that I can use to do that. I'm certainly not going to allow him to destroy my marriage.'

Karen examined the card. 'Go for it then if you're not going to call the police. I would go to the police.' Something occurred to her. 'Do you think he'll go after me next?' Gemma heard the panic in her voice. 'What if he's going after the three of us and you're the first? What about Mattie? I've not heard from her in a long time. I'll try and contact her on Facebook. Have you been in touch with her?'

'No. I hardly go on Facebook, to be honest. Can't stand it. But Karen, you're right you know. I've no idea if he means to go after us all or just me.' She saw a real look of fear on Karen's face now. 'Look, it's probably just me. I was the one who punched him and tied him up. You just danced around in your underwear. I was the one who suggested we strip them.'

'Right. You were, I didn't do much. Let me try and find Mattie. We need to speak with her.'

'Good idea. I'm only asking for curiosity sake, but you haven't seen anyone suspicious following you, have you? I mean now that you know about him.'

Karen looked terrified. 'God, no. I've got kids, do you think he'd try something with them? Jesus, Gem, are we all in real danger?'

And that was when she realised, they all were. 'No. I really don't think so. But it won't hurt to be vigilant.' Karen didn't need the worry and besides she wasn't sure anyway. Jake was fixated on her at the moment and she'd be surprised if he was targeting anyone else. She had to sort this out before he did.

Chapter Twenty-Five

When she got back home as she put her key in the lock of her front door, it swung open. She hesitated for a few seconds before pushing the door open wider and walking in. Oliver had texted her that he'd had a call from the bank saying they needed to see him urgently.

A dog barked. In the distance, she heard the faint sound of traffic. The trees rustled in the gentle breeze.

Her heart pounded, fast, making her a little breathless. Her eyes flicked around the hallway and up the stairs. Was this another of Jake's visitations?

She unzipped her handbag and dug inside feeling for her phone. All the time listening out for any sound that somebody was still in the house.

With her phone in her hand, she wavered about dialling 999. Instead, holding onto it, she made her way along the hallway. She looked around, everything looked the same.

Nothing had been disturbed.

Nothing out of place.

She made her way to the back door through the kitchen and unlocked it – in case she needed to escape.

Everything was as she'd left it. The tall china mugs from breakfast were still in the sink. A twenty-pound note sat on the round kitchen table where she'd left it for Oliver to pick up the dry cleaning. He'd clearly forgotten.

Moving out of the kitchen, she walked into the lounge towards the French doors, unlocking them too. As she moved back towards the hallway, she dropped her coat on the sofa.

Climbing the stairs, she was jumpy as if somebody was about to leap out at any moment.

She pushed the bedroom door open, ready to dart downstairs if there was anybody in there.

There wasn't.

She froze in the doorway aghast at the array of photos on the bed and floor. Shit. Huge A3-size photos. All photoshopped of Jake and her together, cosying up and looking intimate. Not true. What was he up to? There were photos of Karen and her outside the coffee shop, too. She'd have to warn Karen now. She stood for a moment weighing it all up. Something occurred to her. She counted the photos. Eleven.

She stood on one of the photos. With the heel of her shoe she crushed Jake's face until there was nothing but a huge hole in his head.

Bastard.

She checked the other rooms.

All clear.

Back in her bedroom, she perched on the end of the bed. What was she going to do about this out of control situation? The man was clearly deranged.

She paced up and down the room as Jake's face and all the memories of that night and the past few days taunted her.

A lump swelled in her throat. Taking out her phone she called Jake. But as the number dialled a text came in.

Eleven.

The call connected. 'What the hell are you playing at!' she yelled.

'When can we meet?' he responded, ignoring her question.

She screwed up her eyes and tried to speak through her tight throat. 'Now. I want to see you now,' she demanded. She knew there was going to be no reasoning with him: he just seemed intent on destroying what she had.

She had every intention of stopping this. Stopping him. He was doing all this to prove he called the shots. The ghost of her stepfather suddenly appeared moving around her childhood room, picking up her revision notes, her files and dropping them on the floor. She watched him flutter her notes like a pack of cards all over the floor and laugh. *'I could make all this lot vanish. If I wanted to. Then where would you be with your precious exams? So, you'd better stop being an arse when I come to visit you. Understand?'* She watched herself squirming on the bed in front of him, hating every part of him for holding her hostage. For her vulnerability. Her ghost vanished as quickly as it came – she was still vulnerable and still being held hostage.

'Suits me,' he said, his voice sounding full of pleasure. 'Go to The Riverside Country Club. I'll see you there in two hours.'

'Why two hours? Why not now?'

'I imagine you want to have a bath and get yourself ready. You have a debt to pay, and I think I want to collect today.'

She cut him off and threw the phone down. Hundreds of images ran through her head as to what he had in mind this time.

He did nasty so well.

She'd be damned if she was scrubbing up for him.

It wasn't happening.

She slipped off the bed, frantically grabbed all the photos, retrieved a black bin bag from the kitchen and jammed it full. Then she ran to the garden and burnt the lot on a small bonfire at the far end of the garden.

Chapter Twenty-Six

Gemma was adding the last lot of pictures to the bonfire when she heard the back door open. Oliver was home, and she needed to think of an excuse as to why she was burning paper. What bad timing. As always.

She waited for him to find her, nervously.

'Hey, darling, what you up to?' he asked, strolling towards her and staring at the black embers.

She took a sip from her glass of wine, grimacing that he'd caught her with that too. The flames tore through the last photo of Jake's face just as he arrived next to her.

'Aren't you cold out here without your coat?' He took a mouthful of her red wine. Then gave her a kiss on the cheek. 'Should be a cup of tea. Are you nearly finished? Shall I put the kettle on?' She was grateful he didn't bang on about the wine. She stopped drinking. She had to drive later.

'Yes, I'm finished. Let's go back inside.'

She pushed open the back door remembering what Karen had said about twelve being significant.

'So, what were you burning out there?' he asked, locking the back door behind them.

'Just rubbish stuff I found in the office, you know from the move. I was having a bit of a tidy up.' She'd told him that she received an email yesterday with her contract for the virtual secretarial job, which she was supposed to start today. Then she'd forgotten and gone into town. Stupid. Stupid. Stupid.

'I thought you were supposed to be working today, doing your virtual stuff. You were gone ages. You said you only popping into town for an hour. Did you get my text? What a pain that was. Nobody at the bank knew anything about making a call asking me to come in. Can you believe it? Complete waste of time. Anyway, I guess it got me out of the house.' He pulled a banana from the fruit bowl. 'I am sick of all this paperwork. I feel like a bloody mole caged up in that office fobbing off creditors and the bank. You'd think they'd stop badgering us by now, wouldn't you?' Finishing the banana, he threw the skin in the bin. 'So what have you been up to since you got back?'

She pulled the laundry from the dryer and folded each piece diligently while looking at the clock. She'd had to tell him about the contract. The money was running out and she had to start using the rest of the money Jake had given her. Telling Oliver more money had just appeared wouldn't cut it a second time.

'Oh, well I had half a dozen letters dictated that needed sending out. I found them in my inbox when I got back home. Kept me busy and out of trouble.' She laughed a nervous laugh. 'Then I had a tidy up.' She indicated the bonfire outside with a nod of her head.

'Clever how it works, isn't it?'

'I guess.'

'Good idea though, saves money on renting office space. What's your boss like?'

'OK, I guess. I've only met him on Skype, seems alright. But I suppose what you said does make sense.' What the hell did virtual secretaries do, anyhow? She'd spent five minutes googling it and still wasn't totally sure.

'Some virtual secretaries have an answering service, don't they? They transfer the calls to your landline, or you get a dedicated number. For small businesses it's a no-brainer, don't you think?' he asked.

'Yeah, but I don't think he wants that service.' She finished the laundry, glanced at the clock and began to think of a reason to leave the house.

'Oh, by the way,' said Oliver. 'I've hired another firm of accountants – well, not a firm to be exact, an accountant so he can wrap up the business and deal with the creditors. No point in carrying on, we'd be working to pay people off and make nothing and, quite honestly, Gem, I can't do this on my own any longer. It's too much. Besides, I don't want too and I'm drowning.'

'You mean shut the business down and not sell it on? I hadn't thought you were even thinking of continuing? I thought that had been the plan all along.'

'It was just a question the accountant asked. He said we could carry on with the business. Start a Limited Company and use a different name, then either move our suppliers over or begin again. I thought about it for all of one second.'

This was news to her. She'd thought the business was gone for good. Start up under a different name? Carry on? Why not? Could they? 'Could we save losing our home?'

'No, because the house falls in with the partnership. The only problem with the scenario I've just mentioned is neither of us would be able to be directors of the new company because... we'll have to declare ourselves bankrupt.'

The B word. No credit, no borrowing of any kind. For anything! No Next account or charge cards. 'Christ, Oliver, I don't know if I can go through starting over again, I feel so disillusioned with it all.' Her heart wasn't in it any more. 'I think I just want an easy life and get a regular job. Forget the pressure. The sleepless nights. The worry. Staff. No. It's totally burnt me out, and...' She was too focused on Jake and how to get rid of him to think of anything else and lost her train of thought.

He shrugged, opened the bin and chucked the empty envelopes from the post he'd just opened. 'I'd like to have another go, darling, but maybe you're right. Let's tie up this mess then talk about it again.'

Chapter Twenty-Seven

JAKE

He turned right at the bottom of his drive on his way to The Riverside. He travelled in silence preferring not to have the radio on. She was getting too damned sure of herself. So, she'd found Karen.

He pulled into a parking space at The Riverside. Switching off the lights as another car pulled up and parked a few spaces in front of him. He watched the passengers disembark. Police, they all had a look. Something must have gone on in the place. He hoped it wasn't going to affect his meeting. He was looking forward to it.

His little exchange with Oliver the other night had thrilled him. He knew he'd have to work fast to deal with Gemma. Now he'd made contact with Oliver, she'd be mindful of how easy it was to get to him. She had no idea what he had in store.

Walking in through the revolving doors he felt the excitement bubbling in his stomach as he walked to the bar. He bought a drink to quell it.

'Scotch, Thomas, please,' he asked the barman.

Thomas placed a tumbler of the amber liquid in front of him. 'How are you keeping, Mr Challinor.'

'Couldn't be better, Thomas.' He raised his glass to him in a salute. He embraced the smouldering tingle of anxiety, it was one of his favourite feelings.

Jake said hello to the man who came to sit next to him. He wore a beige suit with a green cravat. His heavy brown eyes sought Jake out for company, he must be close to his fifties. Jake had on occasion spoken to him; he was a member of the club. His wife played tennis with Jake's. Today he didn't want to speak with him. Joseph Goldsmith.

Goldsmith was always asking questions and probing into his life. His eyes trying to read him. In many ways, Goldsmith was a decent guy, but he had a big mouth. He was known for it at the club.

All at once, Jake was conscious of the conversation going on farther down the long bar between Thomas and a man and a woman. He caught snippets of the dialogue. Some of the words made him feel hot. It made him catch his breath. Sweat began to pool under his arms and along his forehead. He took out his handkerchief and mopped his brow, surreptitiously.

Goldsmith began talking to him. He pulled at the collar of his jumper to cool down. Most of the time Jake could hide his stress brilliantly, but he had to be prepared first. Something like this, out of the blue, would take him several minutes to calm his heart rate down and assume normality. He swung around on the bar stool giving his back to the barman to hide his unease.

He was about to answer Goldsmith when the couple approached him.

He'd been right.

The couple in the car park were police.

'Mr Challinor? I'm DI Craig Lewis and this is DS Jill Foster. Your wife told us we'd find you here.'

He kept his head straight and firm and put his handkerchief back in his trouser pocket. Every instinct he possessed made Jake want to ask for a glass of water to speed up his cooling down. He knew it would be a sure sign he was agitated.

He felt their eyes probing him. He wanted to glance away but that would make him look suspicious. His peripheral vision picked up Gemma coming through the door. She clocked him straight away. He shifted off his seat as he acknowledged them and moved them all away from the bar to a quiet area a few feet away.

Every moment was agony as he waited to see if Gemma would approach him.

All three of them watched him. He felt like he was caught in a searchlight. He didn't look around; he didn't want Gemma to see he'd noticed her. He needed composure while talking to them. He knew what it would be about. She might decide, in one of her stupid, reckless moments to mention something to the police. He couldn't allow that.

He stroked his forehead to check the state of his perspiration, not too bad. His heart rate had slowed down; he was in control again.

With his back to Gemma, he sensed rather than saw her sit on the bar stool he'd vacated.

Chapter Twenty-Eight

GEMMA

Gemma arrived at The Riverside Golf and Country Club that was situated a few miles out of Knutsford. The car park was busy and she struggled to find a spot for her Mini. It took her two tours of the car park before she found a space between a 4×4 and a Jag. She just about squeezed herself out of her car without banging the door.

Walking past the rows of cars towards the front door she noted Jake's Overfinch. A massive urge to kick the car came over her, but she restrained herself. She'd do herself more harm than the car, she knew it. She'd break a toe, or worse her foot, knowing her luck.

She told Oliver she had met Karen in the village and they arranged to grab some time together. More catching up. Another lie and she hated herself for it. He'd been disappointed after his wild goose chase that afternoon and she knew he wanted to sit and talk. She found it difficult to speak the lie. What choice did she have? She was too frightened of what Jake might do if she didn't turn up.

She was dressed in jeans, boots and black leather jacket with her trademark hair pulled up into a ponytail. Her clothes were to make a point. A statement. She was tough and wasn't going to be messed about. The clothes did not convey her internal turmoil; she wore them like a shield.

Before leaving home, she had a mad idea to check Facebook. Sure enough, there he was, strutting his stuff with a billion photos of all the places he had been. She couldn't think why she hadn't thought of looking him up on it before. Probably because she hated social media. Stalking him without any form of danger had sent a colossal pulse of adrenaline coursing through her veins. His wife was on at least half the photos, a good-looking woman and sane looking too. What was she doing with him?

She came across a photo of Mattie, smiling, joking, and looking unreservedly happy with Jake's arm slung over her shoulder. Her legs had trembled when she saw it. Mattie mustn't know who he was. Was it a coincidence?

The photograph looked as if it was taken at a party and both held a drink, a Mojito. The tiny spiders ran up and down her back. What was Mattie doing with him? She looked closer at the photo to double check it was her. It definitely was. He even tagged her so there was no mistake. She couldn't know who he was, surely. What the hell was going on? What if he was stalking Mattie too? She needed to find Mattie. She needed to tell her the man was dangerous. And who he was. She phoned Karen to see if she'd managed to get hold of her. The phone had felt heavy in her hand as she waited for Karen to pick up. Ring after ring after ring, she waited almost hanging up just as she answered.

'I got your text. What do I do if he turns up?' Karen sounded jumpy.

'I don't know,' she said, sympathetically, 'just be on your guard. Look, I've just found Mattie on Facebook. At a party with him. He's wrapped around her. She can't know who he is, surely?'

'No!' she said, shocked. 'Let me look, was it on his page? I've not got around to looking her up yet. I looked at his page when I found out he was living here. I never saw this. He must have posted this recently. I've not had a chance since I got back to look again. After school activities etc., then making tea. Let me load it... wait a second... God. I see it.' Seconds later she said, 'I see, you're right. They do look cosy. Mattie would never do that if she knew who he was. She hasn't changed much, has she? I thought... well, the last I heard she was working abroad. She must be new to Facebook; I tried looking her up a few years ago and didn't find her. Let me check when she joined. Oh, she joined last year. Do you think that's a coincidence?'

'Do you think that's how he found her?' Gemma asked.

'Maybe. Where are you?'

'Just out. I have to go I'm already late. I just wanted to tell you about Mattie. I think we need to get in touch with her. Find out if she's OK and tell her who she's mixing with.'

Karen agreed.

She hung up; she didn't want Karen to know where she was. It was too complicated to explain. Even she didn't know what the hell she was doing.

She strode into the bar area spotting Jake instantly and walked over to the bar. He was in conversation with a couple and looked irritated that she had spotted him. Who was he talking to that he clearly didn't want her know about?

She found a stool close to him and ordered a vodka and lime in the plush, low-lit bar of the country club and handed over some cash.

She listened to his conversation without turning around. It was obvious he didn't want to make contact with her just yet. Intrigued, she did just what he didn't want her to do and turned around. Making it blatantly obvious she was listening in.

Jake looked ill at ease.

She sipped her drink.

The man he spoke to was around six feet, about the same height as Jake, bald and wearing a black coat. His blue tie was pulled loose from the collar of his white shirt. The woman was dressed in a smart but tired pinstriped trouser suit. She wore her bleached blonde hair pulled into a ponytail and no make-up. Neither of them took any notice of her, but she had the impression they knew she was there. She enjoyed watching him squirm.

She finished her vodka and ordered a soft drink. She had to stay clear headed.

Jake ran his hand through his hair avoiding eye contact with her, and then he brushed non-existent fluff from his shirt. He did that twice. Then he fisted his hand by his side. They hadn't noticed. But she had. She noticed his tell. He was on edge. Why? Who were these people that made him feel uncomfortable?

She asked the barman.

Police.

Right now, she felt the ball was squarely in her court. And he knew it. That was probably why he was avoiding contact with her. In case she joined in. In case she told the police what he was doing to her? She had the perfect opportunity to out him right there. She thought about it. Her body language must have alerted him to what she was thinking. His changed. It was subtle, but he was now on guard in case she did something.

If she did tell the police, they probably wouldn't believe her. He was bloody smart. He might even tighten the net around her, become more dangerous or turn his focus on Oliver. She couldn't let that happen.

He might even twist it, so she was charged with wasting police time.

In the end she sat and listened. She couldn't believe the police were right in front of her, and she wasn't able to do anything to help herself.

'If you do hear anything, we will appreciate any information you might be able to give us. Here's my card,' the blonde said. Jake took the business card. Looked at it then shoved it into his back pocket. 'Like we said, we are anxious to find Matilda Whitehead. So, any leads about her possible whereabouts would come in useful.'

Gemma froze.

At that moment their eyes locked.

She noticed the tiniest hint of a lip curl before it was gone.

'The number of the station and my mobile are on there. In case you wake up in the night with any forgotten thoughts, Mr Challinor. As we said, these are just preliminary inquiries.'

Gemma rushed out of the bar and raced to the ladies. Stepping inside, she almost barrelled into two heavily made up women dressed as though they were going to London Fashion Week. She scooted into one of the smart cubicles.

Sat on the loo lid, she took a lungful of air and let it out slowly to try and calm her racing heart and mind.

What had happened to Mattie?

Where was she?

Why were they looking for her?

Much as she wanted not to, she felt deep down something dreadful had happened to her. The fact the police were questioning him lent weight to his involvement in Mattie's apparent disappearance.

But what? Did he have her locked up somewhere? Or worse... had he killed her? Oh God. Mattie had rejected him. He might... he might... no, she couldn't go there. Not Mattie. Gemma buried her face in her hands to stop herself from crying out.

She googled Challinor Electronics. A mountain of information came up about the company. She scrolled through all the headings, finally finding a link. She should have done this in the beginning.

She read on. *After his arrest for indecent exposure in Chester and the revelation of a violent assault on a woman in a hotel room the previous year. Mr Fergus Challinor struck his son, Jake, from the board and dismissed him from the company. His brother, Mr D Challinor, has been appointed as the new CEO.* May 2003.

Christ. Had they caused all that to happen? It was a prank. Nothing serious, just a bit of a laugh. They'd been kids in their twenties. She bet Karen didn't know this had happened to Jake. She screenshot the page and sent it to her.

Scrolling further she came up with another story about the Challinor family. *David Challinor, the son of Fergus Challinor of Challinor Electronics who had succeeded his disgraced brother, Jake, to the position of CEO in the company, was rushed to hospital yesterday after an accident in their home. Unconfirmed reports today speculate David Challinor has suffered traumatic spinal injuries and may not regain the use of his legs. Mr Fergus Challinor has appointed a non-member of the family as CEO following the resignation of the youngest son from the company who wishes to remain anonymous.* September 2003.

She ran out of the building.

Chapter Twenty-Nine

Back at the bar, she sat on a stool and ordered a glass of water. She'd wanted to run away, but she owed it to Mattie to find out if anything had happened to her. She got as far as her car and turned back – against her better judgement. She was terrified he'd come and find her at the house if she left.

She saw Jake making his way over. He'd been sitting in the brown leather armchair opposite the bar, waiting for her return.

The barman placed a glass in front of her. 'Are you OK?' he asked.

She nodded. 'Yes, fine just feeling hot.'

She needed to find the courage to ask him. *Have you done something to Mattie?* And then she needed the courage to deal with the answer.

Her thoughts tried to assemble all of the pieces to find the significance of the countdown.

What if he'd been keeping tabs on all of them for years? Something must have triggered his appearance in her life at this time. Could it be her fall from grace? But it hadn't been in the papers when she met Jake. Peter. Why did Peter keep popping up in her mind? Was he connected in some way to Jake? And if so, how?

She sensed him behind her. She felt his gaze burning into her back.

He came up close and ran his fingers along the back of her neck. She flinched. 'Hello, Gemma, so glad you made it.'

She needed to tackle this without shooting her mouth off. Too many questions needed answers.

'Come on. I have a room. We need to go upstairs and talk,' he said, forcefully.

'No, no, we won't go upstairs. I'm not going anywhere with you. We can talk here.'

His gaze didn't leave her face. He helped her off the stool. She shrugged him off. 'So, how do you want to play this?' he said. 'Shall I drag you upstairs? Is that what you want?'

'What? No. I want to ask you some questions. Here.'

'Do you? What sort of questions?' Jake said.

'I want to ask you about Mattie.'

He laughed, but the sound wasn't full of joy. Instead it was evil, dark, and menacing. 'Upstairs,' he said.

She sat back on the stool. 'I'm not going anywhere with you. Tell me what you've done with Mattie,' she hissed.

He leant in close. She felt his hot breath on her neck. 'You don't know anything about me. You merely think you know and that's not the same, Gemma. But you will go with me; because right now I have a messenger delivering a gift to Oliver. If you don't do what I want his love for you will be over once he opens the envelope.' He traced a finger across her cheek. She slapped it away.

'Don't touch me,' she said, standing up and putting the stool between them. He pushed her back down.

He opened Google Maps on his phone and showed her a tracker. 'See it moving? Wait, I'll make the map bigger for you so you can see the exact road he's on.'

She watched as the blue pulsing circle moved along the A34 towards her home.

'I thought you might resist and might need some persuading.'

Unsettled, she said, 'Tell him what you like. I'm going to tell him anyway. Really, do you think he's going to believe you over me? You're delusional.'

She made a move to get up from the bar stool again, but he laid a firm hand on her shoulder holding her in place.

She should have confessed to Oliver from the beginning.

She was a mad fool who had lied and now, now it was snowballing into something else. Something ugly. Jake wouldn't have had this power over her if she'd been honest in the first place.

Wary of him she shrugged his hand off her shoulder and stood up. He pulled her firmly back down. 'Sit down,' he hissed.

Frightened she sat still waiting for his next move.

His hold tightened. With his back to the bar he leaned in close. 'You have no proof of anything. Whoever you tell will think you are the head case. After all, Gemma, you are going through a terrible situation at home. What can you prove about me? Look here, you're the one drinking the vodka. You're the one making the scene. The barman has seen it. Probably thinks you're a drunk. What am I doing besides talking to you? There's no connection between us.'

She thought of what might happen here, tonight. What if he was thinking of killing her? He might kill her or make her disappear. She'd never see Oliver again. All those things she loved about him, she'd never experience them with him again. Their love of cooking and eating out, listening to jazz and drinking wine, long walks and talking. They loved talking. They *had* loved talking. Things had changed a little since all this began, but she was hopeful it would come back.

Jake creeped her out, frightened her. She tried to sound in control.

'There's proof, CCTV at the pub and the hotel,' she said, valiantly.

'Proof? Firstly, that's been taken care of. And secondly, who would come off worse if there was? You meeting a stranger there? Or me meeting a beautiful woman? And you haven't even told Oliver, more lies and deceit.'

She opened and shut her mouth.

'Now, look here at this map, maybe the men delivering some paperwork to Oliver have other instructions. Maybe, because I anticipated your reaction today, I put in place some temptation.'

'Temptation? What the hell do you mean?'

'How much *do you want* to save Oliver? That's temptation enough, isn't it?'

'Are you saying you're going to hurt Oliver?' How the hell had all this turned from a Hitchcock movie to a Tarantino movie?

Jake shrugged and pulled away. He leaned casually against the bar looking at his phone and sighed. 'Oh, well, I guess you'll have to wait and see what happens. Look, he's turning into your road. Call Oliver. Ask him who's at the house.'

Perhaps he wasn't bluffing and she should check.

She dialled Oliver, he answered after two rings. 'Hi, darling, everything OK?'

'Mmm, yes everything's fine.' She heard the doorbell ring. 'Who's that?'

'I don't know, hang on let me open the door. Are you expecting anything?'

Her heart thumped so fast she went light-headed. 'Don't think so.' She heard the door open. Then silence. 'Who is it Oliver? Oliver? Oliver?' Then she yelled, 'What's wrong?' She stood up abruptly, pushing the stool away to get some distance from Jake. What had they done to him? She didn't know what to do. All she heard was muffled voices.

'One of them is on the phone, darling.' At the sound of his voice, she let out her breath and squeezed her eyes closed in relief that he was OK.

His voice went hushed and he whispered. 'They look a little weird; I'm not sure what they want, they don't look the type to be delivering.'

She looked at Jake who had his phone to his ear, he wore a nasty grin.

'Take a picture.'

'What?'

'Take a picture!' she yelled and noticed some of the people in the bar turning to look at her.

'I'm not taking a picture of them, Gem, that's weird.'

'Take a picture, Oliver. Just do it, please.' She heard some harsh intakes of breath around them at her raised voice.

Jake smiled broadly clearly enjoying the moment.

'OK. They're leaving, said they had the wrong house. Do you think they're staking out the place to burgle us?'

'Send the picture.'

'Why?'

'Oliver send me the picture, please. I'll explain later.' She sounded exasperated with him. It wasn't his fault. She knew she sounded weird, but she had to see who was at the house.

Oliver sighed heavily, went quiet for a few moments then said, 'Sent. You better explain what this is all about, Gemma. I'm not happy about oddball strangers coming to the house.'

'I will. Later. I promise. Love you.' Her phone pinged. She killed the call and opened the message and the photo. Then she felt a prickle of real danger. They looked like a Polish version of The Krays.

She ran out of the building pulling her hair out of her ponytail – it was so tight it was giving her a headache. Tears streamed down her face, her anger raging like a volcano, her huge hair billowing behind her but she was past caring what anyone thought.

Once outside, she hurried across the car park. She unlocked her car with the fob before she got to it. The hazard lights flashed on and off. She opened the door. Just as she was about to get in, she saw Jake's Range Rover in the opposite parking bay, six cars down.

She looked around. It was dark, the only light coming from the car park lamp posts.

She ran across to his car. With her key in a deadly grip, she shoved it as hard as she could into the paintwork and walked all the way around, dragging the key behind her. She zigzagged her artwork, making as much damage as she could.

When she finished, she stabbed the tyre; it did nothing. She ran back to her car, searching inside the boot for a sharp object. She rummaged through supermarket bags, a rug, wellies, two telescopic umbrellas and two golf umbrellas, a hat, a waterproof and a pair of evening shoes she'd forgotten about. Giving up on finding anything useful in there, she opened the glove box. From here she pulled out a small jar of Vaseline. Running back to the car she smeared the front windscreen with the contents.

Chapter Thirty

JAKE

Jake's anger was a living, breathing thing. A beast he had to tame. Right now, he strove to reel it in and stop himself from running out of the building after her and squeezing the last breath from her body. Just like Mattie. She hadn't resisted, perhaps because she hadn't known who he was until the last moments of her life.

The terror in her eyes when he told her had fulfilled him. She struggled gallantly for the little thing that she was. Petite and delicate, the opposite to Gemma's tall womanly body.

The seconds between Gemma seeing the photo and realising what he was capable of gave him a high. The whole place went quiet. Voices hushed and the bar noises disappeared. In that time frame all he heard was the white noise of his rage rushing through his ears. Gemma stood up, faced him and before running off, their eyes met for a fragment of a second, if that. But in that time, something passed between them. He felt it deep in his gut. He sensed she felt it too. An understanding.

He turned to Thomas, realised he'd placed a drink on the bar for him and was giving him a questioning look. Jake swallowed the drink. Nodded to Thomas a slight *all is OK*, and left the bar.

At the entrance of the club, he pulled out his phone. Walking down the steps to the car park he opened the file marked KAREN. There was a small picture of her, with her new auburn hair colour, wearing a baggy sweater and jeans. She looked tired and held the hand of one of her two daughters. That woman, together with Mattie and Gemma, had not only taken away his standing in his father's eyes but his future. He'd had to create an alternative future, which he'd had to carve out, faced with the ridicule of his peers and friends. The media coverage of their prank had certainly cut deep.

Jake flicked through the pages of the dossier he had on Karen. He had to stay organised otherwise mistakes would be made... and like a tower of cards, it would all come tumbling down. So he focused on Gemma and what he had to do with her first. Karen would have to wait. A woman nudged past him on the steps, she apologised.

Jake nodded giving her a false smile.

Chapter Thirty-One

GEMMA

The next morning Oliver found Gemma sitting at the kitchen table staring out of the window. He switched on the kettle and the kitchen lights. He picked up her coffee cup and placed it in the dishwasher.

'You OK, darling? You were late back last night,' he asked, moving to the thermostat and turning up the heat. It was a grey day with a fine drizzle that got deep into your bones. 'Aren't you cold in here? Not like you to be sat in a chilly room.' He dropped the empty wine bottle by the sink into the recycling bin and said nothing about it.

She turned around and smiled, twisting the foil wrapper from her chocolate biscuit over and over in her hand.

'I'm OK. We lost track of time, sorry,' she managed. She wanted to burst into tears and run into his arms. She wanted to feel his arms wrap her up. She had driven to their old house – which was still empty – after leaving the club last night and sat in the drive thinking of her life and her memories. Anything to stop herself thinking of the mess she was currently in.

'Fancy another coffee? Oh, we're out of coffee capsules,' he said, opening the silver tin and looking in the cupboard for another. 'You must have had the last one, would you prefer a tea or instant? So, was it good catching up?' He eyed her suspiciously.

She hated instant coffee. She dropped her gaze. 'It was fun, yes. Tea, please.'

'Did you forget to order them?' he asked.

'What?'

'The coffee, we're out.'

'Yes, I'll do it in a bit.'

His happy tone irritated her. It shouldn't, but it did.

'Well, if you order before noon, they'll be here tomorrow. Are you going to tell me what last night's phone call was all about?'

She continued to stare out of the window looking for the song thrush. She saw it most days. Had it found somewhere else to favour? Yesterday morning she had bought a fat ball for it, hung it on the back of the garden chair. She loved watching him work away on it.

Her mobile vibrated on the table. She glanced at the screen. She had thirty missed calls from Jake since last night. She'd turned her phone back on half an hour ago and it hadn't stopped going off. She unlocked it, went into settings and turned it off.

She almost expected him to arrive at any time. Screeching into the drive like Jason Statham, leaping out of his trashed car, breaking down the front door and beating the living daylights out of her.

He didn't.

Not yet anyway.

She chewed the skin around her nails. Her thumb was sore and ugly. Would he go to the police? They probably had CCTV of her on tape.

That's when she noticed the post on the table. On the top of the pile sat a circular for pizza delivery. In the black and white headline, highlighted in red against the white background was the number **10**, a smiley face sat above the number.

She watched Oliver bend down and get the teapot out of the cupboard. He was a dab hand at making fresh tea; this was his new thing, he'd read it in the *Mail*, drinking fresh tea kept dementia at bay. The *Mail* came out with such rot sometimes. He warmed the pot, adding the tea and hot water and left it to brew. She idly picked a piece of loose skin from around her nail.

'So, what was all that about?' Oliver asked her again.

'Oliver, the thing is, well the thing is…' The words stuck in her throat. 'I… you see… Christ, I don't know how to explain it.'

'Gemma, what is it? You know you really frightened me last night with your frantic phone call. What is it you're not telling me?'

Her mind raced. Countless excuses flicked past. She discarded them all, her brain like a search engine going from one possibility to the next, to the next, to the next.

'Tell me, Gemma. What the hell is it?' He sat in front of her and held her hands. 'I think I've been patient enough. Now is the time to tell me. What's going on with you? I know you're hiding something from me.'

She looked into those soft blue eyes.

What if the police got involved and came looking for her? She had no justification for what she had done. Not in the eyes of the law. She could get a criminal record. How was she to tell Oliver what she'd done to Jake's car last night! Oh, if only she'd told him everything at the beginning.

She wanted to drop her head into her hands and weep. How capricious life was.

Oliver let go of her hands and stood up. 'This is ridiculous. After everything that's happening with us you can't talk to me? Gem, I know you're troubled. Let me help you.'

When she didn't respond he swore under his breath. 'I can't do this, Gem. Look at you. You look ill. I've waited for you to tell me what the hell is going on but this is the end of the line. Last night scared the shit out of me. Do you know that? Who were those men? And why were they at our house? When you didn't come home when you said you would I was frantic. It's about that money, isn't it? That ten grand you appeared with. Where did it come from?'

She looked worried and felt worse but the words wouldn't come out. They jarred in her throat.

'Gem, I love you. I want to help you. Why won't you let me?'

A banging at the front door brought her back with such a jolt she knocked over the tea.

Oliver flinched and looked at the front door.

'Christ. Who the hell is that thumping on the door like that?' He looked at her. 'More weirdos?'

Instantly on her guard, she stood up. Fairly sure that what was behind that front door she wasn't going to like. 'I've no idea who's at the door.'

Oliver walked towards the front door.

Wait, don't open it. I must tell you something. Please wait. I'm sorry. I'm sorry. I love you. I love you so much. I did it for us. Please forgive me. The words were on the tip of her tongue.

Gemma followed behind. Bracing herself for what was coming through the door. She looked at Oliver as he walked in front, strong, in control. Angry. He grasped the door handle pulling the door open.

She closed her eyes, her mind all ready for the fury about to burst into their home.

Silence.

She waited, not daring to move.

She opened her eyes, one at a time. Oliver was outside, looking around the front garden. Tentatively, she walked out to join him, scanning the area searching for clues. It had to be Jake.

'Some stupid kids, I imagine,' he said. 'Left a dead bird on the doorstep. What kind of a joke is that? I moved it over to the hedge. I didn't want you to see it. Look, go back

185

indoors. I'll sort this.' There was a dull expression in his eyes.

A lump settled in her throat. 'Where?'

'Don't look. It's not very nice to see.'

She walked to where he pointed. There, beneath the hedge was her song thrush. She knelt and picked Robert up, holding his light body in her hand, gently stroking him as her tears came gently, dropping on his soft, lifeless body.

'Oh, Robert, I'm so sorry. This is my fault. You're dead because of me. What could that bastard gain from hurting you?' She wiped her nose on her shoulder.

The leaves crunched behind her. 'Gemma? Are you OK? What's wrong?'

'He's my friend, Oliver. He lived in our garden. I fed him. I bought him a fat ball yesterday. He came every day. Waited for me to throw out crumbs. What kind of person kills an animal?'

'A disturbed one. Come on, let's bury him.'

'No, I want to do it. You go inside.'

'But, Gemma…'

'Go, Oliver, please.'

She waited for him to close the front door. Then, with her bare hands she dug a small grave for Robert. Before lying him down, she placed a soft cushion of leaves and twigs inside, then gently she lay him to rest. 'I'm sorry. The man is sick beyond measure. Anyone who can harm an animal is sick. Rest in peace my innocent.'

She wiped the tears from her face. Stood up. Took a deep breath of fresh air into her lungs and walked back into the house.

Chapter Thirty-Two

When Gemma arrived home from the nail salon, Oliver was sitting in the lounge holding a glass of whiskey, dressed in his suit, waiting for her for quite a while apparently. It was a few days since Gemma had buried the song thrush and thankfully Oliver hadn't continued to question her about the men at the door and what was going on with her. It was only a matter of time before he broached the subject again. He might not have questioned her but his mood clearly showed that he hadn't forgotten.

She eyed him suspiciously. Something was wrong. She knew by the way his eyes, half closed, followed her around the room. 'Why are you dressed in your suit?' she asked, fumbling with her coat, looking at him from out of the corner of her eye.

'Come over here, Gem.'

She didn't go over; instead, she sat on the sofa and pulled off her boots. Too afraid of what he was about to say. 'My feet are killing. I don't know why I wear these stupid boots; they kill my feet every time I wear them. They shouldn't, they're Kurt Geiger, not cheap.' She wanted to scream at him to stop looking at her like that. She didn't. Desperation sat over him like a grim reaper. 'Expensive. Expensive boots should not hurt your feet.' She started to remove one boot. 'What's up, Oliver?' She glanced at him from beneath her eyelashes. Her tone was faux jolly. The strain between them was killing her.

Jake had been off the radar now for a full day, which made her uneasy.

She had spoken to Karen about the golf club and what she did to Jake's car, and what he had done to Robert the song thrush.

'Gemma, you need to make it clear to Jake that it has to stop or you'll go to the police,' Karen had said. 'You should just go to the police anyway. Stop messing about, the man is deranged and might do anything. He might have killed Mattie for all we know, and he could be coming after me.'

'I've tried, but whenever I go over it in my head it sounds crazy. I have no proof. They'll laugh me out of the station.'

'Then try harder. They might and they might not. Especially if they've spoken to him about Mattie's disappearance.'

'It doesn't matter, Karen, however I go about this it's going to piss him off. That's what I'm afraid of. I don't know how to stop him.' Her words sounded hollow even to her.

'Then you need to find something on him. What about that business card you showed me? Have you rung them yet?' Her voice sounded desperate.

'No, not yet. I think I'm scared of what I might discover.'

Karen's voice softened. 'Be careful, Gemma, don't let him know you're contacting that company. I think he's watching you. He might be watching me too; it wouldn't surprise me. If you don't do something soon, I'm going to the police. The man's crazy. What if he tries to hurt my children? Do something.'

Her words echoed in her head, *be careful*. She needed to be. Jake wasn't going anywhere until he got what he wanted. Retribution. She knew that now.

'Can I help you with those?' Oliver's voice broke into her thoughts.

'No, thanks, I can manage.' She pulled off both boots and her socks, rubbed her bare feet, then slipped them into her warm lilac fluffy slipper booties. 'Aah, that's better, wouldn't it be bliss if wearing slippers outdoors wasn't frowned upon.'

He swirled his drink in the glass. He didn't smile. He was quiet. The atmosphere grew thick with unspoken questions. 'Gemma, I know you're in trouble.'

'Trouble?' Her voice carried a trickle of a tremor. 'I'm not in trouble, Oliver.'

He sipped his drink. 'I know I've asked you before, and you somehow managed to avoid answering. But I'm asking again and this time I want an answer. You know we never did talk about that night with the strange delivery men. I haven't forgotten. I've been waiting for you to come and talk to me.'

She knew Oliver; he was on to something and it didn't bode well for her. Oliver had a knack of making her spill her guts. Even when she wasn't prepared to. He was a natural at it. Had a talent. Like being good at ball games. That was why she tried to avoid talking about stuff with him. Information would fall from her lips unhindered if she wasn't careful.

'No, you're right, we didn't.'

'So, tell me, are you in trouble?'

'Of course not, Oliver, the very thought of it! Where would you get such a notion? But about the other night—'

He shook his head. 'Gemma, forget the other night for the moment, just tell me if you are in trouble, please. Be honest with me. I really, really need you to be upfront right now.'

She stood up and drew the curtains. She felt unsafe everywhere. Even in her home. Oliver was digging and she couldn't let him find out anything. She couldn't look at him. She turned on two of the side lamps and switched off the ceiling light. Oliver never could get his head around ambient lighting. It was so important, especially with those new energy LED lights; they gave off an ugly white brilliance like being in a hospital waiting room, not at all cosy.

With her face a little more composed, she turned back to look at him.

He hung his head looking into his drink as if it would give him all the answers he wanted from her. That wasn't a good sign.

Stuck. She was stuck and didn't have a clue how to say any of it. Ashamed of what she had done and the mess she was in. How would Oliver understand?

He swirled the amber liquid in his glass. 'OK I'll start, shall I? I had a strange experience today, Gem.' He didn't look up. 'I went over to The Riverside to book a table for dinner. I wanted to treat you.' He turned his head to look at her. 'You've probably forgotten, but it's my birthday today.'

Birthday? Wordless in the half-light of the room, she saw the sad look on his face and wanted to die. His birthday! She had forgotten his birthday! What kind of wife was she? A shitty one. All consumed inside her head with Jake had made her forget his birthday.

'Oliver, I... I... don't know what to say. I'm sorry. I don't know how I forgot.' She wanted to go to him, but his body language was stiff and closed. She wasn't welcome there.

'It doesn't matter, Gemma, that's not what the problem is here.'

'No?' He was lying, fibbing, she saw he was hurt and right now all she wanted to do was make it all better for him. Christ, she'd be unimpressed to say the least if he forgot her birthday. That would never happen. Oliver would never forget something as important as her birthday. She, on the other hand, was a great big fool.

'No.' He shook his head and took a deep breath. 'You see it was an interesting experience.'

'What was?'

She didn't want to do this. She didn't want to hear what he had to say.

'While I was at The Riverside today, I found out there had been an altercation there the other night,' he said, looking straight at her. 'The night you phoned and those men came to the house.'

Her hand grabbed the sofa. 'Oh?'

'You see, while I was there – at reception – hotel security was looking at some CCTV. There'd been some vandalism in the car park. A customer had his car trashed.'

Her heart skipped a beat. She dropped her head and stared at the carpet. 'Oh?'

She couldn't bring herself to say, *Oh that's terrible, shocking.* Because the bastard deserved it. And you'd agree with me, Oliver. If you knew what he'd done.

'The owner of the car, a Range Rover, came over to me while I was standing at reception. Asked me if I was local and if I minded looking – to see if I might recognise the *criminal*, as he called them.' He went quiet for a moment. 'Then the strangest thing happened. I found out it was the same man that had asked for directions outside our house a few days ago. Remember? What a coincidence. Don't you think that's a coincidence?'

'Oh God,' she muttered under her breath. 'I suppose. These things happen, don't they? And did you? Recognise the criminal?' *Criminal! Is that what she was now?*

'Well, here's the interesting thing.' He slugged the rest of his drink in one go. 'The person or criminal, as he put it...' he looked her right in the eye '... on the CCTV running back to their car looked like you, Gem.'

'What!' she stammered. 'Me? And you think *I*, did it?' She laughed a little too high pitched.

'Jesus, Gem, I saw it for myself, who has hair like yours!'

She brushed her hand through her hair. 'What! You're going with the big hair? Shit. I can't believe you're even contemplating the very idea. Do *you* think it was me?

Really? Scratching a car? Are you mad?' She had the perfect opportunity to confess to Oliver. But she couldn't. She couldn't!

He shook his head. 'I'm sorry but the evidence was right there on the screen and before you ask, I didn't say anything to anyone. But Gem… I never mentioned the car had been scratched.'

Fuck. 'Yes, you did.'

'No, I didn't. I said vandalised.'

Fuck again.

She had no rational explanation.

The truth was out of the question.

She blagged it. 'It's the only type of vandalism which came to mind when you told me. I could have said trashed tyres or smashed the windscreen. Figure of speech or something like that. What? Don't look at me like that!'

'I'm not looking at you in any particular manner, Gem. It's just when I saw it; it hit me like a bolt of lightning.' He thumped his chest for dramatic impetus. 'Your strange behaviour recently. I know you're in trouble. It was either you or you have a doppelganger.'

'Oliver! It wasn't me, honestly.'

He stood up. 'Right, well clearly you're not going to tell me the truth. For the record, the lucky thing is where the *criminal* parked was a blind spot for the CCTV. They're none the wiser who could have done it. They couldn't see their car or registration.'

She wanted to let out a sigh of relief. Rooted to the floor, it struck her. Oliver might well be in danger. After what Jake had done to Robert, would he be crazy enough to do something to Oliver? She couldn't take the risk.

She was vaguely aware of Oliver talking to her.

She had to protect him.

'Gem, what's *wrong* with you? Christ. Tell me what it

is, please? I think I've been pretty tolerant. You owe me an explanation.'

She found her voice. 'Look, Oliver. I know I've been acting crazy lately, but there's nothing sinister going on. I'm just… well, going bloody crazy with worry and the shame of it all. Do you know how humiliating it is when I go to the village? I can feel people looking at me, talking behind my back. The other night… I just overreacted. There was something on the radio, on the news about con men coming around and pretending to be delivering, checking out the house and then coming back later to break in. I lost it, sorry.'

His voice, gentle, considerate, aimed at drawing her in and opening up, said, 'Gemma, I know you. And you're different. Something has happened. You seem preoccupied all the time. Please let me help.'

She shrugged. 'No. Nothing has happened.' She stared at him, eyes wide hoping to impart a look of innocence and honesty.

'You've changed, something is coming between us, I can't believe you haven't noticed. When we make love, you're not there, you're not fully committed. I know something's happened. Have you met somebody else? Is that what this is? Do you want to leave me? Has that man something to do with it?'

'No! Oliver, no.' Her throat constricted, and she wanted to cry from the pain she heard in his voice. 'There's nobody else, honestly. It's just this whole thing, you know, the pressure and the worry. It's natural for a person to change. We've lost everything. We were on the streets. How can it not fucking change a person? Tell me. Go on. Tell me how that doesn't change a person.' She wanted to get off the *other person* topic. She was in a corner, trapped, with no vision of how to get out without hurting him. If she told him, he wouldn't get it. She moved towards him to give him a hug, but he backed away. His withdrawal felt like a physical assault. 'Oliver!'

'It didn't change me.'

She lashed out without thinking. Total meltdown. 'No, you're marvellous, aren't you? Salt of the earth. Steadfast. The man who took it on the chin.' She caught her breath, horrified as the words flew from her lips unchecked.

'Stop it, Gem,' he yelled back. The shock of her words painfully obvious in his face. 'You're going to say something you'll regret. Stop being a bitch.'

But she couldn't stop. The trouble with Oliver was he never forgot. Like an elephant. What a stupid analogy. How do we know an elephant never forgets? Has somebody spoken to one? *Do you remember the time that elephant stole your banana? Oh, yes, I do and I'll never forget!* She hated what she was doing to him and their relationship.

'Bitch! Maybe I am a bitch. Maybe I've always been a bitch,' she yelled back, tears streaming down her face, her words stuttering. 'Maybe you don't know me at all.' She laughed hysterically at the truth of *that* statement. Because he really didn't know her, did he? 'And you don't. You-don't-know-me-at-all. Not really. Only the bits I want you to know. You're probably better off without me.'

'What the fuck does that mean? I'm not listening to this. You've lost it. And I won't fall out with you.'

'That's right, run away from me, go on. Leave me to handle all the shit.'

'I'm not running away from you. I love you, Gem, so bloody much. What shit? I'm handling the shit. It's killing me seeing you like this. You're keeping something from me and it's killing me.'

Oh, God, what was she doing?

She dropped her head into her hands, ashamed. 'God,

I'm sorry. *I'm so sorry.* I didn't mean any of it. I can't cope with all this. I keep telling you. There's nothing else.' *Please, Oliver, let it go, I can't tell you, please, please, please let it go.*

'You're lying. I know you are. There's more to it. Christ, Gem, I saw you on CCTV, don't tell me it wasn't you.' She shook her head violently as his words darted from his mouth striking her painfully. 'Don't lie any more. Just be honest. Tell me what is going on with you!'

'No, Oliver. I'm not lying, I'm messed up. This has messed me up.' She approached him.

He held up a hand to stop her. 'I'm not going to beg you to tell me, Gem. But whatever it is you are lying to me about, it will destroy us if you're not upfront with me about it. Don't tarnish what we have. Don't do it, Gem.'

She began crying all over again. 'Oh, Oliver, what if I told you that I couldn't tell you. That I was sorting it out and you had to believe in me. Trust me.'

'Trust you! How the fuck can I trust you when you stand there admitting to me you are lying and can't tell me why! Gem, why can't you tell me? What have you got yourself into?' He approached her wrapping his arms around her. She fell into him and held on tight.

'I will tell you, but not now, I can't. I just can't. Will you trust me?'

'I don't want you to go through this on your own, whatever it is. Let me help you. I don't know what you've got mixed up with. We're renting now, we're OK, you have a job We're moving in the right direction. Whatever it is you were doing, and I can't imagine what it was, stop it. I want you to stop whatever it is.'

She cringed. 'I will sort it. I promise. I don't want you to worry; it's nothing serious, I can sort it. The thing with the car. I lost my head. I can't explain to you why right now, but I know it was crazy. And like you said they don't know who it was. Can we leave it like that? I will tell you, but not now.' She hugged him tight afraid to let him go. He was stiff in her arms. 'Please, Oliver. Don't leave me, please. I love you so much. I'm sorry, I'm a crazy bitch and I lost the plot there for a while but I'll sort it.'

'If you're in danger, Gemma, you must tell me. Those guys who came to the house, were they anything to do with this?'

'No, no, they weren't.' She bit her lip.

'That money you had in your bag. It's to do with that, isn't it?'

'Stop asking questions. I'll sort it. I know how it looks. Please let me sort it.'

Chapter Thirty-Three

Another few days passed with no further news from Jake until today. Stuck on her windscreen was an eight-inch laminated number 9 like the ones people stick on their bins. She ripped it up and threw it away.

Gemma drove to Chester where she collected a manila envelope from a mailbox that she'd registered a week ago. She had finally taken Karen's advice and rang the number on the business card.

After the other night she watched Oliver's every move, as he watched hers. She imagined telling him, saying the words out loud. The words that would set her free. Sometimes in her head she played out the scenario with Oliver working in the office and she standing behind him. 'Oliver, I'm sorry, I can't keep the lies to myself any more, I have to tell you. Jake paid me ten thousand pounds to spend the night with him in a hotel, but we didn't have sex. We've never had sex... and there's more.' But she never had the courage to continue because it sounded so hollow and cheap and, quite frankly, pathetic.

Then she imagined him turning around, his face broken, crumbling from the impact of her words. His eyes welling up and the love that always glistened in those eyes for her extinguishing like dying embers.

So she kept quiet because it wouldn't be as easy as it played out in her head. He'd use pained words. Words that would describe how she'd destroyed him with her lies. Words that would impale on her heart forever. So she kept the lies inside, locked away together with all the other ugly secrets.

And besides, even if she was brave enough to tell Oliver.

What then? Jake was still in their lives. He wasn't going anywhere. Deep down she suspected it wouldn't matter to him. He wanted to hurt her more than just break up her marriage.

She had to stand firm.

She discussed it with Karen who agreed. She also agreed it was too risky to tell Oliver. Who knew how he'd react. He might love her more than his own life as he professed, but in reality, how strong was that if faced with what she'd done. Innocent or not, she had no way of proving it and he'd always doubt it and that little bit of doubt would erode their relationship over time.

'It would be too much for him, Gemma,' Karen said.

'But he loves me.'

'He loves the woman who hadn't lied to him. You're not that person any more, and that's what he will see.'

'So, what do I do?'

'You get Jake out of your life, and you never tell Oliver.'

'Lie to him forever?'

'Exactly, it's the only thing you can do.'

Back home she perched on the kitchen chair and pulled out the manila envelope from her oversized handbag. She read the covering letter then looked over the rest of the paperwork before folding the papers away and replacing them back into the envelope.

She was faced with an interesting conundrum. If you're damned if you do and damned if you don't – then it becomes a real enigma. So, which would be the more favourable?

Chapter Thirty-Four

She awoke next morning to a text message from him.

8

I'm not playing your games any more. She wrote back not acknowledging his message.

8!!!!!!!!!!!!!!!!!!!!!!!!!!!!!!

What about 8? she asked because it was no use ignoring him, he'd just keep texting again and again until she acknowledged him.

8 days left.

For what?? she asked wanting him to spell it out to her what the countdown was for.

You need to try harder. You're not trying hard enough to work it out.

For what? Not interested in your games. You need to explain. I don't understand. Anger consumed her as she wrote. *I don't care what your 8 means. I'm not afraid of you any more.*

☺ I think you are. You need to be.

She switched her phone off and threw it in the bedside drawer.

He'd clearly lost his mind. What he was insinuating was stuff out of movies not little villages like theirs. And not because of a small prank she played years ago. The whole thing was madness and he was driving her mad.

She made her way to the shower without waking Oliver, to try and wash away the anger inside her. She got herself ready then woke him up; she didn't want to stay in bed after the text, lying next to Oliver with all that anger made it impossible for her to be near him.

They were spending the day shopping and promised each other that today they would do lots of romantic things together. Like going for a walk in Tatton Park and taking a picnic with a flask of hot tea. The weather was dry and they were well wrapped up. Oliver had asked about her job again. Again, she had to lock herself in the study for a couple of hours pretending to type out letters. Stuffing them in envelopes and posting them to made up addresses. Each day he didn't press her for more information on what was bothering her was a bonus. He wanted to, she saw that, but he kept true to his word and said nothing.

Her body ached with pent-up fury and fear.

In the car on the way to Booths supermarket, Oliver sounded cheerful while she struggled with the banter. Once there, he said he was popping to the bank and that he'd meet her back at the supermarket while she picked out some snacks for their walk.

'I'll text you when I get back here,' he said. 'You know since the accountant has taken over all that paperwork I feel lighter and I think I can see a light at the end of the tunnel. I'm so glad we did it.'

'Oh, I haven't brought my mobile.' She smiled, pleased he was under less pressure. As for his tunnel and the light he saw, she suspected it was a train coming straight for them and Jake was driving.

'Why not? That was dumb. OK I'll search for you inside the supermarket.'

She didn't want to read any more texts or see any missed calls from Jake. But what if he had something in mind and was preparing to do something? What if he tried to take her or do something to her? She'd be unable to let Oliver know. She glanced around, unsettled by her own thoughts.

Too late now. Her phone was in the drawer of her bedside cabinet.

'Oh God,' she said, unable to believe her eyes when she

walked back to her car with the shopping. 'Oh God. Oh God. Oh God.'

People began milling around her, talking under their breath, muttering to themselves. The supermarket car park was jammed full.

The colour rose in her face.

Wrapped up in her coat, scarf, woollen hat and gloves, she bounced between rage and mortification. Unable to believe what she saw. Following on from that text this morning it was clear that things were moving quickly towards the end of the countdown and the implications of what that meant. Surely, he couldn't be planning to kill her? But what if it did mean that? After all, Mattie had vanished.

Clicking her fob, she released the boot lid of her second-hand Mercedes Benz SLK. On a mad moment a week ago, she'd been driving past the Mercedes garage in Macclesfield when an uncontrollable urge had come over her and she swung in. When she swung back out, she had traded in her Mini and bought the car on finance. A stupid and idiotic thing to do and one which Oliver had not stopped going on about. Every day, morning, noon and night. Blah, blah, blah. She got it. It was stupid. But the sensible part of her brain hadn't been switched on, only the pity party part of her brain. Stupid. Stupid. Stupid brain. She thought before she was black listed she might as well. Completely irrational. Now she regretted it.

Grabbing a packet of wet wipes from the car door, she pulled a handful out and rubbed at the lipstick on the windscreen. Instead of clearing it, it just smeared all over the glass making it worse.

Oliver would be here in a moment. Christ. There was disquiet in the air. What if he was out there watching her? She couldn't shake the feeling he was close by.

Nobody approached to help her.

They would have done if they'd smashed the windows, or if some other words were written on the glass. But *bitch, liar, she-devil* seemed to put them off. In a way, she was grateful. She didn't need to explain to anyone, least of all nosey passers-by.

'What the hell is going on?' Oliver said.

'No idea, I just got here,' she said, stuck in an impasse for what to say.

'I'm going to check the CCTV in the supermarket. Who would do something like this? I can't believe it. Why?' he said, full of indignation. 'This is what comes from having a flashy car, Gemma. I told you no good would come of this.'

Oh God. 'It's nothing to do with having a flashy car, Oliver. Have you forgotten where we live? Look around. There are more flashy cars in Knutsford than there are people.' It was a figure of speech, but he got the message.

Somewhere along the way with all this, Jake had lost his mind if he was prepared to do something so public. He was getting bolder and she was really starting to get the feeling he was unstoppable.

Oliver made a grunting sound deep in the back of his throat. 'What the hell possessed you to buy this?' He shook his head and stomped back towards the supermarket. 'Can't imagine what you'd have done if I had turned up with a car like this.' He looked around. 'Shit. Maybe it's someone we owe money to. Have you thought of that? They see you driving this and go crazy. It was so stupid of you, Gemma.'

'I'm coming with you.' She threw the wipes onto the driver's seat and locked the car, following him back inside the supermarket. 'Stop going on about it, Oliver, it's done. It's only for two years.'

He rolled his eyes as if that made it all better. 'Two years! Christ, I think you were right the other day when you said I didn't know you. I really don't. Thank God you have a damned job. Not that it'll make any difference if they end up taking it away. They've taken everything else.'

He had a point. In total, Jake had given her thirty thousand pounds. They should be able to manage on that for a good while. She hadn't actually taken more money; he'd shoved it in her bag and she'd found it later. Even though she wanted to bin it or send it back, she hadn't. She needed that money. It was as if he knew she'd keep it. How could she send thirty thousand pounds back to him when they had nothing? It was almost as if she was losing all her principles in the hope everything would turn out right in the end. She hated the fact she found it so easy to keep the money. By the time they got inside the supermarket, she couldn't stand the accusing voices inside her head. 'I have a fourteen-day cooling off period if I want to cancel, so I will. I'll take it back.'

'Good. Do that.'

She pursed her lips. She didn't want to. But she would. It was a mad, reckless thing to have done.

'You stay here. In fact, go to the coffee shop over the road, Cha Bar, and wait for me. I'll come for you when I've had a look at the CCTV.'

'No, I need to see this too,' she said, firmly. 'It was directed at me, Oliver. You are not going alone.'

'Why would anybody do this? It's as if they hate you. Why use those terrible words?'

She shrugged. *Because he's a disturbed, mentally ill freak*, she wanted to say.

She turned around looking at the gathering throng of people around her car. He would be here. Watching. She knew it. Like those terrorists who stayed to see the calamity of their actions.

She imagined him watching them from a good vantage position. Laughing at their disbelief. Enjoying seeing Oliver concerned about who could want to hurt his beloved, Gemma.

'I'll get you for this,' she said, angrily, though not loud enough for anyone to hear.

It took them half an hour to wait for security to find the right place on the CCTV. Of course, it was a waste of time; you couldn't make out the figure. And they left on foot. Apart from the fact you could tell it was a male, there were no other giveaway signs.

Oliver became a little paranoid after seeing the footage. 'You can't go out on your own, Gemma. I'll have to go out with you everywhere.' He looked around the office exaggeratedly like a bad actor auditioning for a role.

She shook her head. 'You can't go everywhere with me, Oliver. It was probably some random act. You know, because of the car. Jealousy, that kind of thing.' As soon as she saw the tape, she recognised him in an instant.

'But it was a man, Gemma. I have a bad feeling about this,' Oliver said. 'What about that car you damaged? It could be him?'

'Oliver stop it. It won't be him. He didn't even know it was me!' she said, as they left the office and walked to the car. She had to clear Jake out of her mind and devote her time to putting Oliver's fears to rest.

'But what you haven't grasped, Gemma, is that he wrote with lipstick.'

She took off her hat to cool down. The heat and seeing that arsehole on CCTV had made her feel dizzy. She knew where Oliver was going with this. But pretended stupidity. She could see his mind working around things. Any minute now the perpetrator would turn into a serial killer. And perhaps he wouldn't be too far off the mark, although she'd never say so. She had to work out a line of attack.

'Don't you see?' Oliver continued later after they had

cleared the lipstick from the windscreen and drove away from the supermarket. He peered at her with those intense blue eyes, his hands gripping the steering wheel. 'A man does not happen to be carrying lipstick in his pocket. Therefore, he had intent.'

She was already ahead of him. So far ahead it made her feel sick.

She bent down and tore a chunk of bread off the French stick from the shopping bag in the footwell to avoid speaking.

'Gemma, will you look at me, for Christ's sake; this was premeditated. The man is dangerous,' he yelled. She had no choice but to look back at him.

'C'mon, Oliver, don't start, please.'

'I'm not starting. I'm trying to get through to you the severity of this. *Please* take this seriously. Why are you not hysterical? Do you think those men who came to the house have anything to do with this? Or maybe it's someone we owe money to. Angry people can do stupid things. They could be following us right now. What if they already know where we live?'

She choked on the bread. Oliver pulled out a bottle of water from the cup holder. She drank greedily, her fingers holding on tight to the bottle. She saw he was worried about her and sending himself to hell and back thinking of her safety.

'Gemma, we need to go to the police. Don't you understand what this could mean?'

'OK, OK, Oliver, I get what you're saying, but I think going to the police with this one incident is wasting their time.'

'No, Gemma, it isn't. The next one could have serious consequences. We could tell them about those strange men that came to the house, too. Gemma, why aren't you concerned?' He paused. 'I find this a little worrying, more than a little worrying, in fact. In fact, I'm wondering if you know who did this.'

'Oliver, No! Of course I don't know who did this.' The last thing she needed was the police getting involved. She turned to face him, her knee bent, tucked beneath her other leg. She breathed in sharply. The police could not put Jake and her together. But what it could do – if later on something was to happen to Jake, is provide them with a link back to this incident. Linking her to him and from there they'd surely find out about their stay in Oxford. No. She had to have no ties with Jake. And *she* had to get rid of him by herself. Nobody could ever know. A secret is never a secret if somebody else knows. She knew it was madness, but it was the only way out.

Guarded, she shrugged inside her big coat. 'I am concerned, Oliver.' She kept her voice calm and level, masking her true feelings of rage. Oliver went to speak. She raised her hand. 'Let me finish.' She spoke quickly. She wanted to get it out and wanted to stop talking about Jake. The more they spoke about Jake, the more she wanted to stab him in the head with a sharp instrument. 'I know what you're saying, and I see your concerns. *But* I think this was a prank and I am not prepared to waste police time. *If* anything else happens then, yes, we'll go and speak to the police and tell them about this incident.'

'I suppose there's some logic in that. I still don't get why you're reluctant to go and let them know about the two incidents just so they have a record of it. But if anything else, I mean absolutely anything else, even the tiniest thing happens… you will tell me, won't you?' He rubbed his hand over his face the way he did when he was struggling with something.

They arrived at Tatton and had a quiet walk and even

quieter lunch sat on a bench, by which time the drizzle had stopped. Jake's erratic texts consumed her thoughts. She felt a twinge of guilt at the way she'd put Oliver off going to the police when all he wanted was to protect her. She wished she could make it all go away, to sit Oliver down and tell him everything and that what she'd done was because she loved him. But she couldn't.

Chapter Thirty-Five

JAKE

Something about scrawling insults all over her windscreen was satisfying. He felt strangely gratified when he finished. She still taunted him with her calmness and her togetherness with Oliver. Although he saw Oliver was flustered, it didn't tear them apart. His concern and protectiveness towards her unnerved him. It propelled him to the next stage he so eagerly awaited.

Oliver's reaction almost made him laugh, his anger and irritation towards the vandalism was predictable. She had steel running through her that he wanted to break. And he would. Anyone else would by now begin to show signs of breaking. Not her. She was a bigger challenge than he expected. He'd stood at the back of the car park, too far for her to see him, but with his binoculars he saw their reactions in minute detail. She even scanned the crowds and looked right at him unknowingly.

She just didn't realise yet how much she was dancing to his tune. All her threats of going to the police. Telling Oliver. Threatening that she was not having any more to do with him was nothing but rubber bullets fired in his direction.

His annoyance that she wasn't working out the significance of the countdown was beginning to put a strain on his patience, and he needed to impress on her that when zero day came, she would indeed be sorry.

He learnt a long time ago that there were several stages to a good manipulator. Three, in fact. The first was to convince the target they needed your help. The second was to convince them there was no way out. The third was to convince them they had fallen so far down your rabbit hole they were totally at your mercy.

Her prevarication had gone on long enough. He was about to push her to her extreme. And he hoped she would rise to the occasion. He'd waited all these years to collect. And collect he would.

Chapter Thirty-Six

GEMMA

She had a lousy night's sleep. Her mind churning over what she planned for today.

She focused on the task ahead, putting aside her concerns for the possible dangers involved. Sean had given her all the information she needed and now she would act on it.

Sean Evans owned Fast-light Intelligence, a company offering security, private investigation and specialist photographic support. She found him through the business card in the newsagents.

The only thing that could go wrong was if someone changed their mind. She hadn't asked Sean how he found out Jake's movements for today or that of his household. She didn't want to know. She paid him and he delivered.

She dressed quickly. Black jeans, black jumper and boots. She pulled her hair into a tight ponytail and wrapped it up inside her black woolly hat. She took a long look at herself in the wardrobe mirror. She looked gaunt and troubled. She wore no make-up, just mascara. She couldn't go anywhere without mascara. She grabbed her black quilted jacket from the wardrobe. Took a deep breath and headed downstairs.

She heard Oliver on the phone. She bobbed her head around the door; he had a stack of papers on the desk. Why were there still so many? She thought the accountant dealt with all that? Not that she wanted to ask. It made her shiver. She mimed that she was going out. He nodded, blew a kiss and gave her a short wave. She moved, quickly, wanting to be out of the house before he came off the phone.

11.00 a.m. She sat in her car waiting for the windscreen to demist. She pulled on her black leather gloves, put the car in reverse, turned it around and drove out.

She was exhausted from the emotional rollercoaster Jake was putting her through.

She was heading for revenge.

She had to focus.

Turning out of the drive onto the main road, she made her way towards the A34 heading for Alderley Edge. She drove fast, going over in her head what she needed to look for. She remembered she hadn't turned off her location services on her phone. She scrolled through her phone with her left hand, narrowly missing a couple of cyclists. Idiots, why did they always have to ride side by side on narrow country lanes? Didn't they realise how dangerous that was?

Her Mercedes SLK travelled smoothly along the A roads. She didn't put the address into her satnav. She had memorised the route.

Turning off the A road onto a back road, she put her foot down racing along the clear road. Turning a bend, she came head to head with a tractor coming the other way. She hit the brakes narrowly avoiding a collision by mounting the verge.

Soon she was cruising down *his* road. It was quiet, apart from the odd 4×4 trundling by. She drove past his double fronted Victorian house on her left. Noted the in and out drive and the gravelled driveway. The house had several extensions turning the once modest house into a grand home.

On the opposite side of the road were open fields as far as the eye could see. Except for the odd house in the distance.

She ran through her routine, speaking it aloud as she parked thirty yards up in a small lay-by. She was going to intrude on *his* territory and didn't care if he found out.

She felt the effects of adrenaline racing through her veins causing her stomach to twist and tighten, making her heart race. She was hot and wanted to take off her hat, but she couldn't leave any trace of herself behind.

OK. So, according to Sean, Jake was out this morning. He'd taken the early train to London with his wife and the housekeeper didn't come in today, it was her day off. God, let's hope she hadn't changed it.

She could have asked Sean to do this but because she didn't really know what she was looking for, she thought it best if she did the snooping. Besides, the less involved Sean was the better. It irritated her that she had to use him to begin with but some things she wasn't able to sort herself.

She was almost at the front door, the gravel drive crunching underfoot, when she heard a car slow down. She dropped back down the four stone steps that lead to the front door and hid behind one of the two large planters. The car continued past the house.

She bent down, moved the stone cat by the front door and pulled the spare key from beneath. *Sean, you're a star.*

The glossy black Victorian stained-glass door opened easily.

She made her way down the black and white tiled hallway. The third door on the left was his study, passing a large gilded console table with an onyx top and huge gold-framed mirror behind. The wide mahogany staircase led from the hallway opening onto a sizable landing. Black and white framed photographs of family members lined the wall that followed the rise of the stairs. Her footsteps amplified in the quiet house. She opened the door and slipped inside.

Leaning against the door, she waited until her heart resumed a normal beat while looking around the very archetypal male study, all leather and wood. A mahogany Victorian partner's desk with a faded green and gilt-tooled leather top, moulded edges and cock-beaded drawers, dominated. The drawers were raised on plinth bases with concealed casters. The entire wall space was full of books. She went over to see what he found interesting to read. Her finger passed over the spine of old tomes, clearly bought to impress. She'd bet her right hand he'd never read any of them.

She mused if he might sense somebody had entered his inner sanctum. If suddenly in London, he stopped what he was doing and felt that creepy feeling down the back of his spine.

She had to be careful to leave things as she found them. She suspected nobody came in here without Jake.

Where to begin.

There was a wooden filing cabinet near the window. She started there. She pulled the top drawer out. It was full of files, buff coloured ones, so stuffed some caught on the top of the cabinet as she pulled out the drawer. She flicked her finger along the top of them, nothing stood out. She pulled out the second and third followed by the fourth drawer. Again, nothing shouted at her that was worth investigating.

Chewing her lip and drumming her fingers on the top of the cabinet, her eyes scanned the room. Where would he hide something that he wanted to keep secret? Where? Where? Where? She pulled out his big black leather chair and sat on it. There wouldn't be anything in the desk drawers. Nobody would be that stupid to leave anything secret in such an obvious place.

Quickly and with deft fingers she went through the six drawers on her side of the desk. Then moved to the other side of the desk, knelt and searched the other six identical drawers.

Nothing.

She needed that indefinable something that linked him

to something she could use against him. She wouldn't get another chance like this. She sensed Jake would somehow know somebody had been snooping. Not necessarily her, but he would lock this room after today. She'd put money on it.

She was nervous, hot and sweaty. Sweat trickled between her breasts. She longed to rip off her woollen hat but feared dropping a stray hair and alerting Jake that she had been snooping.

She looked around the room from where she knelt. She got up and pushed at the bookshelves not really expecting them to open like a James Bond movie. They didn't. Sighing heavily, she strode to the filing cabinet, again. Yanked the top drawer out so forcefully the whole lot wobbled. She put her hand against it to stop any further movement, then, for the second time checked through the files. Once again, nothing.

Except that this time when she came to close the drawer, it wouldn't close fully. *Oh, shit, she'd broken the bloody thing*. She pulled it out then pushed it back in checking the runners. Everything looked, as it should. She ran her hand down the back in case something had come loose and that's when her hand fell on another file. Grabbing it, she pulled it out. It was fat and stuffed, held together with two fat red rubber bands. A beatific smile covered her face.

Sometimes luck just happened.

There had to be something juicy in here. Oh, yes, there had to be.

She pulled the file out reverently, holding it in both hands as if it was fine crystal and would break with the slightest movement. She carried it to the desk and sat on the leather chair. Carefully, she removed the rubber bands one at a time. She placed them to one side. Aware she mustn't lose them.

Slowly, she opened the file whilst stuffing a stray hair back under her hat. At first her heart sank. It was full of boring letters from the bank talking about bank loans and interest. *Oh, Christ! Why would you hide this?* Furiously, she carried on turning each page, slowly to make sure she didn't miss anything. Her heart sank so low it virtually lay on the floor when nothing stood out.

Then she turned the next letter and recoiled so violently into the chair it rolled backwards and smashed into the wall behind with a loud thud. A framed picture crashed down off the wall above her head landing right on top. 'Oh, Christ!' she yelped holding her head to ease the pain.

Chapter Thirty-Seven

Oh God! Fixated on the file, she turned each page with the tip of her fingers not wanting to touch the disgusting pictures. Not wanting to see any more, but she had to, she had to carry on. Who were these women? What about their families did they know what had become of them? They wouldn't have closure. A voice inside her head pushed her on, telling her she had to see all of it.

And then Mattie stared back at her.

Vomit gurgled up her throat, she grabbed the pocket of her coat and threw up inside. She would have preferred throwing up in his precious filthy, disgusting, depraved study.

She could publicly disgrace and humiliate the bastard. Her hands instinctively grabbed the photos ready to screw them up, get rid of them. Would he notice? How often did he look at them? But for what end? Dead bodies, smashed up, beaten. *Oh God, what am I going to do?*

She had to find that recording from Le Manoir aux Quat Saisons too, and she was running out of time.

An hour later she had photographed all she needed. She pulled off her hat when she got to the car and was horrified to see it soaked in blood.

As she got back in her car a text message came in.

7 ☺

Fuck you

☺ *Not if I fuck you first.*

Back home she raced up the stairs to their bedroom, flung off her clothes. Hid the blooded hat in the bottom of her wardrobe and jumped in the shower, washing the crusted blood from her hair. Her mind running through the images she'd seen and unable to stop them. They were in danger. All of them.

The hot water ran lovingly over her body, her long hair clung to her back and thoughts wavered in complete disorder. She thought back to a time when she met Jake and thought ten thousand pounds for companionship was a good deal. Christ, how naïve had she been.

She dressed quickly.

Downstairs she shoved her clothes in the washing machine. She heard Oliver on the phone in the study. He must have a call list as long as the Mersey. She listened at the door, he was talking to his mother from the sound of things. That was going to be a long conversation. She wasn't ready to face him yet. She thought about leaving. The two of them catching a plane and flying off somewhere faraway. But he'd have too many questions and would never stop asking. Eventually, she would have to tell him and that would be the end. She wasn't going to lose Oliver.

She went out into the garden for privacy and called Karen. As her phone dialled out, she heard a few birds chirruping in the bare trees. She looked at the back of the houses that backed on to the open field directly at the end of their garden and yearned for their inhabitants' non-complicated lives. She'd give anything for a life like that right now.

She needed the original of that film. She hadn't found it and it suddenly occurred to her to ask Sean to find it; after all that was his job. She frowned, it meant letting him into more of her secrets. But she saw no other way around it. She had to get hold of it. And Karen? Was he planning the same for her?

'Gemma, is everything OK?' Karen asked, after picking up on the third ring.

'No.' She told Karen what she'd found and her desperate need for a way out. Her hopes laid bare at her feet she hoped Karen would come up with a magical solution to the horrors unfolding.

'You have to go to the police.' Her voice was urgent. The panic clear in her tone.

'I can't. How can I? I broke into his house.'

'You'll have to take that risk. Christ, Gemma, he's a murderer not only of Mattie but also of other women. You can't not go.' She heard her crying. She was right. Of course she was right. She knew that. It just wasn't the sensible thing to do.

'It's easy for you to say.' Hearing Karen crying made her well up, the tears running down her face. Christ. She forced herself to stay calm.

'It is. But if you don't, then I will have to go and tell them everything I know.' There was a pause. 'Gemma? I have to ask.' Another long pause then the words tumbled out. 'Do you think he's coming for me?'

Fuck. This was one question she hadn't wanted to answer. 'I don't know, to be honest. Maybe.' She struggled not to break down as the anger and panic surrounding her exploded inside her. 'Karen, listen to me. I know you're scared. I'm in the middle of doing something about him. Please. Please let me try and sort this.'

'I'm going to the police, what you're asking is putting my family in danger. You can't ask that of me!' She was becoming hysterical.

It hardly came as a surprise that she would feel that way. Karen's family against her marriage. She knew which she'd choose.

'Gemma. Face it. Only the police can help. He's out of control.' She sobbed trying to get the words out. 'He's out for revenge. Now. Next week. Next year. We can't hide.

He will come for me. I'm going to the police.' Her crying subsided a little.

'No! No, you can't...'

'Gem, I can. I can't risk my family for your marriage. Sorry that sounds harsh, I know, but think about it. If he killed Mattie over this stupid prank, he's clearly deranged, and God knows what he will do to us. To my family and me. I'm not prepared to risk it.'

'Please, Karen. Give me a few days and I promise I will sort this. Take your family and go away somewhere he can't find you. Please, Karen. Promise me.'

'OK, Gemma, OK. But take care and stay in touch.'

Gemma covered the few yards to the back door and raced to her car calling Sean on the way. Oliver called out to her but she fled in no mood to talk to him.

'It's not what I usually do,' Sean said.

She grabbed her handbag off the chair in the pub she'd arranged to meet him in out towards Staffordshire. Sean stood out at six feet four with a ginger mop of hair, thin and dressed in a high fashion black suit. The trousers tapered and came above the ankle making his feet appear huge.

'How much will you do it for?'

'I'll bill you when we finish. You know once he realises it's gone; he'll know it's you.'

'Do you think I give a toss what he thinks?'

He laughed at her bravado.

She wasn't going to allow him to have that power over her any longer, pulling her strings whenever he wanted to.

'He'll come after you. Seeing those photos, I'm not sure he's going to let you sit back and crow. You should go to the police with the information you have. You're in danger, Gemma. The man's a psycho.'

Another limp proposal, just like Karen's.

'I don't give a shit, Sean. I know you think I don't mean it. You're wrong. I need that recording before I can go to the police with the photos. I don't want that bastard being able to get off with any excuse. And he will. Believe me, he will say I've got it in for him then he will be mental with rage. Imagine! Christ. I'm not risking it. I need to be sure when I do go to the police that he's got nothing on me to wheedle out of it.'

'Those photos will be proof of what he's done.'

'Oh yeah. What do you think they're going to say when they ask me how I came to be in possession of these colourful photos? Shall I tell them I broke in and stole them? His lawyers will throw it out. They need a warrant to get into his house and proof of some crime to get one. They won't be admissible because I broke into his house to get them. And he will implicate me if he can. No, I need to get rid of everything and… that includes him.'

He nodded. 'I've got a suggestion. If you do anything to him, they're going to find a connection somewhere to you. Why not let me handle this?'

She shook her head. 'No way. No. I… I'll deal with *him*. You're not to get involved beyond getting me that recording. It must be on his computer. I need you to remove all trace of it. The photos I took I need you to make sure there aren't any copies anywhere else and destroy the ones he has. I can't be linked to him in any way.' The last thing she needed was another man able to blackmail her. It was bad enough he knew this much.

'You'll need access to his phone and to his iCloud. I can get that for you.'

As Sean pulled out of the car park, she decided to walk for a bit to gather her thoughts before going home. It was all going so quickly and she had to decide on her next move. Did he already know she'd been snooping in his house? No. She suspected she'd know soon enough.

Chapter Thirty-Eight

JAKE

Suspicion was a permanent state of mind for Jake. From the moment he walked into his study on Thursday morning, he had a strong hunch that something was different. He texted his wife, who was at the other end of the house, to come in and see him.

His wife, Katy, wore her hair short, framing her face. She arrived with a coffee for the two of them. She perched on the edge of the desk, her skinny legs dangling. Katy was a divorcee for a year when she met Jake. They got on like a house on fire. She presented the dutiful wife and did her own thing, never bothering him. He likewise. It was the perfect marriage. She never worried about his lady friends. She never questioned his whereabouts. He liked that. It suited him. He always knew she was in it for the money but that was fine with him. She made him look respectable. In turn as long as she was discreet, she had free rein to do as she liked.

'I thought the cleaner was off yesterday?' he stated.

'She was,' Katy said, tartly.

'So, *who* was in the house yesterday while we were away?'

'Nobody, Jake. The house was locked up.' She blew on her coffee to cool it down. 'Don't you want your coffee?'

He scowled at her and placed a coaster under the coffee. 'How many times have I told you to use bloody coasters, Katy?'

'So many I forget.' She smiled at him and pouted.

'Did you set the alarm when we left?'

'No, because you know it's not working, they're coming out today to fix it.'

Jake looked distressed.

'They were coming out yesterday, but *you* didn't want them in the house when we were away. Remember?' she said.

He nodded and reclined in the leather chair.

'Why? Is something wrong?' she asked.

'I found a picture on the floor.' He turned to show her.

'For God's sake, Jake. You're so paranoid.' Katy walked over and looked at the broken picture.

He pushed the chair backwards with his heels out of the way so she could have a better look, his face grim.

'Is there anything missing?' she asked, looking around the study. 'It all looks the same to me.'

'Me too. But I can't get my head around how that picture fell off.'

Katy sipped her coffee walking back to the door. 'Well, let me know when you work it out. I should imagine it's one of those freaky things. I'm off to get my nails done. Don't go out, will you. The alarm company is due any time.' She smiled cheekily and left.

He gave the filing cabinet a cold-eyed glare. Coolly, he walked towards it, a slow anger emerging within him. He pulled the top drawer open and reverently pulled the file from the back. He dropped it on the desk and pulled off the red rubber bands.

And that's when he saw it.

If he hadn't pulled them off slowly, he'd have missed it. His back stiffened. He pulled a long blonde hair from the rubber band.

The bitch had been in *his* study. In *his* house. Something insidious inside him swelled up. That she dared to do this made his anger boil. He flicked through the file and found the photos of her were missing. Logging onto his computer he scrolled through until he found the downloads folder.

Nothing.

She had definitely crossed the line.

'You fucking bitch,' he said, his voice hard. He walked to the filing cabinet and replaced the file. She was laughing at him. How dare she. Who the hell did she think she was?

Chapter Thirty-Nine

GEMMA

By early Thursday evening, she was assured by Sean that as far as he could make out there had been no other copies made. Certainly not from his computer and those had been deleted.

Gemma was running around getting herself ready. They were dining with friends of Oliver's who were stopping off in Knutsford for a day to see Oliver on their way to their son's house in Oxford. Oliver had invited them over for a meal.

'Why did you invite them, Oliver?'

'Because, Gemma, we can't hide from everyone, we have to start to integrate with people again.'

Bridgette and Luke were in their late sixties. They had known Oliver since he was a child. Luke was a retired chief inspector. Gemma had met them a few times over the years, there was a sort of great uncle and aunt relationship between them although they were unrelated. Luke was an old school friend of Oliver's dad and had known Oliver all his life. There had been a time when Oliver had wanted to join the police.

'What am I supposed to cook at such short notice?'

Her worries that Oliver had not put the car park incident behind him were soon realised during dinner. The three of them, relaxed by the free-flowing wine, suddenly stared at Oliver when he brought up the incident and slapped it on the table like a huge, ugly, scaly dead fish.

He confided in Luke his worries about Gemma's safety and her lack of concern about the incident.

The landline rang.

Gemma went to answer it in the lounge glad to get away from them. She put her glass of wine down on the occasional table next to the phone. 'Hello? Hello?' Silence on the other end. She put the receiver down and walked away. It rang again. 'Hello? Hello? Who is this?' Silence. She put the receiver down and unplugged the phone from the wall, suspicious it was him.

Sitting down again around the pine dinner table in the cosy cottage kitchen, it was difficult to hide when Oliver put the spotlight on her and laid it out to Luke, who suddenly took on the demeanour of his past occupation. Although it was hard to see him in the role of chief inspector wearing a maroon tank top, grey trousers and black Velcro fastening shoes.

'It could be it was a one-off attack, Oliver. Kids, you know. No particular rhyme or reason for it. On the other hand…' His brows knitted together. He coughed and his voice changed, became deeper as if he was back in his police role. 'It could be more significant. Have you felt as if anyone is watching you, Gemma?'

Had she? Only as if she had a heat-seeking missile locked on to her, would be her honest answer. She played with her food and shook her head.

A text message came in. She saw Oliver look at her phone in front of her. She felt rude reading it but she had too.

Did you think I'd forgotten to text you today? LOL. Sorry to disappoint. 6.

Knowing her face would reflect the anguish inside her; she kept her face down and pretended to eat her food until her composure returned, fully aware Oliver watched her. She left the table moments later.

'I'll put this out of the way,' she said, taking it to the lounge and placing it on the mantelpiece.

Her ears picked out the sound of a car engine in the distance, slowing down then stopping.

When she returned, Luke continued. 'You see most attacks of this nature come from someone the victim knows. This type of attack is rarely random.'

A sudden blast of air funnelled into the kitchen from the hallway. Oliver got up. 'I mustn't have closed the front door properly when you arrived, sorry about that. It's not the warmest house at the best of times.' He went to the front door and closed it. Gemma heard him put the chain on.

'We did hear there might be a bit of a storm coming this way tonight,' Bridgette said.

Gemma slumped in her chair. She toyed with her necklace. Luke sat next to her and clamped his hand on her shoulder. 'You mustn't blame yourself. These occurrences can come out of nowhere. Any little thing can sometimes trigger irrational behaviour,' he told her.

'I *don't* blame myself, but I do think Oliver is building this thing up to more than it is.' She squirmed on her chair and tried to change the subject. She didn't like Luke touching her. Shouldn't he know better being a copper? 'Anyway, let's not talk about me. How are you enjoying retirement, Luke? Is it all it's cracked up to be?' She shrugged his hand off.

Luke blinked several times. 'Err... well, yes and no.' He cleared his throat, embarrassed.

Oliver glared at her.

She glared back. Her mobile rang. She looked around the kitchen.

'I think you left it in the lounge, darling? A few moments ago?'

'You two carry on, I'll go see if it's important, then turn it off,' she said, seeing Oliver wanting to yell at her to leave it alone, believing whatever it was could wait.

She walked into the lounge and saw her mobile on the

mantelpiece flashing with a call. When she went to pick it up, it stopped. Unknown caller. It rang again. She answered. 'Hello?' Silence. 'Hello?' Silence. A chill fell over her skin. Then she received a text. And another. And another. And another. And another. Text messages lit up her phone, one after the other. Freaking out, she opened some of them and all there was displayed was a single: ? All of them the same. One single question mark. They continued bombarding her phone. Alarmed Oliver would come in and see them, giving him a perfect reason to call the police, she switched off her phone.

'Luke, don't you agree she should go to the police about this? She may not have noticed anyone watching her.' Oliver was on a roll, egged on by Luke's encouraging nods and serious face as Gemma walked back into the kitchen.

Gemma settled back in her chair and nibbled at her food, spaghetti carbonara. She'd found the ingredients in the back of a cupboard and defrosted the bacon in a bowl of hot water. It wasn't bad for an on the spot meal. She was annoyed Oliver was back on the same subject.

'Think hard, Gemma. Is there anyone you might have crossed lately?'

She said, her patience running out of steam, 'Look, I haven't upset anyone apart from the obvious ones. Nor have I had an altercation with anyone, or road rage... nothing at all.' She gave Oliver a look, warning him not to say any more.

'Well, I'm going to keep a close eye on you, Gemma, and see if anyone's watching you,' Oliver said. They glared at each other across the table.

She shoved a forkful of spaghetti into her mouth.

'Look, Oliver, you'd better stop this otherwise Luke is going to think I have a stalker,' she said, swallowing her mouthful.

The tension round the table had gone from casual dinner party conversation to a grilling. Gemma stabbed her food. Bridgette just sat there drinking and looking from one to the other. Gemma's glass was empty. Knowing it was rude and not caring one jot; she leant over and grabbed the bottle of red, pouring herself a glass. She ignored Oliver's gesture to fill his glass and slammed the bottle back down next to her. Now he would have to get up or ask her for it.

He thumped his glass down lucky not to break the stem. 'Well, I bloody well think there is something to worry about. Stop trying to be so casual about it, Gemma. I know it bothered you.' He turned to Luke. 'If she won't go to the police, can you get somebody to drop by the house, Luke?'

'No! Oliver!' she protested. Clearly, Oliver was not giving up without a fight here. She turned in her seat to face Luke. 'I hear what you're saying, but I don't agree. I don't mean that to sound rude.' She did. She meant it to sound very rude indeed. 'I know you're the police. Well ex-police, but what are the chances from this incident the person who did it would harm me?'

'Massive, I should say,' interrupted Oliver. He looked intently at Luke and avoiding eye contact with her, he reached across for the bottle of red, poured himself a full glass then offered Luke some.

Stammering, Luke replied, 'Well, the chances from this incident that it could escalate to physical harm are pretty small.'

'See,' she said, jumping in, then turning to look at Oliver. Her face flushed with colour, hoping this would put a stop to it. She gave him another look that said, *how many different ways do you need to hear this!*

Oliver opened his mouth to say something then hesitated.

Gemma flashed him a smile thinking he'd finally got the message.

'Let's make a deal,' he said. Gemma scowled at him. 'If Luke thinks it's OK, do it for me, please. I would like somebody to come to the house to talk to you and give you some advice. You know the kind of things to look out for… just in case there is some crazed man out there.'

She had to admit, he was a stubborn bugger, but that couldn't happen. 'No, let's not, Oliver,' she informed him. 'Luke said it was highly unlikely this would escalate to the level you are thinking it would. *So*, I suggested if anything else happens we then speak to the police and not before.' She put her knife and fork down on her plate.

Chapter Forty

JAKE

He pulled up outside the cottage and walked slowly to the front door. Through the diamond shaped glass he saw them sitting at the kitchen table entertaining. Music played in the background and candles flickered in all the downstairs rooms.

He pulled a key from his pocket and tried it in the lock. He smiled; he suspected she wouldn't have changed the lock from the last time he let himself in. What excuse would she have without worrying Oliver?

He slipped in quietly. In the living room he saw her handbag tossed casually on the sofa. He opened it and looked at the contents. He took an envelope from his jacket and placed it inside. Standing behind the heavy red curtains in the lounge, he adjusted them to see through the gap and dialled her landline.

Gemma walked in holding a glass of wine, she put the glass down on the occasional table by the sofa next to the phone and picked up the receiver. 'Hello? Hello?'

He watched her take a sip of wine and scowl at the phone before replacing it. She walked out of the room and he rang it again.

She answered it the same as the last time. He looked her up and down, she turned her head and he loved the way she scowled when she realised it was him calling. 'Hello? Hello?' If only she knew how close he was. The thought caused his blood to race through his veins giving him an instant high. Then she unplugged it and went back to the kitchen. He smirked knowing how agitated it was making her.

Quietly, he walked from behind the curtains to the lounge door and peered through the crack between the door and the frame. His grey eyes watched her, his expression one of having to tolerate an unpleasant smell. He watched her movements. Pouring wine, eating, deflecting the conversation.

Intrigued, he listened to them and a smile crossed his face when he heard Oliver's concerns for her after the terrible supermarket ordeal. That was when he sent her the text. Oh, how delicious her face looked when she read it. He darted back behind the curtains when she came in to leave her phone on the mantelpiece.

How long would she be able to hide him from Oliver? If there wasn't a chance of being heard, he'd laugh with the pleasure it was giving him. He could barely hold it together knowing she had been in his house. He moved farther back behind the curtains. His hands fisted.

A blast of cold air suddenly burst through the front door blowing it open. He clearly hadn't closed it properly.

He waited for Oliver to get back to the table and dialled her mobile blocking his caller ID. It rang on top of the mantelpiece.

Gemma walked in and answered the phone, but just as she picked it up it cut off. It rang again. 'Hello? Hello?' When no one answered she put it down.

Jake sent her a text with a question mark. He heard the beep and wished she would turn around, just a little, so he could see her face when she opened it. Oh God, he would give anything to see her face. He grinned and sent it again. And again. And again. And again. And again. He kept sending it until he must have fired off at least thirty. She looked distressed as she fumbled with the phone to turn it off. Another tremor of pleasure went through his body, but he was getting bored, he needed to ramp it up. She deserved better. He hadn't thought she would have it in her to break into his house.

It was becoming more and more difficult to hold back and not hurt her and see her pain, but he did. If he did it now, he wouldn't be able to stop himself and he wanted to see her suffer.

Before he left, he sent a final text. *Very nice jumper with the tiny hearts you're wearing tonight.*

He slipped through the door taking the chain off and closing it quietly.

Switching on the ignition he looked back at the house. A new plan already formulating in his mind.

Chapter Forty-One

GEMMA

Gemma and Oliver arrived home late afternoon the following day from the court hearing for their bankruptcy. They travelled back in silence. Neither knowing what to say after the dismal time spent in the courtroom.

Big dilemma, though. The judge, in his crisp navy Savile Row suit, perched high above them in his intimidating chair, pronounced they were going to hell unless they pulled a magic bag of money out of thin air. Not his exact words but the meaning was the same. He added they would be able to keep their house because fifty per cent would go to the court appointed trustee to pay off their debts as they had enough equity to do that. And if they could keep up the mortgage payments, they could continue living there. But for that to happen they would have to prove they had jobs. Proof. Payslips. And, of course, she had none of that. She hadn't been able to mention her job. They'd have to raise the fifty percent too, which wasn't going to happen. If they showed they had any money coming in, they would have to give a percentage of it to their creditors.

Oliver spoke, at last. 'I don't understand why this boss of yours pays you in cash with no proper payslips.'

'I don't know. I never questioned it. It was a job and he offered cash. I was hardly in a position to say no, was I?'

'No, but didn't you think it was suspicious that he wanted to pay you that way? And besides, you said you've only met him on Skype. So how do you get the money?'

She shrugged. She didn't need this right now. She pulled her lipstick from her handbag to give her time to think.

233

How had she been so dense and not thought this out? She breathed in and out slowly. Christ, what was all the nitpicking, it was money. A job. What did it matter? They had no time for integrity. They couldn't *afford* integrity!

'No, Oliver, I didn't care. We needed money and I didn't care where it came from. What would you have preferred that we nip around to the back of Currys and pinch a cardboard box we could both live in together?' Sometimes Oliver really tried her patience with *wanting to do the right thing*. They wouldn't have found a cardboard box anyway, they all got crushed nowadays. Recycling! The thought of it made her want to scream. She didn't want to talk about where the money came from, but he'd think it strange if she didn't. Her outburst made him look at her in that questioning way he did regularly these days.

'So?'

'So, what?'

'When did you meet your boss and why haven't you told me?'

She had no idea if he would believe her, but she had to say something. There was no hint of a smile or softness on his face. He waited. 'I met him in the Cha Bar coffee shop.'

'And you didn't mention it? Why?'

'Why?' She was good at hiding her emotions. Lying was beginning to be her forte. A sudden image of her stepfather flashed in her mind and suddenly all visible emotions vanished from her face. She looked at Oliver, calmly and in control. 'Because when I met up with him you'd had that meeting with the bank. Remember? You came home so deflated. I forgot. It wasn't as important as you, Oliver.'

He was quiet for a moment or so. 'And after that?'

'After that, I really forgot all about it.'

When they arrived home, she saw a parcel for them by the front door. Gemma stared at it, suspiciously. The text she received this morning after turning on her phone had frightened her. He was spying on them. She didn't come out of the house yesterday evening for him to see her jumper. He probably had binoculars trained on their house as they spoke.

Climbing out of the car, she picked up the parcel addressed to her. In bold marker pen in the bottom left hand corner was the number 5.

'Who's it from, do you know?'

'Not a clue,' she snapped, leaning against the gate for support. She hoped he wouldn't start asking questions and relating it to the stalker incident. 'I imagine it's something I ordered a while ago and forgot about. You know how it is with some of these deliveries. They take ages to come unless you pay extra carriage charges.'

Oliver threw her a look as he got out of the car and locked it. 'Well, open it then.'

She sighed. 'No, I'll do it later.'

'Gemma...'

'DON'T!' Gemma exclaimed, tense that he was putting pressure on her. 'Please don't.' They'd come to an agreement not to mention the stalker incident again. She'd managed to get Oliver to promise he would back off unless anything else happened. They had a God almighty argument last night after the dinner finished and Luke and Bridgette left. 'It's not from your so-called stalker. It will be something I ordered online. You're being paranoid.'

She headed into the house and up to their bedroom. She wanted to disappear and not have to face Oliver's questions. She'd promised herself she would not take it out on Oliver and here she was breaking her own promise.

She took one look in the box and booted it across the room.

Was he in their house last night? She was sure she'd

heard Oliver put the chain on after the door blew open. But it wasn't on when Luke and Bridgette left. She walked over to the box feeling detached as she picked it up and took it into the bathroom. She opened the box and dropped it. 'Oh my God.'

She opened the toilet lid and dropped the dead bird inside. He was sick. She pulled off some loo roll and threw it on top then flushed. She stood still waiting to see it all disappear. He was making his point to make sure she knew he'd killed Robert.

He was moving fast and she had to move faster.

He wasn't the first man to push her to the edge.

In her early years she almost set fire to her mother and stepfather in their beds, such was her pain and anguish at the time. But the worry of getting caught held her back. The plan, to light a cigarette and drop it on the sofa on one of their many drinking nights was a good one. Nothing ever woke them. She chickened out.

Other times she'd crushed aspirin and sprinkled them over their battered fish from the chippy on a Friday. All that did was make them sick. She even cleaned the inside of the loo with his toothbrush. But his insides were so corroded that nothing happened to him. Such was her misery. The best one. The one she was most proud of was the morning after she asked John Sweeney, who was training at the local garage to be a mechanic, to tinker with *his* brakes. It cost her a blow job at the time. She watched from her bedroom window as her stepfather drove off, her heart thumping, only to see him crash into a parked car and scare one or two pedestrians but nothing more. Although it was a failed attempt, he became wary of her. Not until she knocked him down on that final day did she feel she'd had her justice.

Chapter Forty-Two

OLIVER

Two days later Oliver sat in the outside lane of the M56 heading north to Manchester in the early morning rush hour. Something had niggled him for a long time. He didn't tell Gemma of his plans. She'd go ballistic.

The traffic was fierce and the idiots on the road irritated him. He drove impatiently, weaving in and out of lanes in the Mercedes. He came off the M56 onto the Parkway straight into a gridlock all the way into Manchester town centre. He could have left later and avoided all this stress, but he was too impatient – he needed to find out.

He promised her long ago that he would protect her. Nothing would stop him doing that. Nothing else mattered to him. He was losing everything else, but he couldn't lose her. Of late, she was so preoccupied it made him nervous. His life was with her and he couldn't shift the feeling she was hurting. He could tell she was nearly out of her mind with worry about what would become of them. She kept it tight. Bottled up. There had to be more to it than the financial problems they were going through. He'd never seen her like this. Then, the other day, he happened to mention her family and she very nearly garrotted him with his tie. She apologised and cried, begging him to forgive her.

He needed to get inside Gemma's head, needed to know her past and to do that; he needed to find out about her past.

Forty minutes later he drove the Mercedes slowly along Upton Street in North Manchester. The row of terraced red brick houses all looked identical. The street was lined with parked cars and vans, there was nowhere to park. A few young people, smoking, dressed in hoodies and joggers, congregated outside one house on the opposite side of the street. They looked over, checking him out to see if he was a threat to them. He was nervous and felt out of place and hoped that wasn't the house he was looking for. He'd made a mistake coming here in the Mercedes.

He squeezed the car in between a rusty old VW Golf and a Renault Clio with the back window ledge covered in children's soft toys.

Last night while she slept, feeling concerned for her state of mind, he'd gone into the loft. Amongst her boxes full of stuff, he remembered seeing one marked *school*. He thought somewhere amongst that lot there might be a home address. It could of course be a waste of time, who's to say her family still lived here? He had a hunch and he was following it. Although she told him her family were all dead, somehow he never quite believed her.

He stepped out of the car and looked around the street. It was quiet, apart from the group across the road the only other people were two young mums with buggies, chatting. She'd certainly come from humble beginnings. He would never have guessed it. All the streets were alike; two-up, two-downs. There were no front gardens. You walked straight out from the front door onto the pavement. He imagined that once they would have all worked in a nearby mill in the times when North Manchester was rich in cotton manufacturing. Farther along the street a front door opened, he turned and saw a woman in a sari and four kids step out.

He pulled the collar of his blue overcoat up against the chill wind. The gathered crowd down the street watched him. They didn't look very friendly; he hoped to be away in no more than ten minutes. It was colder here than at home in Cheshire. You wouldn't think twenty odd miles could make such a difference. Everything around here looked grim. The low cloud didn't help much.

He stood in front of number 1 Upton Street, Salford. He noticed how grubby the front door was. There was no knocker or doorbell; he used his knuckles. Then wiped his hand on his coat and pushed them in his pockets. He stood back and looked at the two houses on either side. Both well maintained and clean, this was the scruffiest in the row.

Inside he heard coughing. When the door finally opened, he faced an undistinguishable looking woman. He couldn't hazard a guess at her age. Her features melted into the multitude of deep lines crisscrossing her face. She was bent over with arthritis, a pronounced hump on her back. Her short dark hair was flat against her head with grease. She coughed again, her false teeth loose in her mouth, clicking.

'Waddya want.' She spat phlegm into a grubby tissue she pulled from her sleeve and screwed her eyes up to look at him. Her glasses dangled round her neck on a length of dirty string. She fumbled with her hand to find them, then shakily put them on and stared at him. 'Well?'

Unfazed, he forced himself to stand there, though his instant reaction was to back away. The smell of cigarette smoke escaped the house and circled her like a bad smell cloud on cartoons.

'Mrs Weids?'

'Who wants to know?'

He wanted to yell at her, but she'd probably slam the door in his face and the crowd down the road would approach. So, he asked again.

'Are you Mrs Weids?'

'I heard ya. And I asked ya, who wants to know?'

'I'm looking for Gemma Weids's mother.'

She gave him a cold look. Her mouth pursed, wrinkles

surrounded it like the tie-up end of a balloon. She pushed her glasses further up her nose and leaned forward to get a better look at him.

'Who are you?'

'A friend.'

She honked up more phlegm and spat in the same tissue, then screwed it up into a ball and closed her fist around it. Oliver held down the nausea that threatened to overcome him.

'She ain't no friend of mine. She's a WHORE.' She slammed the door.

Oliver put his foot in the way and it bounced open. 'I just want to talk to you, Mrs Weids, please.'

She walked off back into the house. 'Fucking bitch, I ain't got nothing good to say 'bout that one.'

He followed her in closing the door behind, noticing the crowd across the street watching. That was why she let him in, knowing they were there keeping an eye on things.

She walked to the back room where an electric bar fire blasted out dry heat. The condensation dripped down the windows. As soon as they walked in the heat hit him. He removed his coat but there was nowhere to put it, so he hung it over his arm. He loosened his scarf. She sat in the armchair nearest the fire.

'Sit if ya wanna.'

Taking one look at the other chair, he eyed it suspiciously perching on the end. The stench of smoke filled his nostrils. She lit a cigarette. The ashtray on the table next to her overflowed with cigarette butts.

'Where is she then?'

'Oh, err... living in London.' He didn't want to give Gemma away.

She scoffed. 'Thinks she's a fancy thing, does she? You 'er husband then?'

'No, just a friend, like I said. So, Mrs Weids, what happened?'

'Waddya mean what happened? She say something happened? She was always a bloody liar that one. Ungrateful. Thought she were better than the rest of us.' She scoffed again, and her teeth nearly fell out. She pulled them out then pushed them back in. Oliver looked away. If he puked on the carpet would she even care? The room was a disgrace. Plates with mouldy food lay around her chair. He counted four half-empty glasses scattered about the room.

She picked up her teacup, then hesitated. 'Want a drink?'

'No, no, thank you,' he said, quickly.

She frowned, creasing her face even more. 'So?'

'Well,' he replied. 'I wondered that was all. She never speaks about her past and I presumed something had happened to stop her from wanting to talk about it.'

She contemplated this for a few minutes. Coughed, but this time didn't bring up any phlegm. Instead, she puffed on her cigarette that lay smouldering in the ashtray.

Oliver cleared his own throat and said, 'Well, Mrs Weids, did anything happen?'

'Aye, sumut happened alright.'

'Go on,' he said, wanting her to elaborate.

'Bitch lied, told everyone her stepdad raped her all the bleeding time. Lying cunt.'

Oliver recoiled at the use of that word, horrified that she could use it for her own daughter. He found it hard to believe this was Gemma's mother.

She tapped the cigarette on the side of the ashtray. 'Not surprised she said nowt about it to you.' She took a long drag on her cigarette and then blew the smoke at him. 'Oh, aye, bitch kept quiet.' She nodded her head, her eyes glazed over as if watching a replay in her mind. 'She hated him from the start. Made it clear he wasn't welcome. Made it hard for me. Made him cross at the lies she told.'

Oliver physically flinched, his fists balled with anger that Gemma had put up with this home life. 'Did it ever occur to you she might have been telling the truth?' he said sarcastically. Clearly this woman wanted an easy life, brush it under the carpet and shut up.

She laughed a cackling laugh, which brought on another coughing fit and a productive cough. She picked up a dirty tissue from the table next to her and spat into it. She fiddled with her dentures and scowled at him, indicating she was angry by his statement. She looked hard and selfish, and he thought she deserved the harshness life now dealt her. He wanted to get up and leave the grubby stinking home. It made him feel unclean, but he needed more answers.

'Well did it?' he prompted.

She drew deep on her cigarette and stubbed it out in the ashtray. He could tell by her body language she was about to say something foul. She pulled another cigarette from the packet. Clasped it between her lips and lit it with a blue Bic lighter, all the time looking at him.

'No,' she said, her face rigid. 'She got ya all fired up, hasn't she? She's good at that. And lies. She tells good lies. Comes across all innocent like, and folks believe her, butter wouldn't melt, that sort of crap. But I knows her, I gave birth to her, I know what she's capable of.' She narrowed her eyes. 'Did she tell ya she killed her stepfather?' She roared with laughter, which brought on another coughing fit. At the sight of Oliver's shocked face, she cackled. 'Na, thought not. She thought she had, but she just busted his hip. Mind you he never mended proper like, and he spent the rest of his days in a bloody wheelchair. Made my life hell that bitch did. She reversed her car into him. Knocked him down. Then she got out the car to check. He was unconscious.

Bitch got back in and reversed again crushing his hip like a melon. We had never married. When he couldn't work I got no benefits for him.' She ignored his attempt to butt in and carried on. 'Council didn't know he lived here, ya see. Anyways, I saw it all from me bedroom window.' She pointed with her cigarette to the ceiling. 'Then she laughed when I came running down shouting at her. Told me she didn't see him.'

Oliver sat, stunned. 'What about the police? Did they look for her?'

She tilted her head. 'Bastard police. No point involving them,' she said, looking away from him.

No, Oliver thought, they wouldn't want the police investigating the reasons why Gemma would knock down her stepdad.

The conversation went quiet for a moment.

'She has a side to her. Mind, ya do have to push her some, but when ya do and she sees no way out, she does what she wants. Dunt care neither.' Another hacking cough came over her.

Oliver didn't know what to say. It wasn't what he was expecting to hear. From what he'd heard he wasn't sure he knew Gemma at all. This didn't seem like the Gemma he knew. His Gemma.

'She's very convincing, ya know. Ya can't believe what comes out her mouth. She'll lie to save her own skin.'

Oliver wasn't prepared to believe her side of the story. 'Why didn't you believe her when she told you her stepfather was abusing her?'

She coughed and then drew deep on her cigarette. ''Cause she's a fucking liar.'

This woman repulsed him. 'But surely as a mother you must have had a moment when you thought it might be true?'

That didn't appear to shock her into maternal warmth towards her daughter. 'Gemma never got raped. Her stepdad would never have done that.'

The room so filled with smoke hurt his chest and eyes. She took another couple of drags blowing them in his direction.

'Maybe it was an accident. Maybe you couldn't see clearly.' *Maybe there was so much smoke in the room it was like looking through fog*, he wanted to say but suspected this would antagonise her.

'I saw well enough. She wanted to kill him for sure.'

He moved on. Knowing he wasn't going to get any remorse from this woman towards her daughter. Her mother preferring her man in her house than defend her own daughter. It disgusted him. He wanted to punch her. 'Where's her dad? Her real dad?'

'I dunno, loser he was.'

Much like you, he wanted to say. 'Haven't you ever wondered what happened to her?'

She tapped her cigarette on the ashtray. 'No, wouldn't piss on her if she were on fire, nasty bitch.' She picked up the teacup again, slurped, and wiped her mouth with the dirty tissue. 'After he died, I never found another fella. Folk thought we were bad on account of her. Ruined me life that bitch did. Should have had her terminated when I found I was up the duff from that loser.'

Oliver had heard enough. He got up from the chair. She laughed at him, hawking up more phlegm. 'You scared of her now?'

'No, Gemma is nothing like you say. But you're a disgusting human being and an insult to mothers around the world. I feel sorry for Gemma having been subjected to you for even one second, never mind years.'

'Bloody hell, ya got it bad. Go on fuck off then, get out.'

She laughed. 'She got you just as messed up as that other fella what came here.'

'Who?'

'I dunno, do I. Never let on. Didn't ya know she had another chasing after her?' She laughed the same cackling laugh that brought on another coughing fit.

'What did this man look like?'

'Dunno.' She shrugged.

'Did he give you a name?'

'Might have. How much do ya wanna know it?' She put out her hand.

Chapter Forty-Three

GEMMA

Gemma woke the next day to the sound of a text.

3.

Three days left until he did what? She didn't need reminding any more. What did he have in mind? Some sort of accident? Torture? Turn up at the house and kill them both? She got out of bed and showered. Through her exhaustion she was struggling to find a way out.

Oliver acted strangely the moment he woke up. He persisted on talking about their childhoods.

Suspicious that something else had happened to garner this sudden interest in her past, she went overboard with love and attention. She even cooked him a full English and cocooned him in a blanket of love to steer him away from childhoods.

She said no to going down memory lane. She was fine. She didn't need to dredge up her past. But he insisted. Besides, as far as he knew, the past she'd spoken about was boring and simplistic. A simple, made-up fabrication of a pretend childhood. He told her it would be good for her to open up! Why would it be good for her? She'd dealt with her past long ago. She maintained it was too painful remembering her parents' death in a car crash. In her head, she had no intention of travelling that dark, grim path again. And how did he know it would be good for her? He didn't know anything about her past, only what she'd wanted to tell him. Her past was where she wanted it to be. In the past. Where it belonged.

But he persisted, like a damned dog with a bone. Why

now? After all this time, why start questioning it? It was a taboo subject for her and he'd been happy to go along with that. Until now.

He carried on regardless of her remonstrations, painting her colourful pictures of his upbringing, the close relationship with his parents and extended family, all of which she already knew. She revelled in the descriptive pictures he drew for her of Christmas family gatherings, family holidays and Christmas plays. All the things she never had. She already knew most of it. She lived through his memories; she always had, absorbing it all and immersing herself there. Imagining how it must have felt to have that love and security around you. But it still didn't mean she wanted to open up about her own upbringing. She maintained it was too painful.

'Your turn, Gem, tell me about your childhood again.'

She stood up. 'No! I don't want to talk about it. You know that. Why are you doing this? No. You promised me you'd respect my wishes on this. Stop it. You promised.'

He threw up his hands. 'Christ, because we need to talk about what is going on here. I know whatever is going on has something to do with the things that happened to you a long time ago. The death of your parents?'

She narrowed her eyes. 'Really! And you've come to that assumption, how?'

'I just have.'

'You just have? You just have! What are you, some kind of therapist? Oh God, you haven't gone to a therapist about me, have you?'

He shook his head. 'No, of course not. Look you can't see it. You can't see the irrational way you are behaving. Christ, you vandalised that car and you won't tell me why you did it. You're drinking and buying a car we can't afford on finance! And you said you'd take it back and you haven't.

You met your boss who pays you in cash and you forgot to tell me? I would say all that is pretty bloody irrational.'

'I will tell you about the vandalism, just not now. I thought we got past the car.'

'You might have thought I had, but I haven't. I haven't brought it up again because I can't stand arguing with you. But you must see how mad it seems to me and then you say you'll tell me, but not now! Just what does that even mean, Gem? You tell me you've stopped drinking, but I still see the bottles. This boss of yours is worrying me.'

'Oh my God, only a little drinking. I've cut down massively. You make me sound like a drunk! My boss is no big deal. So I forgot to mention him! Shit. You're making a huge thing out of this, Oliver.'

'Well, however much it is, it's too much for my liking. Something has stirred you up. You never drank like this and don't say it's about losing our home. Please don't patronise me. You think you're clever, don't you but I notice it on your breath every day. I notice the bottles in the recycling bin hidden beneath boxes and tucked inside boxes.'

She was not going to stand there and take this abuse from him. No, she wasn't. She had put them in the bin that way to stop them clanking together. Any sensible person would do the same. You can't call someone a lush because they organise their bottles correctly in the recycling bin.

'Are you going to stand by that? Because I did that to stop them clanking. It's sensible.'

'To stop people hearing them clanking? Is that why?'

'There's nobody next to us, Oliver, we're detached,' she screeched. 'Why would I give a stuff about anyone hearing? No, it was to stop them smashing.'

'Smashing? Clanking? Christ, it's all bullshit. It was to stop me seeing them.' He gave her a look of derision.

He was delusional. She wasn't hiding anything! He was

imagining it all. Why was he trying to hurt her like this? He said he loved her, but this wasn't love, this was abuse and harassment. Yes, that's what it was. She felt a flutter of panic that everything was beginning to unravel between them. She tried to relax her screaming nerves. Now. Now was the time to tell Oliver the truth. Right now. Confess. She'd put it off long enough. It was never going to get any easier. Just the opposite.

'Why are you trying to make out I'm a drunk, Oliver? I thought you loved me.' She felt a stab of guilt for having a go at him when all he was doing was trying to help her.

'Can't you see, Gem? I do love you very much, and that's why I need you to talk about your childhood. That's where all this drinking is coming from.'

Mad! Raving mad! He was off his trolley. How the hell had he come to that fucking conclusion? She had her childhood under control. It had nothing to do with the little bit of wine she drank. She drank a *little* wine, here and there. Always with a meal. Sometimes without, granted, but only a little. She wasn't falling over drunk. Pissed. Smashed. A drunkard.

She hissed, she couldn't help it. Bringing up her past was really getting to her. 'It-has-nothing-to-do-with-my-childhood.'

'I won't judge you, Gem, you know that.'

You would. You would if you knew. Everyone would. Wait, what is he talking about? Judge? Why would he say that?

'Don't be angry, Gem, but I went to see your mother. I know she's not dead.'

She recoiled and glared at him accusingly as if she'd misheard him. Shaking her head, she shouted, 'WHAT! You did what?' She couldn't believe her ears. 'HOW DARE YOU. How... how did you know where to find her? I never spoke about her.' Then she realised her mistake and quickly backpedalled. 'You couldn't have. She's dead. They're both dead. I already told you that.'

'No, she's not. You're lying again. Stop it. Stop fucking lying to me!'

She didn't know how to get herself out of this or how she was going to save them. Not now. Not if he was telling the truth. 'I'm not. You've made a mistake. You've been to see someone else. You've got me mixed up with someone else, that's what you've done. They're dead. Why? Why would you do that without telling me? You shouldn't have done that. You shouldn't have done that,' she screamed at him.

'She told me another man had gone looking for you.'

All the way down her back the spiders crawled. What man? No. Not Jake!

She felt a sense of hopelessness at being unable to stop the imminent collision that was about to engulf her. Her overriding emotion of shame that after all this time and all they had shared, those few words he uttered were about to derail them.

'Gem, you misunderstand,' he interrupted her. 'I don't know exactly why I felt the need to dig deep, I just did. Call it a hunch, but I think it has to do with your childhood. I remembered you had old schoolbooks in the attic and old school paperwork. I got the address off them. One thing led to another.'

She kept shaking her head unable to stop. The pressure beginning to take its toll. Everything around her was crumbling. She wasn't sleeping. She wasn't eating. All she did was drink to keep her thoughts from going around in circles. Oliver was right about that, although she'd never admit to it. But it had nothing to do with her childhood.

Sean had given her ammunition against Jake but she was at a loss how to use it. Scared what Jake might do if she threatened him. Scared how it might backfire. Scared he might hurt Oliver.

'One thing led to another? Knowing how closed I am about my fam— my childhood,' she stuttered on the word *family*. She had no family. 'You decided to go behind my back and see her! Find her! How could you?' She backed away from him, repulsed that he knew. He knew! He knew about her. Where she came from. Her mother. All of it. Christ, the shame of it. He knew about the abuse. The rapes. The beatings. Shame. Shame. Shame. It flooded through her, immobilising her. Traumatised, she froze, her body trapped, unable to move. His words were her kryptonite.

Gemma vividly remembered the horror of her childhood. Oliver had opened the sluice gates and the visions flooding in made her blood turn cold. All the work she'd done to lock them away and now he'd unleashed them.

'How the hell can I misunderstand? You went to see my mother; how can I misunderstand that? You shouldn't have done it, Oliver. You idiot.'

She couldn't bear the thought that he knew what happened to her. Damaged her. She hated that Gemma, the one too scared to fight back for fear of getting a beating. She realised she was doing it again. She was too scared Jake would hurt them to fight back. The strong Gemma took control the day she killed her stepfather. That's what she needed to do now. She needed to take control. She had left her mother and that life behind. And now, Oliver, her Oliver, knew what that filthy bastard had done to her. God, she felt dirty. She wanted to scrub herself clean. Goosebumps spread all over her body making her want to tear off her clothes and scrub her body with bleach.

'I suppose you think I will think the worst of you now I know more about you,' he said.

She regarded him steadily. Her whole body shook. All

these years she had managed to hide her past. Now Oliver was raking it all up. Utter humiliation. This was her personal hall of shame where the memories were seared closed and now burst open tormenting her again. All over again.

'I can't bear that you know,' she said, outraged, unable to hold back the tears. She needed space. To wash, scrub, disinfect her body. Oh God, how dirty did she feel? She could almost feel *him* near her. She cringed at the visions in her mind. Her mind ablaze with memories. Vile, disgusting memories. Why wouldn't they stop? They raced in her mind's eye on fast forward. Make them stop. Make them stop. Oh God, make them stop. She clutched her head. She didn't want to see him. Didn't want him to see her.

Oliver grabbed hold of her wrapping her up in his arms. Oblivious to what she was doing, he trapped her arms by her sides to stop her from ripping her skin off with her nails. Raking her nails across her skin as if to shed it. When she couldn't self-harm, she dropped her head on his shoulder and bit his jumper. A deep animal scream erupted from inside her. He held her tight against him.

'Let it go, Gemma, let it come out. I'm here. I won't let anyone harm you ever again. I have so many questions, Gem, but seeing you crushed like this, shame spilling out of every pore of your skin, it isn't worth the knowing. I won't ask you again. I'm so sorry, please, believe me, I'm sorry, I'm sorry.' He tightened his hold against her fierce desire to escape him.

Gemma couldn't speak, her throat tightened, her body so wracked with pain it shook uncontrollably as though she'd been tasered. She had never ever let it out. Never freed herself. She was unable to stop. It poured out of her.

She cried for so long by the time she finished she was exhausted and the only thing she wanted was to be held close in Oliver's arms.

He carried her to the sofa wrapping her in his arms. He sat down with her, stroking her hair, comforting her, making her feel safe.

Sobbing, she murmured, 'Oliver, I can't bear that you know. I feel so dirty. So, grubby...' she hesitated '... I... I need to tell you something else.'

'Gem, it's fine. I don't think any differently of you. You don't have to say anything else.'

Her mouth was dry, her chest tightened as she thought of the unthinkable. Would he *really* understand? Could she *really* tell him?

'Oliver, did she tell you I killed my stepfather?' There was no guilt. No remorse. He deserved it and more.

So many memories drifted back. Recollections of so many times her bedroom door opened in the night. The stinking smell of alcohol wafting in her face. The bed sheets pulled off her. And her loathsome mother turning a blind eye. Calling her a liar when she went to her and told her what was happening.

'Oliver, I can't redeem myself in my eyes now that you know. I will always know that you know my dirty little secret.'

'Gem, you didn't kill your stepfather, you crushed his hip and he survived.'

'Oh. No, no, you're wrong, I killed him. I crushed him with my car. I wanted to kill him.'

'I know you did. But you didn't. He lived his final days in a wheelchair.'

'Oh God,' she groaned. 'All this time I thought I'd murdered him.'

'You left that day, didn't you?'

'Yes.' She remembered how anxious she was waiting for the police to find her. When they didn't come, she thought she was incredibly lucky and had got away with murder.

'There was nothing to follow up. You never made contact

with your mother, so you never knew. They didn't tell the police what happened. I guess they didn't want them to find out what had been going on.'

She wilted in his arms and looked ready to collapse. 'Oh God, Oliver, I wanted to kill him. He deserved to die. I really wanted to kill him.'

'I know, babe, and he deserved it. But from what your mother said he suffered plenty afterwards and she did too. You made their lives very difficult.'

'I wanted to kill him.'

'Hush now, it is in the past, Gem.' Oliver kissed the top of her head.

Her voice quivered. 'Oliver.' She couldn't look at him. She snuggled close to his warmth for comfort. 'Oliver, you should never have gone. Never.' She pulled herself out of his arms. 'I don't know how we can carry on? You knowing all about me. About what happened to me.'

'What are you talking about?' Alarm crossed his face.

Too ashamed to look at him, she stood up. 'I have to go.'

'What are you talking about?' he said, jumping to his feet. 'So you had a crap upbringing. You're not the only one. But you have me now, we have each other. It doesn't make any difference to me. None of it does.' He moved in front of her, blocking her exit. 'You can't leave, we will come through this, Gem.'

'Oliver, please. I can't talk about it any more. I don't *want* to talk about it any more.' She faced him with a granite-like expression as he stretched out his arms to hold her. She backed away.

'Gem…' His voice faltered. 'Gem, don't do this, please. I know you feel dirty and ashamed…'

'Don't you dare tell me how I feel. You have no idea. You never will,' she yelled and looked away. 'Oliver, why did you do it? Don't you see? Don't you see we can't move forward now?'

Chapter Forty-Four

OLIVER

Oliver didn't think he needed to persuade her. He thought she would be over the moon that he wanted to love her despite her past. It wasn't her fault. She was a victim.

He felt he was losing her. She was pulling away from him like an unravelling cotton reel. This wasn't what he wanted.

'Don't you see?' she cried out, the sound she made was so full of pain it tore his heart out. 'You know.'

She stood in front of him, tears flowing uncontrolled, her body shaking with pain and sadness.

He muttered, quietly, 'Gem, these things happen to people. It isn't your fault. You must believe that. You're a victim of abuse.' Afraid he might spook her to run away, he stayed calm hoping to bring her round.

'Sadly, Oliver, it's not that easy. Don't you see? If you didn't know, I could pretend it never happened and be happy with you. But you *do* know. And I can't pretend any more.'

'Gem, please...' Panic made him move back to block the doorway. 'Oh God, please don't do this, Gem. Don't go.'

'I have to,' she said.

'No!' He put his arms up to stop her, pushing her backwards. 'You stay here, please, please don't leave me. I'm going. I'll stay in a hotel tonight, give you time on your own and tomorrow we'll talk some more.' He held her gaze. 'Please, promise me you won't leave the house tonight. Please, Gemma. Say it. Say you won't leave.'

She heaved a huge sigh. 'OK, I won't leave... tonight. But I don't see a way round this.'

'Just stay here tonight, please. You promise?'

'I promise.'

He wrapped her in his arms and gently kissed her lips. 'I love you so much, Gem, you're everything to me. Give me a chance to help you.'

'But I—'

'Shhh, don't say any more. The universe has ways of making things right if they're meant. And I believe we're meant to be together. I know you believe that too.'

Chapter Forty-Five

GEMMA

Her knees trembled when she opened the front door not long after Oliver left and found Jake standing on her doorstep. The blood rushed through her veins making her disorientated. She nearly collapsed from shock.

'What are you doing here?' She stood in the doorway leaning against the frame and pulling the door towards her, placing her foot behind it to stop him pushing it open.

'Oliver home?'

'No. Why?'

He smiled calculatingly. 'I know. I saw him leave. Gone shopping?'

'Maybe. Why?'

'Just wondered. Can I come in?'

'No.'

He edged forward, she felt his breath as he pushed his face closer and whispered in her ear. 'I'm your landlord and I've come to do an inspection. By law you have to let me in.'

'Fuck off, Jake,' she whispered back, but her words had a sting in them. 'Tell your friendly estate agent lovey to come and do the inspection.' She tried to close the door, but he put his hand against it. Retreat would show weakness; it would give him an inlet to surge forward and take control. She let nothing in her face divulge her panic.

'Now, now, Gemma, this is not the way to behave. I've told you before. You have to follow my rules and you're doing it again.'

'I told you to get lost.' She pushed the door.

He pushed back. 'Don't. You. Dare. Speak. To. Me. Like. That.'

'Why? What are you going to do? This is my home and you're trespassing. Go. Away. I don't want to see you again. I'm sick of you. I'm sick of your games.'

'Oh really?' He pulled himself up to his full height, took a deep breath and looked down on her. Then, before she had time to react, he thrust the door open. It bounced back and slammed into her shoulder. He strode into the hallway, propelling her backwards with the force of his entry, slamming the front door closed.

She stayed where she landed.

'Let's have a drink, Gemma, and you can tell me about your day? How did Oliver get on with your mother, by the way?' He walked to the kitchen, pulled open the fridge and poured out two glasses of wine. 'Come, sit down.'

How did he know? She didn't go. She stayed put. He paced the floor.

He could do anything to her and nobody would know.

'I said come here. Join me in a drink.' His voice chilled her.

Her eyes wary of his every move. His every nuance. 'How do you know?'

He stared at her in astonishment. 'Because I know everything about you. Everything. I thought you knew that?' He stretched, placing his arms behind his head, smiling at her casually. 'I met your mother. Charming lady.'

She remained fixed to the spot. Unable to speak. Unable to think coherently. Christ, him too. So it was him, not that it surprised her. What should she do? What could she do? Running was not an option.

'Oh, are you working out how to get rid of me? Tut tut, Gemma, so antisocial of you.' His face twisted in sympathy at her expression of surprise. He stretched out his long legs.

'Tell me, Gemma, have you and Oliver broken up? Such a shame. Dreadful, when people go snooping, isn't it?'

She didn't answer.

'Oh, come on then, tell me if you got a kick out of your snooping? I bet it wasn't what you expected to find?'

'No, it wasn't. What do you want, Jake?'

'Want? I want you to suffer, like I did. Oh, I'm going to drive you mad and in the end you will drive yourself mad. I must say, I've enjoyed watching you. Have you any idea how pleasurable it is to watch someone when they don't know they're being watched? Oh, by the way did you appreciate the envelope I left for you?'

'I saw that picture of Mattie.' She changed the subject.

'I know! And that surprises me. I thought you might have done something about it. You know, gone to the police. Why haven't you?'

'You know why.'

'Ah, yes, because you broke in. Criminal offence, didn't you know.'

'You broke into my house. What's the difference?' she said.

'Did I? Do you have proof?' he said.

'Oh, shut up, Jake. Just shut up,' she yelled. 'What happened to Mattie? Did you... did you... I have the photo; I can still take it to the police.'

'Kill her?'

'Did you?'

He laughed and drank his wine. 'Come and have a drink. You know you want to. How long has it been today? Eight hours? Mmm must be getting to you by now. And with Oliver gone there's no one to stop you. I've been watching you, and I would say that eight hours is the max you go without a drink.' He slammed his hand against his mouth in shock pretence. 'Oh, you're surprised I know you down to such detail.'

'Tell me what happened to Mattie.'

'No. Tell me why you haven't been to the police.'

'I want you out of my house. Get out.'

'No. Tell me. Is it because it will reveal what you've been up to?'

The house was silent around them. The drumming in her ears the only sound she could hear.

'Get out of my house or I will call the police.' How did he know so much about her? Why was he here? Had he stopped the countdown? Was this it? She wanted to tell, of course she did. It was Mattie! But… but nothing would help her now. Christ! She owed it to Mattie to do something. But she was scared. Was that selfish? What would he do to her if she did go to the police? She was behaving like the old Gemma. The scared creature afraid to do the right thing.

He mimicked her. 'Get out of my house or I will call the police. You haven't got the balls to go to the police, have you, Gemma? No, because you're too scared of everyone finding out about you, especially Oliver. Tut tut. He doesn't believe much of what you say anyway.'

She grabbed her phone off the hall table and dialled 999. 'Go or I finish the call.'

He slammed his chair backwards. It crashed into the kitchen cupboards bouncing to the side. 'Dial that number and I will kill you.'

She ran to the front door as she hit call, put it on loudspeaker and before she knew what was happening, he was there, grabbing the phone from her hand. He killed the call and wrapped his other hand around her throat pushing her back against the door.

'You stupid bitch, you think you are so fucking smart. It isn't time for you, but I need you to know you are MINE!' With his free hand he slapped her across the face. Her head swung to the side with such force it slammed against the door. 'Maybe you're so dense you need a lesson. No, you don't,' he said, as she grabbed the doorknob.

'What are you going to do? Rape me? Beat me up?'

She would have trouble remembering what happened later. Because in one fast movement he grabbed her by the shoulders and threw her up against the front door. Her head hit the wood so hard it knocked her out for about thirty seconds or so.

When she came to, her head spun and ached massively. She heard Jake yelling at her. His voice a distant sound, as if underwater. A loud ringing in her ears drowned out all other sounds. Unable to move her head or speak she was completely paralysed. Her brain, like a computer had switched off trying to reboot itself. Her limbs weak and floppy.

She lay face down on something hard. She tried aligning her thoughts to what had happened. A strange taste in her mouth caused her to cough and gag. Each movement unnatural and difficult to function. The bang to her head made her want to throw up.

She was manhandled, then picked up and draped over the granite worktop. Her head spun like a fairground ride. There was a rocking motion on top of her from behind, firm hands gripping her shoulders pinning her down. The cold hard feel of the kitchen worktop dug into her face and chest as he forced himself inside her. Pushing deep. Again. And again. And again.

Was the outlandish risk she had taken for money now going to cost her her life? It was laughable if not so tragic. To escape a terrible situation, she was now immersed in a much worse one? It was the cruellest of ironies that wasn't lost on Gemma.

'Jake, don't,' she said when she realised what was happening, but her words came out fuzzy and incoherent.

Why couldn't she speak? She began to panic that something terrible was wrong with her.

The rocking stopped and she slid to the floor, falling in a heap on the cold tiles. She managed to look over at him. He zipped up his trousers, smiling down at her. 'You're a fucking bitch and this is only the beginning. This is what you promised, it's payback.' He kicked her in the stomach. She doubled over vomiting over the kitchen tiles. He picked up her head by her hair and poured wine into her. She choked and spluttered, shaking her head from side to side to stop him. 'Drink it. Don't you need it? You fucking lush. I will destroy everything you have. Have fun telling Oliver all about this. I look forward to meeting up with him soon.' He let go of her and she doubled over cradling her stomach. Hot tears coming fast, dripping into her mouth and the floor. The small pool of salty water stung her cheek where she'd grazed it.

Gemma woke to find herself still on the floor. Dawn was streaking through the dark sky. Groggily she came to.

Woozy when she tried moving, she propped herself up against the cupboard behind her. Her head throbbed. Her body ached. If he was capable of doing that to her, there would be no limit to what he could do to her. But she knew that already. She felt numb. Maybe this was what she deserved. Maybe her mother was right after all. Maybe she was trash. But then she stopped crying, angry the way her thoughts were going. She drew in a deep breath. 'No, Gemma. She isn't right and this is wrong and you will put it right. You will,' she said aloud to herself.

An envelope lay by her side. It was empty. On the front, written in bold marker it said, **You're not worth it.** She tore it up and headed upstairs to her bed.

Chapter Forty-Six

She slept the whole of the day and into the next day. When she awoke, she saw the bruising on her arms and legs beginning to bloom, soon she would be covered with purple and mauve welts. A new text message from Jake showed on her phone.

2.

She rose unsteadily from her bed; it hurt to breathe and she wondered if there was something broken. Sitting was awkward, her back hurt to sit up straight, she had to slouch. When she stood up and looked in the mirror, she saw her swollen cheek was beginning to bruise. She pulled a brush through her hair wincing. Was it something in her that caused men to rape and beat her? Maybe, subconsciously, she gave out something like a scent that dragged them into her pool of life. Maybe her ballsy attitude provoked them and they couldn't help it. Maybe she drove them to hit and rape her. She reprimanded herself for thinking that way.

She had to think of an explanation for Oliver. She'd fallen down the stairs. No, that wouldn't explain her badly bruised stomach. She'd fallen up the stairs after having too much to drink. Still wouldn't explain her stomach.

A random memory came to her from about three years ago, it was winter and they were having a cosy time in the local coffee shop. It had snowed, thick and crunchy underfoot. They'd wrapped up and walked from home to the coffee shop in the village, with all the lovely old penny-farthing bicycles hung on the walls and the real log fire, enjoying the brisk walk and laughing at their breath steaming from their mouths as they spoke. There hadn't been snow like that for many years. It was magical and romantic and ever so cosy sitting by the fire.

The fire crackled and spat as they hunched up close, watching the sparks and dreaming of emigrating somewhere where the seasons were all complete, like New England. They planned and planned, and planned how they might achieve their dream and spoke about the sort of house they'd have. A real fire. A wrap-around porch to sit out on in the hot summer months. A screen door to stop the mossies getting in in the summer. And snow. Lots of snow in the winter.

The sound of wheels on the gravel and footsteps put a stop to that. She looked out of the window to see Oliver pulling into the drive. Grabbing her dressing gown, she pulled it tight around herself.

She took a deep breath to stop her hands from shaking. Her mind in a whirlwind as she pulled nervously at her hair trying to get the hair clip to fasten. She let some of it fall across her swollen cheek. Biting her lip and taking one last look in the mirror she dabbed a little blusher to hide her paleness and foundation to dull the bruising.

She sat on the end of the bed facing the door, waiting. Twirling some loose hair around her fingers to soothe herself. All the time thinking feverishly that Jake could have killed her last night. This was all a hideous game to him.

Everything had changed.

She now had a plan.

She wasn't proud she was going to lie to Oliver yet again. But better to lie to him than tell him the truth and have him going after Jake.

She knew Oliver would want some kind of reassurance from her, which she wouldn't be able to give. Not right now. Not until Jake was out of her life for good.

Oliver's step was fast and fluid up the stairs. She knew he was looking for her, thinking that perhaps she had left.

When he walked into the bedroom he stopped abruptly as though an invisible rubber band had pulled him backwards.

Ambushed by the sight of her and taken aback for a few seconds before he flew at her and held her tight.

Her voice came out broken, more so than she intended, 'Sorry, Oliver, I'm sorry, for what I said to you. I didn't mean to hurt you, really I didn't.'

'It's OK, darling, I'm not cross with you, but what's happened?' He pulled back to look her over and gently touched her swollen cheek.

His endearment and gentle touch caused her to weep all the more. She didn't meet his eye.

'I had too much to drink; I'm sorry. I know I keep promising. But with you leaving last night, well, I couldn't stand the thought of you alone somewhere. I tripped on my dressing gown coming down the stairs; I was carrying the tin box containing all our photos and fell on it.' She showed him her bruised stomach.

Oliver winced then looked back at her face, stroking her cheek again. His intense blue eyes full of pain and worry and love for her made her hate herself even more. She had to look away.

She imagined Oliver was silently thinking his actions last night had caused her to drink, which led to her falling down the stairs. She ought to tell him it wasn't his fault. That she should have had more self-restraint. But the paradox was she hadn't drunk anything and had to pretend she had loaded up.

Horrible thoughts from last night flashed through her mind like strobe lighting. When she moved on the bed, it hurt.

Like on so many occasions making up was the best part of falling out for them. But today she could not let that happen.

Freeing herself, she glanced at the standing mirror in the corner of the room.

'I do look a fright, don't I?'

'You do. Maybe we need to go to A&E and get you checked out. I'm worried about your stomach. It's badly bruised. You must have taken a real tumble.'

'I did, but I don't want to go to A&E. I think it looks worse than it is.'

'I'm so sorry, Gem.' He ran his hand over his face. 'Look, I feel guilty about all this. In the hotel, alone in bed, I missed you not being next to me. But I had time to think things through.' He looked closely at her. His face had a pinched expression she recognised. 'You're such a wonderful person and I don't want to lose you.' He exhaled. 'I think I must be more stressed than I thought. And not coping as well as I thought either, taking it out on you and… well, just getting ludicrously paranoid day by day.'

Oh God, she didn't know what to say, seeing Oliver like this, losing his strength made her weak. He had to be strong so she could feed off his strength. If he wilted, she wouldn't be able to go on. He was her rock. Oliver never showed weakness. He was blaming himself when none of this mess was his. And she had to let him continue to do so. For now.

Later that afternoon, while she lay wrapped up on the sofa having endless cups of tea, a knock on the front door rattled through her bones like a train. Mid sip, she stalled, her ears pricked up and fear consumed her. She knew that knock. Three knocks followed by a smaller one.

'Gemma, your boss has come to see if you're OK. Didn't you call him to say you wouldn't be available today?' Oliver said as he walked in with Jake.

Her voice was croaky and scared. 'No.' She lay still unable to look at them.

'Well, I've explained what happened, and he's happy to leave you for a few days, isn't that right, Mr Challinor?'

'Heavens! Gemma! That must have been a hell of a tumble you took? You look as if you've had a hell of a beating, never mind a fall down the stairs.' Jake sounded really concerned and put on a great display of being appalled by the bruise on her cheek.

'I told her we should go to A&E but she won't have any of it. Stubborn, very stubborn is Gemma. Can I get you a coffee or a tea?'

He shook his head. 'Please don't worry about getting back to work too soon, get yourself better and then we can catch up where we left off. I thought something was wrong when you weren't answering your emails. I hope you don't mind me popping over. You living out here always worried me.'

'Would you like to sit down?' Oliver signalled to the armchair opposite Gemma. 'I didn't realise Gemma had told you where we lived?'

'No, I won't stay, but it's very kind of you to offer. Yes, I was curious. I live in Knutsford too. I've heard a lot about you, Oliver. Gemma often drops little snippets of conversation when we Skype.'

'Yes, it's probably best if you leave right now,' she said.

'Gemma! Sorry, she's feeling pretty rotten, I'll see you out.'

'Not to worry, I understand she doesn't want to see me. When you've been through something like that you just want to stay home and recover. Wait a minute, were you at the Riverside Hotel the other day? I think I spoke to you. I had my car vandalised and asked you to look at the CCTV,' he said to Oliver.

'Now you mention it, yes, I do recognise you,' Oliver said and shot her a look. 'Did you find out who did it?' Oliver walked to the door to show him out.

'No, sadly not. I was very angry.' He laughed. 'You know what men are like with their cars. I love mine. I guess I have to hope the culprit will get what they deserve.'

Oliver nodded and dropped his head. 'So, you have the Overfinch, don't you? Lovely, I'd love one of those.'

'Take it out for a spin, why don't you.'

Oliver held up his hands. 'Oh God, no, I couldn't. But it's kind of you to offer.'

'Perhaps another time.' Jake stuck out his hand. 'A pleasure to meet you, Oliver.'

Chapter Forty-Seven

From somewhere deep came a sound – a hideous noise as if something was dying in great pain. Gemma curled up on the sofa, hiding behind the cushion, how had he managed so effortlessly to destroy her? Every part of her hurt but her chest more than anything. The pain was as if her heart had been wrenched out with a blunt instrument. Can you really die from a broken heart?

She closed her eyes and pummelled the cushion against her head trying to bang some sense into her. 'No, no, no, no,' she said in time to the pummelling.

Oliver lifted the cushion off her. She looked at him and the pain in her chest twisted. She pushed back into the sofa. Oh, if there was a hole for her to fall into. Even if it was into hell. She would gladly drop through. Anything was preferable than seeing the look on Oliver's face a moment longer.

As soon as the front door closed Oliver knew. He rested his forehead on the door and all his strength poured out of him through his feet and pooled on the floor. He heard muffled sounds coming from the lounge.

He should feel relieved he knew, finally, what was going on with her. He'd suspected, but couldn't quite believe it of Gemma. They had a great thing going. He believed the whole shebang she told him. He'd tolerated her weak explanations for everything that had been happening lately. Now the pieces were dropping into place. He'd sensed it between them the moment Jake walked into the lounge. She was having an affair. With her boss. With her rich boss. He had nothing to offer her but debt and struggle. He would never have believed it if someone had told him that Gemma would sell him out for money. God, what a fool he'd been.

He must have wanted to break up with her and that was why she wrecked his car. It all made sense now. Her behaviour all made sense.

For a few moments he stayed by the front door correlating his thoughts. Then he went into the lounge and pulled the cushion off her face.

Was he sorry? No. She looked worse than he expected and the other amazing thing was Oliver opening the door to him. But, oh, what a shockingly brilliant twist of fate.

Back home, Jake stepped into his office locked the door and made his way to his safe, whistling a happy tune he'd just heard on the radio. Hidden behind a row of books, he began the combination. Two to the right, eight to the left. Click, click, click.

Where the fuck is everything? He knew it was all there a couple of days ago because he checked. He started yelling and throwing books around the room.

'Katy! Katy!' he yelled, pulling books off the shelves and drawers out, sifting through papers.

'What is it?' She came running to the door and pounded on it for him to open up. 'Jake, are you OK? Open the door.'

He turned the key and stood in the middle of the room amongst all the mess.

'What the hell is wrong? Have you lost your mind?' Katy said.

'Shut the fuck up and tell me if you've been in the safe.'

'Me! No! Why would I go in your safe? I don't even know the combination.'

'Are you sure?' he demanded.

'Yes, I would know if I had, Jake. What's gone? What's happened?'

Chapter Forty-Eight

GEMMA

Gemma was meeting Sean in Yorkshire tonight. He had a job up there and thought it best they meet as far away from Cheshire as they could. Urgent, he said on the call.

She made excuses, informing him things were bad at home and she couldn't make it. That Jake had turned up at the house and now Oliver thought she was having an affair with him. Crying, she told him Oliver had left her and she hated everyone and she didn't know what to do. Jake had won. He'd destroyed her just like he said he would. Sean told her she was to drive up and meet him this evening without fail. And to tell no one. Not even Oliver.

The text from Jake had come in bright and early that morning.

1.

7 p.m. that evening she set off. It was a dreadful night to drive across to Yorkshire. The rain lashed down as though it was the end of the world. Her wipers couldn't keep up. A light mist came down over the moors making visibility terrible on the motorway.

After an hour the rush hour traffic began easing. As she climbed up over the moors, her petrol warning light came on. In her haste to get out of the house, she forgot to fill up. She punched into her satnav a search for petrol stations. She was going to be late. To make it worse there was no phone signal. She had a nasty headache and reflux. Reaching into her handbag on the passenger seat, she popped a Gaviscon into her mouth.

Jake had played on her mind all day. Her emotions ran

from rage to out of control psychotic thoughts. She couldn't let him get away with what he did to her. The thought that Oliver believed she was having an affair was enough to drive her over the edge. He'd turned his phone off. She'd left him a mountain of voicemails and text messages begging him to call her to let her explain he had it all wrong. But all she got back was silence. She didn't even know where he was. She rang around all the hotels and B&Bs in the area, but nobody was able to help her. Oliver had vanished.

She would have to leave it to fate to show her the way. One thing was for certain, Jake was going to pay for this.

Pulling off the motorway following directions for fuel, a finger post pointed for petrol off to the left. The mist grew thicker making it difficult to make out the road. Her satnav showed no signs of a petrol station. Maybe it was an old sign that hadn't been taken down, directing her to an abandoned petrol station or it might be a real sign pointing to petrol via a shortcut?

She took it. Realising as she pulled into the abandoned so-called petrol station that she'd made a bad decision. The other thing was her desperate need for a wee.

The satnav told her she still had one hour to her destination. Her onboard computer told her she had under ten miles of petrol left. The next real petrol station was roughly seven miles according to the satnav. Well, one thing was for sure, she would need the toilet before she went any further.

Taking her phone with her, she put on her full beam and stepped out of the car. She turned on the flash light app to see where she was walking to relieve herself.

The darkness was thick and impenetrable. She hadn't seen fog like this for years; it seemed to settle where she was. Stepping gingerly, one foot in front of the other, she moved forward, slowly, then realised it made no difference where she peed.

Finally, arriving at the real petrol station some fifteen minutes later she filled up, bought some chocolate and at last found she had a phone signal. She called Sean to explain she was running late, then set off. Before she left, she asked the attendant about the old petrol station.

'Ooh, you're lucky you're alright,' he began in a thick Yorkshire accent. 'That there hasn't been used for a long while. It's a fly tip more than anything. Dangerous too. A couple of teenagers fell down the slope a few years back, lucky to get out alive. We've been asking for it to be barricaded off but nothing comes of it.' His words echoed through her head all the way to the hotel.

Sean was waiting for her in the lobby as she came through the swing doors.

'What happened to you? I thought I was going to have to send out a search party.'

She told him about the abandoned petrol station and what Jake had done, and how Oliver had walked out on her. All she wanted was for Jake to pay for what he'd done to her. She filled Sean in on why Jake had targeted her in the first place and how he blamed her for losing his position in the family business. She told him what she'd read in the papers about his brother's accident, and that she believed Jake had been involved. She also told him that he confessed to killing Mattie although they already knew that from the photographs they found. Lastly, she told him about the rape. Letting it all out was a relief.

Sean was silent throughout her monologue; she saw a nerve twitch in his jaw. 'Oh my God, what a nightmare for you. I can't believe you've had to put up with this on your own and, to top it all, Oliver thinks you're having an affair with him. Does he know about the rape?'

She shook her head.

'I thought Jake Challinor was nasty from the bit of

investigating I did on him, but I have to ask… has he done this to you before?' His eyes roamed her face, taking in her bruises.

She shook her head. 'He's been abusive but not rape.'

Sean blew out his breath through clenched teeth. His face taut, his lips pulled in a grim line pressed together as though holding back his words.

'I bet you're ravenous,' he said, walking her over to the restaurant. 'I've told them we're going straight in to eat, is that OK with you? I reckoned you'd be starving and, frankly, I think you need to eat something before I tell you what I've discovered.'

'No, I can't eat. I haven't had any appetite since that night. Tell me, don't soften it up just tell me now, I really don't want to eat anything,' she said.

He lowered his voice as they entered the restaurant. 'I need you to be calm and fed. I won't tell you unless you eat. You look awful, Gemma. I can't believe he did this to you. It makes my next job all the easier.'

Now she thought about it; she was ravenous, still, she didn't think she'd be able to stomach much. What was all the cloak-and-dagger stuff about anyway? Surely there weren't more dark secrets in Jake's past.

There was only one other table in the restaurant, the hour was late. The waiter sat them at the opposite end of the room. They ordered and their food arrived promptly.

'Right, fire away. Tell me,' she said, halfway through her main course.

'Eat, just relax, Gemma, the wait will be more than worth it.'

She smiled at him quizzically. He was an odd one. She hadn't thought there was anything more he could do for her. After she paid him for his help in breaking into Jake's, she thought that had been it. But he seemed worried for her and dropped the occasional text asking if everything was OK and did she need him for anything else. As she endeavoured to get through the food on her plate, she tried focusing on what he was saying.

'Sean, sorry, my head is buzzing and I'm all over the place. Can you tell me now?'

Sean nodded. 'OK.'

She folded her napkin and dropped it on the table, sat up straight and said, 'Just tell me why you've made me drive all the way over here.'

Sean put a buff coloured folder in front of her. 'Open it.'

She looked at him then the folder.

'Open it,' he said again.

'What is it?'

'You'll see.'

She slowly opened the file. It was full of papers, some with date stamps, some official looking. She picked one up and all the colour drained from her face. Little black spots danced in front of her eyes. Heat blazed up her torso like a freshly lit petrol doused bonfire. The room spun and the next thing she knew she was lying on a sofa with Sean fanning her with the menu.

'Gemma, are you OK? How do you feel? I'm sorry, I thought the information would shock you, but I never thought it would knock you out.'

'Is it true?'

Sean nodded. 'Yes, yes, it is.'

'How did you come by it?'

'Something niggled in my mind the last time I was at his house. I couldn't shift the thought there was more to be found. So I went back there yesterday.'

'I feel sick.' The thought that Jake had played her so well and orchestrated the whole thing left her stunned. It had all been a game, from beginning to end. 'That means he planned everything.'

'Everything. The man is deranged and out for vengeance.'

'Do you think he would—'

'Yes, I do. I believe he killed Mattie. With the evidence you have there you can go to the police.'

'Can I? But… won't they ask how I got all this?'

'They will, you don't need to elaborate. They will be more than happy to have proof he killed Mattie. The rest will be the icing on the cake.'

No, she had to be careful. She'd seen this type of thing in the movies. 'I can't, Sean. His lawyers can get it thrown out. I broke in. You broke in. The best I can do is get him to invite me to his house then I can say I took them. No, I'm not doing that either. I don't want to be near him again.' She sat up abruptly. 'Oliver!'

'What about him?'

'Christ, he'll do something to Oliver. I know it. I must get home. Oh my God, Sean, once he knows this is missing and I'm not around, he'll go for Oliver.'

'I'll come with you.'

'No,' she said and suddenly she knew exactly what she was going to do. 'I need a drink. No, no I don't, I need to get home.'

Chapter Forty-Nine

Arriving home in the middle of the night, she went straight to the study and pulled out one of Oliver's paper maps of Yorkshire. She had laughed at him for keeping them when they had satnavs, thankfully he hadn't listened to her. Lying on the bed she studied it until she had the route imprinted in her mind. She recited it to herself over and over. She didn't know where Oliver had gone yesterday, and he still wasn't answering the phone. For now, she wanted him away from her in case Jake was watching. She hoped Jake wouldn't know where he was either. She fell asleep exhausted and still clutching the map.

The expected text arrived.

0. D-Day.

The M60 was clear for a change. Gemma checked over the map again to make sure she knew exactly where she was going before leaving.

She put the papers from Sean in a safe place. Peter The Bastard was Jake's cousin and together they had embezzled from at least twenty companies. He was no more an accountant than she was. She wanted to scream. Jake had planned this for a long time. What mugs they had been. She wanted desperately to tell Oliver, but the time wasn't right.

Sean told her he would search again for the passwords to their bank accounts. In his line of business, he knew people with the know-how. Sean had contact with hackers who worked on the Dark Web advertising their skills. If anyone could hack the passwords she had no doubt they could. 'What you need to do is steal the money back, and I can help you with that. That will hurt them more than anything else,' he'd said to her. She agreed, but she personally wanted to hurt Jake. She didn't say that to Sean, though.

Pulling off the motorway, she followed the route she took last night, taking the same turning that took her off the main road. When she came to the finger post, she followed the road arriving at the deserted petrol station.

She parked up close to the steep embankment. Climbing out of her car she saw last night's tire marks. She wore flat brown knee-length boots, jeans and a soft dun leather jacket. Looking down the embankment, it was full of used car parts and tractor tyres. A burnt-out car, shopping trolleys and twisted, dangerous looking pieces of metal. Black bin liners and clothes littered the area. She spotted a washing machine amongst the detritus. A man-made landfill from all accounts.

If somebody was to fall deep into the mire of the landfill, the steepness of the ridge would make escape pretty much impossible. Especially if injured. Remembering that the old man at the filling station had told her that nobody came here made this just perfect.

Travelling back home the motorway was free flowing. Her mind tormented her by the different possibilities it threw up of how this might end or go terribly wrong.

She turned the music up as loud as she could stand without blowing her eardrums. It helped drown out the thoughts.

She pulled into her driveway slamming on the brakes.

Parked up in her drive stood a black Overfinch Range Rover.

The booming sound of The Rolling Stones blasted through her Bluetooth on her car stereo. Their lyrics and moment of delivery couldn't be better timed. 'The Doom and Gloom' lyrics resonated an uncanny synchronicity with her life right now.

As she sat listening to Mick, only one thought pierced her mind.

She knew she had to kill Jake.

Chapter Fifty

She checked the Range Rover. Empty. Then she saw a light coming from the lounge.

Irate he had let himself in, again, she opened the front door, gingerly, expecting him to be behind the door with a baseball bat or something similar.

Walking into the house, she caught sight of herself in the hall mirror. Staring back was a woman, the colour faded from her face, her eyes, lifeless. Dread set her face like rigor mortis. Her natural instinct was to run away. But he would find her. She wanted to face him now that she had this new information on him. Even though she felt sick to her stomach, she wasn't going to let him get away with what he'd done to her.

He must know she had the papers and that was why he was here. Was that it? She badly wanted to reverse her steps, but an invisible rope pulled her along. She had to be the strong Gemma and do this.

For some stupid reason she wanted to see his face when he asked her about the papers. He wouldn't hurt her, not yet, not until he knew who she'd shown them too and where they were.

She was frightened of being alone with him after the last time. If only Oliver was here. She had to stop thinking like that. Oliver wasn't here and it was a good thing. He needed to be far away out of Jake's reach.

She approached the lounge where she heard his voice talking and stopped to listen through the closed door. He must be on his phone.

Reluctantly stepping inside, she paused in the doorway. Jake and Oliver turned to look at her. Her face flooded

279

with heat, instantly. Her first reaction was to run to Oliver. Instead she stood rooted to the floor, she only had eyes for Oliver.

'Oliver!' she said, helplessly, unable to believe he was home. He must have come here in a taxi. But why? And why was he talking with Jake? What had Jake told him? She tentatively smiled making her way towards him, unsure how to be with him.

Had Jake told him anything? Fabricated everything, telling Oliver she was having an affair with him? She wouldn't put it past him, the bastard. It was what he'd threatened to do after all. But she was no longer the passive fool. She'd made a decision and she was taking control.

She had no choice.

None whatsoever.

'I just came back to collect some things. I'm not staying,' Oliver told her, 'I happened to be here when Jake arrived.' His voice was cold, despondent. He wouldn't meet her eyes. His tone hardened when he said Jake's name. She had never seen Oliver like this, his face was unreadable.

Jake relaxed in the cream armchair in the corner of the room, its timber legs slightly off the floor as he rocked back and forth. He'd made himself at home, loving the tension between them.

She wondered if he did know the papers were missing. She couldn't tell. And didn't want to look at him more than necessary. He made her flesh crawl.

Jake watched her like she was his prey, waiting, never taking his eyes off her.

'What's going on? Why are you here, Jake?'

Jake tilted his head to the side. 'Oliver, we should tell Gemma what we chatted about. I think she should know, don't you?'

'Jake has told me the whole thing,' Oliver said. He

breathed in deep and let it out slowly. 'I seem to have misunderstood. Everything.' He still didn't meet her eyes.

Gemma looked confused. She stared at him hard, willing him to look at her as if by sheer force she could somehow mentally communicate with him.

Jake smiled, rocking back and forth.

'Oh,' was all she managed, waiting for the punchline. Jake didn't do nice.

'He says they've caught the vandal that trashed his car. Apparently.' The last word dripping with sarcasm. Oliver turned to face her now as if trying to read her thoughts. 'The man was wearing a mask and false hair. One of those Halloween type masks, easily mistaken for your hair, I guess.' There was no warmth in his eyes when he spoke. She said nothing. 'A friend of Jake's overheard a conversation in the pub and reported it to the police.' She could tell he didn't believe what he was saying.

'I see,' she said. That was convenient. Gemma shot Jake a questioning look. He shrugged standing up. What was he up to? The dread in the pit of her stomach slowly built like a train approaching from a distance.

'So, that's basically it, Gemma. It's all cleared up, right?' Jake said looking at Oliver who nodded like a man who'd clearly heard enough bullshit. 'Look, I'm thinking to make amends for the terrible mix up and the awful problems it's caused you both, why don't we go out for a drink. I'm still Gemma's boss after all and I bear no grudges.' He looked directly at Oliver waiting for a reply. 'Come on, let's put it down to a terrible misunderstanding. What do you say, Oliver?' He pulled the keys from his pocket. 'Oliver, mate, come on, let's go. Forget about it. We'll have a pint and put it all behind us.' He smiled the smile of snake at Gemma. 'She's a lovely looking woman, your wife. I'd be protective of her too. All's well that ends well, don't you think?

Gemma, you come too. You drive, Oliver; I've already had a drink, don't want to push my luck.' He laughed. 'Besides, you took a fancy to my car the last time you saw it.' He threw the car keys to him. Oliver caught them and lay them on the table next to him.

Her anger surfaced, but she kept a lid on it. How dare he patronise them.

'You know as soon as I heard from the police about the arrest of this man, I couldn't wait to tell you, Gemma,' Jake said. 'That's why I came over here and to see how you were doing too. I knew you'd want to know, but your phone was turned off so there was no option but to come over, but you weren't here. That's how we got talking and... well... Oliver told me what had happened between you. It upset me so much that he'd imagined we were having an affair. Crazy, isn't it, how people can interpret the wrong thing from just a few simple mistakes.'

Gemma fixed her eyes on him.

'Why do you look so worried, Gemma? I'm sure you were off doing important stuff, am I right?' He didn't wait for her to respond. 'Do you know, I think we may have a friend in common. He was talking about you the other day, but his name escapes me.' His eyes were piercing when he said the words.

'I doubt we move in the same circles as you,' she said.

'Mmm, I guess. Well come on, Oliver, let's go for that drink. Maybe you'll love the car and put it on your bucket list. It's a good idea to have one; you never know when your time will be up and you'll regret all the things you wanted to do.' Jake shot her a cold look.

She knew he was pleased to be getting under her skin.

'What are we waiting for? Oliver, you look too stressed. You mustn't let things get you down. Cheer up. Whatever's been bothering Gemma you can sleep tight it's not an affair.'

'You're right,' Oliver said.

'What!' Gemma shook her head.

'Maybe we should go, Gemma. I think we could do with getting out. Before you say anything,' he held up his hand, 'I know what you said the other night, but we really need to talk about it. Come on, let's have a drink with Jake, then we can have a meal and talk things through after he's gone. We'll have one drink, Jake, you can leave us at the pub and we'll get a taxi back.'

She'd had enough of Jake's manipulating. He knew there was nothing she could do right now. He'd put her in a tight spot with Oliver, again. And she had no idea what Oliver was playing at.

What was his game now? To abduct them both? Then she had an idea. She'd show him, coming to her house, charming Oliver into believing he was a good guy. Lying, thieving bastard. If Oliver knew he was behind their problems he'd kill him. Now was not the time to tell him. Oliver would get hurt, she didn't think for a second Jake wouldn't kill him first.

'Let's go,' she said, infuriated, grabbing Jake's keys and striding out of the room.

'Gemma…' Oliver called out, but she was already racing through the front door to the car.

She jumped into the driver's seat full of frustration. Altered the seat and the height of the steering wheel to her preference. Oliver and Jake joined her. Jake's stare from the back seat burnt a hole in the back of her head. She wanted to punch the smug bastard. She got a sense of foreboding as she got into the car. She told herself he would be really stupid to try anything with both of them in the car. That wasn't his style. That meant nothing. He was mad with her. He could turn. But everything else he'd done was calculating, he liked control and right now he didn't have that.

She slammed the car into reverse. Her heart thumped. She did a fast, tight, three-point turn in the driveway sending gravel and dirt flying.

Before she pulled out onto the main road she turned around. Looking him in the eye, she said, 'In the immortal words of Bette Davies, "Buckle up, Jake, this is going to be a bumpy ride."' She had no intention of going for a bloody drink with him. She was going to race his damned car to an inch of its life.

'Gemma, are you OK?' Oliver asked. 'You seem a little hyper?'

She gave him a cheesy grin. 'I'm good.'

Gemma slipped off the main road down a familiar country lane, she drove the Range Rover, fast. Taking the corners, tight. Racing into them at speed before breaking, then putting her foot down as she came out of the bend. She heard a sharp intake of breath from the back and smiled. *Fuckwit.* She then came out of the lane onto the main road and pulled into a lay-by, heavy on the brakes.

'Mind if I put some music on? I *love* driving to music.' She felt a little crazy. A little out of control. But she wanted to scare him because she was scared. She wanted to show him she had something about her and that he should be worried about what she was capable of. She Bluetoothed her phone with the Range Rover and hit her music icon on her iPhone. Found her favourite track, 'Doom and Gloom' by The Stones, and pressed play.

The guitar solo came first, quickly followed by the drums, loud and pacey. She turned up the sound. Mick screamed through the speakers. She pulled out, fast, took the turning for the motorway and floored the car. Awesome. She caught Jake looking at her in the rear-view mirror; she joined in with Mick on the lyrics. In control and with so much revenge piled up inside her ready to burst, she took both Oliver and

Jake on a nightmare journey. Sliding between the lanes. Cutting in dangerously. She didn't care how reckless she was. She almost wanted something to happen. But her desire to live prevented that. She only wanted to shake him up.

Back at the house, Gemma climbed out of the driver's seat. She opened the rear door and threw the keys at Jake smiling as she walked back towards the house. As an afterthought, she turned her head and said, 'Thanks. That was so much better than I thought it would be.'

Safe behind their front door, Oliver finally spoke. He hadn't said a word in the car. 'Bloody hell, Gemma, what the hell was that all about? Were you trying to put us both into an early grave?' he yelled. Totally perplexed by her behaviour.

'Nope, I just had a rush to see what that car could do. A mad moment, you might say.'

'This whole situation is mad. When he turned up today, I was convinced he was going to tell me you'd left me and had gone to live with him. When you weren't here, it made sense.' He slumped against the wall. 'I accused him, and he laughed at me, denying it. Then he told me about the car vandalism and told me I had it all wrong. You see, I thought you'd done it because you'd fallen out. Lover's tiff – that kind of thing. I felt so relieved when he told me you weren't having an affair. But he's lying, isn't he, because you did trash his car. So why would he lie?' Oliver's contained fury was like a force field around them.

'If you thought that why agree to go out for a drink with him?'

'I wanted to see what you were both like together. Read your body language.'

'So you still think something is going on?'

'Something is not right between you two, that much I do know. What else can I think, Gem? That you've both robbed a bank or are going to rob a bank? It's the only thing I can think is going on.'

'I do need to tell you something, and you won't like it, but maybe you'll understand once you hear me out.'

'So how does Jake know we're looking for Peter?'

'I told him,' she said. 'What did he say to you about him?'

'I didn't understand what he said, to be honest. He mentioned that you had asked him to find Peter. Had you? And that he might know where he was, but it would be tricky getting him back because he'd covered his tracks and there probably wouldn't be a link between the money going missing and him.'

Oliver was aggravatingly silent after that, folding his arms across his chest, waiting for her to reply.

She told him everything.

She had to.

That was the moment right there and then.

'I don't believe it! You lied all this time to me? How could you! Gemma!' His hands flew in the air, then he grabbed his hair and shook his head. 'I don't believe this about Peter! It must be a coincidence. He can't have planned this. It's mental, have you heard what you're saying? Shit. Are you telling me the truth? How can I believe he paid you for companionship? No sex? No sex at all?' His voice resonated off the walls.

Squinting at him she asked, 'What were you hoping I would say?'

She didn't shout back. What was the point? He wasn't taking it well. But seriously, how had she thought he would take it? Offer her a cup of tea and a sit down and say *clever girl, Gemma*. She omitted the rape; he didn't need that information.

'I'm shocked. Hurt. You lied to me. All this time, you lied. Just like you lied about your mother.'

'Look, Oliver, I'm not working for Jake any more. I think he's… unhinged, but I have found out—'

'Unhinged? You think? And what about you? Gem, I thought I knew you. I thought I knew what went on inside your head, but you're a mess.' He drew in his breath, still pulling on his hair he turned to face the wall and banged his head against it. Thud. Thud. Thud. Thud. Then the worst happened. He started to cry. 'I don't believe you. I think you slept with him. Nobody would pay you ten grand a time to be a *fucking companion*. How stupid do you think I am!'

He went quiet. She didn't dare speak for fear of saying something else to hurt him. Then he bellowed again. He really bellowed. 'You are so fucked up. I can't bear being near you.' And with those final words he left, pushing past her, grabbing his coat and slamming the front door making the entire frame shake.

Chapter Fifty-One

JAKE

He'd won. He knew Oliver hadn't believed him, what man would? And he knew she would tell him everything. He pulled the earphones from his ears and laughed, but it was a hollow win because for him she still hadn't paid enough. Had she actually thought that car exhibition was going to scare him? Fool. She had a long way to go before she scared him.

He watched Oliver slam the front door and leave the house. It wasn't enough for him. She had to disappear. Then Karen. The three of them had to pay the ultimate price for the years of misery he'd had to endure.

He parked down the lane and got out of his car and moved closer to the house. Dusk was falling, and the trees hid his movements.

He brought the binoculars up smoothly to his eyes and waited. He felt disappointed when she drew the curtains. Perhaps she suspected he was watching her. His muscles flexed. He allowed his mind to drift to what he was going to do to her and how slowly he was going to do it. He touched the single bladed knife in his pocket and thought of the wounds it would inflict on her beautiful body.

After all these years was it possible that tonight he was going to get full satisfaction?

A car pulled up in the drive. He watched Karen get out and ring the doorbell several times. She pulled her phone from her pocket and called. She must have heard Gemma's mobile ringing inside because she suddenly looked up at the house. She peered in at the windows, but the curtains were drawn so she looked through the letterbox. She rang the doorbell a couple more times.

It would have been easy to grab her. No. All in good time. The victims each had a place in his timeline. And Karen had such lovely children to play with.

He watched them arguing on the doorstep. Karen yelled and poor Gemma tried to comfort her. Annoyed he was unable to hear their conversation, by their actions, he suspected Karen was probably going to the police. He had to move fast now.

The adrenaline sang through his veins giving him a rush. He fought down the excitement by smashing his fist into the tree. The pain gave him an outlet.

Once again composed, he stroked the blade of the knife in his pocket with his thumb. He left. At home he would finalise his plan for her demise.

Chapter Fifty-Two

GEMMA

Gemma heard the doorbell. She looked out of the window and backed up when she saw Karen. She wasn't ready to speak with her and, besides, it wasn't safe for her to be here. She ignored the phone calls too and didn't bother reading the text.

Then she thought she owed it to Karen. Opening the door, she came outside.

'Can't I come in?'

'Better if we talk out here, I think he's bugged my house.'

Karen looked dreadful. Hearing her house might be bugged freaked her out even more. 'I've come to tell you I'm not waiting. I'm going to the police. I'm so frightened, Gem. I can't bloody sleep. Gavin's taken me to the doctors, he thinks I'm having a nervous breakdown. Which I bloody am.' She stared crying.

'Karen, please don't go yet.'

'No, Gem, I have my kids to think of. The man is deranged. You don't have kids. I can't wait and then find it's too late. I'm driving them mad taking them everywhere. Picking them up. Questioning everyone they speak with in case they're connected to Jake. I'm going. I just wanted to warn you,' she sobbed.

'No. Karen, please. Look, give me twenty-four hours. Please, Karen. Honestly, I have a plan. If I haven't sorted it in that time, go then.'

'No, Gem. You're asking too much.'

Gemma grabbed her arm and brought her in close so

only she heard what she said, 'Karen, please, I have a plan. I'm doing it tonight. I have help. Please.'

'Shit, you're as insane as he is.' She shook herself loose. 'I'm going to the police. He's going to kill you too if you're not careful.'

She left without saying another word. Ignoring her calls to wait a little longer.

She had five text messages and a myriad of missed calls from Jake when she got back inside. She opened and read each one.

Call me.

Call me, now.

You better call me asap.

What the fuck are you playing at? Call me now.

????????

She didn't call. She lay on the bed and waited for another twenty minutes before she replied.

With her heart beating a thousand times a minute, she texted back.

We need to talk.

Bloody right we do. Meet me in Sainsbury's car park in Northwich at 1 a.m. tonight.

She had to get him to follow her tonight. She had to provoke him enough for him to want to get his hands on her. She fought the reflux as it rose in her throat. It was getting worse; she was living off the damned tablets now. He would be so angry tonight, she feared for her safety. She had to get him out of her life. He had no shame. No remorse. He would never, *ever* stop.

She stared at the wall in front of her, replaying her plan over and over. It seemed perfect. She knew what to do. How to push his buttons.

The drive from Sainsbury's to where she wanted to lure him was too far. She needed to find a meet closer to where she needed him. She clicked Safari and googled the nearest Sainsbury's within ten miles.

I won't be here tonight. Can't meet there. Meet me at this Sainsbury's at 2.00 a.m.

She sent him the postcode. He'd take the bait, because he needed to. And she knew he would.

Gemma arrived half an hour early. A torrential storm had started as a miserable drizzle when she left home. She circled the deserted car park, turning her car around, so it faced the exit. Her stomach churned. Her wipers battled with the rain.

She plugged in the postcode of her next destination. Her Mercedes SLK purred as it idled. It locked automatically once you went over five miles an hour. She felt safe locked in her steel cage.

The empty lit up car park looked eerie. At the far end, behind her, what looked like an abandoned car stood close to the store. She looked at it a couple of times considering whether to check it out in case anyone was asleep inside. Looking at her watch, she had twenty minutes. Probably not.

She sat and waited looking in the rear-view mirror every few seconds. Her head bobbing up and down as though bobbing for apples. That car really bothered her. There was something about it she couldn't put her finger on. From where she was parked, it was impossible to make out the model.

'Goddamn,' she hissed, turning the car around to cruise by and take a better look. She drove, feeling anxious, putting on her full beam, cruising past, craning her neck to see if anyone was inside the Audi. Something told her to get out and check it properly. She didn't. The torrential rain hammered on the roof of her car and her wipers were on full speed, she didn't fancy getting soaked.

Parking back in her original spot, she checked her watch.

That had taken her about two minutes. It bothered her the abandoned car should be an Audi. Something gnawed at her brain why that car troubled her.

She could do with a vodka and lime right now to steady her nerves they were stretched so thin you could play a tune on them. Her heart raced, raising her temperature. She turned the heating down and opened her window ajar. She finished her coffee, opened the door and tossed out the empty cup. Closed the door. Unbuckling, she leaned into the footwell to get her iPhone from her handbag. No messages from Oliver or Jake. Maybe he wouldn't turn up.

Glancing once again in her rear-view mirror. She froze.

Did she just see something moving inside that car?

She let out a breath a few seconds later when nothing more happened. God, she was losing it. But now she couldn't take her eyes off the car. There was definitely something about that car that didn't feel right. She checked her phone once again.

Something fleeting caught her eye in the side mirror. The hairs on the back of her neck and arms stood on end. The spiders raced all over her body. When she looked more closely there was nothing to see. The rain made visibility out of the windows distorted. Then the creepiest thought came to her – what if Jake was already here? Stalking her? It would explain the car and why she was sure it had moved closer. She leaned over the passenger seat, pressing her face against the glass to get a clearer view, but the rain distorted everything. The rain, coming down so hard made it impossible to be sure. Shadows played in the car park as the trees along the edge swayed in the wind.

As she bent down to check her phone, her door was wrenched open and she was dragged out by her collar. At first, she thought she was being robbed it all happened so quickly.

She twisted in agony as she hit the tarmac. Her head was jerked up by a strong hand clamped around her neck, then she stared into Jake's raging face dripping with water. Directly under a street light, the reflection made him look evil. He wrapped his other hand in her hair pulling her up onto her knees. She cried out. Her scalp burned, her hip where she landed wouldn't take her weight. She crumbled to the side. He forced her up. Fire burned in her leg. He held her up in place. Bending down, he got within inches from her face, let go of her hair and slapped her. She dropped to the ground and rolled over in agony. The rain pounded in her face, her mascara ran into her eyes.

She couldn't see properly and tasted blood. Screaming out when she tried to move. He laughed, kicking her in the back of the leg. The pain jack-knifed through her leg. She grabbed hold of it in agony.

'You fucking bitch. Did you think you would scare me today? I know what you think. I know what you're planning, and I know you stole those papers.'

She tried to get up, but he shoved her back down. Her head hit the tarmac. Hard.

'You think you're a fucking smart-arse, don't you?' His voice was cold. 'What were you going to do? Run me down in the dark empty supermarket car park?' He laughed in her face. He bent down closer to her. 'Stupid bitch,' he spat.

There was a whooshing sound in her ears as if she was under water.

'You think you can stop me? You think I'm going to let you get away with what you did to me, how you destroyed me?' he yelled.

She writhed on the floor, mentally pushing away the shooting pain in her hip. Willing it to take her weight. How did he open the door? It was locked... stupid, stupid, stupid.

The coffee cup. She saw it lying on the ground. How could she have been so stupid?

More pain as he savagely picked her up by the front of her jacket, shaking her violently, then throwing her back down. She landed on the same hip. She screamed out in pain. Her head hit the ground for a second time. The pain shot through her leg like a red-hot poker. Vomit rose and she puked. She was on the verge of passing out. Her vision blurred.

A primal wildness rose inside her.

Her mind began racing.

He was going to kill her.

This time he would not turn the tables on her.

This time she would kill him.

She was in control of her destiny.

He bent lifting her face up to his. Terrified he would strike her again, she didn't show her fear. He wanted that. He wouldn't get it. She showed no fear.

She looked him dead in the eye.

'You're wondering how I sneaked up on you, aren't you?' he said.

'The Audi...' she said. Now she remembered seeing it at the house when she broke in and on the lane. It all added up. Blood filled her mouth making it difficult to say any more. She pushed it out with her tongue. It dribbled down her chin.

'You should be more aware, Gemma. I thought you might remember seeing it at the house. Parked up the lane. I thought it might blow my cover.'

Now she knew why it had niggled her. She should have trusted her senses.

'You're trash, Gemma. Nothing more than trash. You come from trash. You destroyed my life and the bond I had with my father. You and your fucking friends. Did you honestly think you wouldn't ever pay for that? It's called karma or revenge, you choose. Nobody messes with me.'

She tried not to cry. If she cried, she'd become weak. He would know he had power over her. She had to stay strong. She had to stay conscious. She had to get back into her car.

'Did Sean give you the information you wanted?' He laughed a grim chilling sound she could barely hear through the torrential rain.

'How…?'

He lifted her up, but her leg gave way. He dropped her. She let out a piercing scream as the pain shot through her leg.

'I know everything you do. Every move you make.' He wiped the rain off his face. 'You're mine, Gemma. Don't ever forget that. You'll meet Matilda very soon. Remember her? Oh, how concerned you were about her? But you're stupid and the deadline has passed.'

She looked at him wanting to ask what the countdown stood for. He must have seen it in her face.

'Haven't you worked out the twelve days? It was twelve days from getting arrested to my life going public and my ruination. Twelve fucking days of worrying if the papers would print it. Twelve fucking days of dodging my father. Twelve days of hell.'

She kept quiet, letting the rain hammer down on her. Crouched, to protect herself, she thought and focused on what she had to do. After what seemed like forever, she managed to pull it together. Her car was no more than fifteen, twenty steps away at the most. She closed her eyes and forced the pain away from her hip. *It didn't hurt. It didn't hurt. It didn't hurt. Don't be scared. Get to the car. Drive. Drive. Drive. Get to the car. Get to the car. It doesn't hurt. It doesn't hurt.* Every part of her body hurt now. Pain ran through her like an electrical current. She forced herself to put the pain out of her head by pushing it out of her mind.

It was the only way she would escape. She told herself there was no pain over and over until it began to ebb away. When she moved and felt it, she gave it no space in her mind. She saw her car still running. *Get to the car. Get to the car.*

'You'll never be able to leave me. Never,' he yelled like a madman. The rain plastered his hair to his head. He looked bald. He'd hate to think he looked bald.

She wanted to tell him. But she had no energy for that, only enough to survive.

She remained motionless. Holding her breath. Harnessing her strength. Her body in agony and trembling with adrenaline. Her thoughts focused on what she had to do. She had to make her move quickly. He ranted on beside himself with anger. She stopped listening and concentrated. She waited for him to come up to her face one more time. He kept screaming in her face, then standing up and yelling to the skies.

She waited.

He didn't disappoint her.

She didn't know how or where the strength came from. One second, she was crumpled and crouched in a heap, the next she head butted him.

FUCK! The pain webbed through her head splintering throughout her skull at the shock of the impact. Nothing prepared her for this pain.

He fell clasping his head in his hands.

Clutching her own head, she got to her feet and tried to run to the car. Her senses on high alert. He was still down. She dragged her leg weaving towards the car, she had ten steps left, no more. Her hip seared with hot pain. *It doesn't hurt. It doesn't hurt*, she kept telling herself, dragging her leg behind her, Christ, it was so heavy. She pushed herself on with blind determination.

As she was about to reach the car, she heard him get

up, shuffling on the tarmac. She didn't dare look back. Desperation, anger and real fear for her life pushed her on the last few steps. Her heart pounded in her ears, her chest hurt to breathe growing tighter by the second. She heard him swear behind her. The rush of blood in her ears together with her heavy breathing focused her mind. The rain hindered her way. She wiped her eyes with the back of her sleeve and slipped, letting out an animal whine.

'You fucking bitch. You'll pay for that.'

Her leg crumbled at the last moment. 'NO,' she cried out frustrated with herself. She pushed on, hard with her right leg, pulling the door wide and landing on the driver's seat on her bad leg. 'FUCK,' she cried out, gritting her teeth to stop the pain paralysing her.

She heard him running towards the car, his shoes slapping the wet tarmac. She slammed the door and, in a panic, forgot where the lock button was. Her fingers fumbled blindly over the inside of the door. As he reached her, her hand landed on the picture of the padlock. CLICK, just as he pulled the handle.

With the back of her hand, she wiped the blood from her mouth, refusing to look at him. He pressed his face up against the glass, shouting obscenities at her. Rainwater dripped down her face, into her eyes, she brushed it away with trembling hands refusing to look at him.

He banged on the window trying to smash it with his elbow. She put the car in D, released the brake and drove out of the car park, wheels spinning. In the rear-view mirror, she saw him run to his car, slipping before he reached it.

Come on, Gemma, come on. Hold on. You have him now. Drive. Drive. Drive.

Against all her instincts, she slowed down and waited for him to start the Audi and move towards her. Water continued to drip into her eyes from her wet hair.

Then she took off.

With an unsteady hand, she pressed 'Start Route Guidance' on the satnav and drove quickly out of the supermarket, concentrating on the unfamiliar dark road, sporadically wiping the water dripping into her eyes from her wet hair. She knew where to go for a while, but that was all. She couldn't afford to get lost. 'Come on, come on,' she shouted at the satnav as it loaded. 'Come on, why is there no signal,' she yelled. Her brain, so jumbled, she couldn't think of the journey without the satnav beyond the next bend. She wiped her eyes while racing along the twisty country lanes, through the bends, she was all over the road, praying nothing would come the other way. *In two hundred yards, turn left onto the A550.* Thank God. She took the turn without stopping or looking. Skidding onto the A550, her back-end snaking. Managing to keep control, once she was on the straight, she pushed her right foot down. Allowing the AMG engine to do what it was built for and like a Rottweiler straining on the leash it took off. The throaty exhaust sound breaking the silence of the night.

The journey was only a few miles. She took deep breaths as she drove to calm herself, she couldn't afford to have an accident. The weather wasn't letting up, if anything it was getting worse. Her wipers, on full, struggled to clear the windscreen. She leant forward to see the road. She had to stay calm, get in control or she wouldn't survive tonight. She knew that for sure. He was off his head with rage.

Turn left in eight hundred yards, then turn immediately right and you will arrive at your destination.

Gemma followed the map on the screen. She swerved left into the turn and directly right, slamming on the brakes and skidding on the loose gravel, her back-end fishtailed. It was pitch black, no street or car park lights here. She drove to where her headlights picked up her marker.

Parking with the lights facing away from the embankment, she switched her engine off and slowly stepped out of the car, wincing with pain. She put her keys in her pocket in case Jake tried to take them.

Seconds later he turned in skidding to a stop. She stepped closer to the edge. He drove slowly towards her. Revving the engine for effect. Intimidating her. His face inside the car, illuminated by her headlights took on a devilish look. Trying to fill her with fear that he would run her over, he edged closer to her. He wouldn't, that would be too easy for him, she banked on that. She stayed still, very aware what was only steps behind her.

With his front bumper virtually touching her, he stopped and got out of the car.

It all happened in a daze. She wanted to speak but nothing came out. Her head throbbed, and the pain in her hip and knee seared with fire. Her leg quivered with the strain of keeping her upright. She willed it to hold on. To not let her down. The pain intensified, and she could feel it begin to give way, she leant on the other leg to take some of the strain off her injured one.

He moved towards her, his face drawn with intent. His body language clear to read. She stepped backwards until she felt the edge of the embankment beneath her boot. Jake rushed to grab her, arms outstretched. She threw herself to the side. In the blink of an eye, he was gone. She heard him falling then a few seconds later the dull sound of a thud.

Dragging her leg, she got back into her car, turned it around, put on her full beam and looked over the edge of the embankment where she saw his still body.

Poetic justice.

Or was it karma.

A feeling of peace descended upon her. 'That's for you too, Matilda,' she said letting out a deep breath.

Without wasting any more time, she reached into the boot of her car, pulled out her leather gloves, balled her hair into a hat then sat in Jake's car and positioned it to drop on top of him. *God, I better get this right.* With the car door open, she put it into drive. Moved the car towards the edge jumping out before it toppled over. The car crashed into the metal and junk below and hopefully, as planned, on top of Jake.

Climbing back into her car. She sat, shaking, for what seemed like ages before the tremors finally subsided. He wouldn't hurt anyone else ever again.

Chapter Fifty-Three

It was a few days later that she pulled out her phone, flicked to her emails and read.

Good Morning,

We can confirm the account numbers are correct.

We can confirm that the monies are in said account and the password has been obtained.

We can confirm a new Swiss bank account has been set up in your name.

We can confirm the monies will be transferred upon notification from yourself.

We can confirm the individual has been located, and a plane ticket is attached to the confirmed destination.

We can confirm the individual is residing at said location.

Please contact us upon arrival and with exact time of transfer to take place.

Chapter Fifty-Four

She asked herself the question, did she miss Oliver? Of course, she did, but she was a different person now. How can you do what she had done and not change inside? Oliver would forever think she had slept with Jake. It would always be between them.

Oliver had come over to the house after it all happened and she tried to convince him. But there was that little bit of doubt and he found it too difficult to overcome. They hadn't shouted or cried, both of them oddly had stayed calm. She always knew the wedge Jake had driven between them was never going away. Before she met up with Oliver she already knew that.

Miami Airport buzzed with colourful people. Dressed in white jeans, high heels, and a long linen orange shirt, she perched her sunglasses on top of her head. With her handbag swinging from her hand, she walked over to the large window. A small private plane waited on the tarmac ready to pick up its passengers. What a way to travel. Champagne. Delicious food. Attentive staff. Why would you travel any other way if you didn't have too?

She'd made a phone call to Peter, earlier, giving him the shock of his life, she imagined, and left a message asking him to call her back.

She sat down in the back row of the seating facing the information desk, took out her compact and applied fresh lipstick and waited. He wouldn't be able to resist getting in touch with her.

Ten minutes later, her phone rang. She smiled and answered. 'Hi, there. Are you surprised to hear from me after all this time?' she said in a cajoling voice as she drew him in. Curiosity would be bursting from him.

'Yes, how did you find me?' His weariness thrilled her, she smiled to herself.

'Oh, your cousin gave me your whereabouts. He sends his regards by the way. But he won't be able to see you, he's gone down under, probably for a long time.' She smiled at her smart choice of words.

'Where are you?' he asked, bewildered.

'He told me everything, Peter. We got on very well, if you know what I mean, and he confessed everything about his plan and your involvement.'

'Where are you?' he asked again. She heard the panic in his voice begin.

'I must admit you had us both fooled, but especially Oliver, he really thought you two were best mates.'

'Christ.' He laughed, nervously, she noticed the little quiver in his voice. 'Why hasn't Jake rung me?'

'Have you tried his mobile? Is it turned off?' Her smile grew, and she began getting strange looks from passengers sat nearby. She was loving this moment. 'He said he lost his phone and would be getting a new one with a new number, too many people had his old one. Going to start afresh, he said.' She pulled out Jake's phone from her handbag and saw Peter's call flash up. He had left it in the cup holder of his Audi. Peter had tried Jake a dozen times it would seem while talking to her. She had taken it from his car on impulse at the last minute.

She held up her hand and admired her manicure; she'd made the right choice in going for red. Blood red always made a statement. Then she saw him, dressed in black jeans and T-shirt. Hair bleached by the sun, looking around the lounge area.

'I'll call you back in a moment. Just wait where you are.' She cut the call.

She dialled another number; it rang three times before

they picked up. 'In five minutes do the transfer,' she said. She cut the call. Stood up and started to walk. Sean and his hacker had accessed Peter's Cayman Island account and were ready on her call to transfer all the funds into her new Swiss account. All she had to do was give them the signal.

As she walked, she checked her watch. Four minutes after the previous call, she made another call. A few seconds later she heard the tannoy. *'Could Mr Peter Hayes please come to the information desk. Mr Peter Hayes to the information desk.'*

She watched as he was handed a letter. She checked her watch, thirty seconds to go. She was too far away from him to see, but she could picture the colour draining from his face. His heart rate going off the scale and a sure thick sweat engulfing him as his stomach hit the floor and he realised what was happening.

'Thank you,' she said to a member of staff as she went through the gate, she turned one last time to see him grappling with his phone. She walked out into the hot Miami sunshine and walked along the tarmac towards the little plane. Looking up she saw him at the window. Searching. Checking. And... aah, yes, finally understanding.

Her phone pinged.

She opened her message.

Transfer successful.

She could feel him watching her as she climbed the steps to the plane. She turned and smiled as he pounded on the glass.

Now he knew how it felt.

She thought she'd been kind and at least gave him an explanation, which was more than he'd done for them. Bastard.

All the money they had embezzled was now in her account. She should have given it back. She wasn't going to.

She had Sean set up an account for Oliver and sent him half. She left instructions not to tell him for about six months. By then, he should have calmed down and she hoped would accept it. If he knew about it now, he'd give it away.

Dear Peter,

By the time you read this, your life, as you know it will be over. A terrible feeling, one of which I can empathise with having experienced that very same feeling the day you stole all our money.

You're probably wondering what I've done to you. May I suggest you check your Cayman bank account.

Five hundred thousand pounds probably wasn't a lot compared to the mass you amalgamated from the other poor sods you tricked and stole from. But it was enough to destroy us. Now I've taken ALL your money.

Your actions together with those of your cousin were the catalyst to my relationship with Oliver imploding. You cannot begin to imagine how that action plunged our lives into a nightmare. A nightmare from which I have emerged a very different and changed person.

Oliver has more integrity, sincerity and love in his little finger than you or your cousin could ever have.

You'll probably read this last bit later after you've checked your bank and after you've called me lots of disgusting names. Had a tantrum. Screamed. Cried. Tried Jake, again. Wondered how this stupid girl managed to get one over on both of you.

You fucked me over, Peter Hayes.

But I fucked you up.

So, I will say only one last thing... isn't karma a bitch.

Gemma

Epilogue

They never did make it. She confessed everything to Oliver and told him the reason why she had to do what she did. He never understood although, she guessed he did, a little. But Oliver was too pure of heart to ever consider killing anyone.

She wanted to try again to get their relationship off the ground, but he couldn't contemplate what she'd done. He might go to the police. He might not. She told Sean to take the file to the police, keeping her name out of it.

She would always worry who was knocking on her door.

If only she'd understood that money could not fix everything before it was too late. Oliver always said honesty was the best way to stay true to a person. *Once the lies begin, they never stop*, he said. *It changes what you once had.* He believed in that. But she grew up without a moral compass and, for her, survival at any cost was her compass.

Knowing she destroyed the only good thing in her life was so much worse than knowing she killed a man. She'd failed herself, and had failed Oliver and would have to live with that for the rest of her life.

Yet nothing compared to the pain she knew she'd caused him, and the pain that he would never know how much she truly loved him. She would love Oliver for the rest of her life.

Thank you!

Dear Reader,

I hope you enjoy reading my second novel and thank you so much for buying it.

It's always lovely to hear what readers think of books they've enjoyed reading, I know I love reading reviews when I'm looking at books to buy. So, if you have enjoyed reading my book and feel inclined to leave a review on the platform you bought the book from or on Goodreads, I would be ever so grateful. You can follow me on Twitter @The_SadieRyan or drop by my website www.sadieryan. co.uk or on Facebook. I'd love to hear from my readers.

Sadie

x

About the Author

Sadie Ryan is a British author with two grown-up children. She lives with her daughter, adorable rescue dog and cat in a small village in leafy Cheshire in the North West of England. She writes psychological suspense/domestic noir novels. When asked where she gets her ideas from, she says, 'From observation, inspiration and lots of wicked thoughts'.

Find out more about Sadie here:
www.twitter.com/The__SadieRyan
www.sadieryan.co.uk

More Ruby Fiction

From Sadie Ryan

Behind Closed Doors

She's in your house, now she wants your life …

Tina Valentine has it all: the loving family, the beautiful house, the successful career.

But then Megan Pearson starts work at Tina's law firm and with her arrival the perfect world Tina has built for herself starts to collapse as it becomes clear that the newcomer is intent on infiltrating every aspect of her life.

Something is obviously wrong with Megan but nobody else seems to see it. As the mind games and manipulations continue, Tina comes to the sickening conclusion that now she's opened the door to Megan, it's going to be impossible to make her leave …

More from Ruby Fiction

Why not try something else from our selection:

Keeper of Secrets
Lynda Stacey

**Deadly secrets lie
beneath the surface ...**

For as long as Cassie Hunt can
remember, her Aunt Aggie has
spoken about the forgotten
world that exists just below
their feet, in the tunnels and
catacombs of the Sand House.

When excavation work begins
on the site, shocking secrets
are uncovered and danger is never far away, both above and
below ground...

Who Cares if They Die
Wendy Dranfield

Did she jump or was she pushed?

It starts with the hanging woman in the Maple Valley woods; the woman with no shoes, no car and no name. On paper it's an obvious case of suicide – but to Officer Dean Matheson, something doesn't add up.

Then there are the other deaths, deaths that also look like suicides – but are they? The victims are all women living on the fringes of society, addicts and criminals. Who will miss them? Does anyone really care if they die?

Dean Matheson is making it his business to care, even if it means he becomes the target …

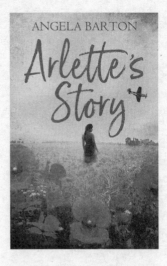

Arlette's Story
Angela Barton

One woman's struggle to fight back against the enemy in order to protect the ones she loves.

When Arlette Blaise sees a German plane fly over the family farm in 1940, she's comforted by the fact that the occupying forces are far away in the north of the country. Surely the war will not reach her family in the idyllic French countryside near to the small town of Oradour-sur-Glane?

But then Saul Epstein, a young Jewish man driven from his home by the Nazis, arrives at the farm and Arlette begins to realise that her peaceful existence might be gone for good …

Visit www.rubyfiction.com for details.

Introducing Ruby Fiction

Ruby Fiction is an imprint of Choc Lit Publishing.
We're an award-winning independent publisher,
creating a delicious selection of fiction.

See our selection here:
www.rubyfiction.com

Ruby Fiction brings you stories that inspire emotions.

We'd love to hear how you enjoyed
When He Finds You. Please visit
www.rubyfiction.com and give your feedback or
leave a review where you purchased this novel.

Ruby novels are selected by genuine readers like yourself.
We only publish stories our Tasting Panel want to see in
print. Our reviews and awards speak for themselves.

Could you be a Star Selector and join our Tasting Panel?
Would you like to play a role in choosing which novels
we decide to publish? Do you enjoy reading women's
fiction? Then you could be perfect for our Tasting Panel.

Visit here for more details ...
www.choc-lit.com/join-the-choc-lit-tasting-panel

Keep in touch:
Sign up for our monthly newsletter Spread for all the latest
news and offers: www.spread.choc-lit.com. Follow us on
Twitter: @RubyFiction and Facebook: RubyFiction.

Stories that inspire emotions